Pisgah Press was established in 2011 to publish and promote works of quality offering original ideas and insight into the human condition, the realm of knowledge, and the world around us.

Printed in the United States of America

Published by Pisgah Press, LLC
PO Box 1427, Candler, NC 28715
www.pisgahpress.com

Book & cover design: A. D. Reed, MyOwnEditor.com
Cover painting and illustrations by Jake LaGory

Library of Congress Cataloging-in-Publication Data
Burgess, Barry
Mombie/Burgess

Library of Congress Control Number: 2014955489

ISBN-13: 978-1942016038
Fiction

First Edition
First Printing
July 2015

This is a work of fiction. Any resemblance to actual events
or persons living or dead is coincidental.

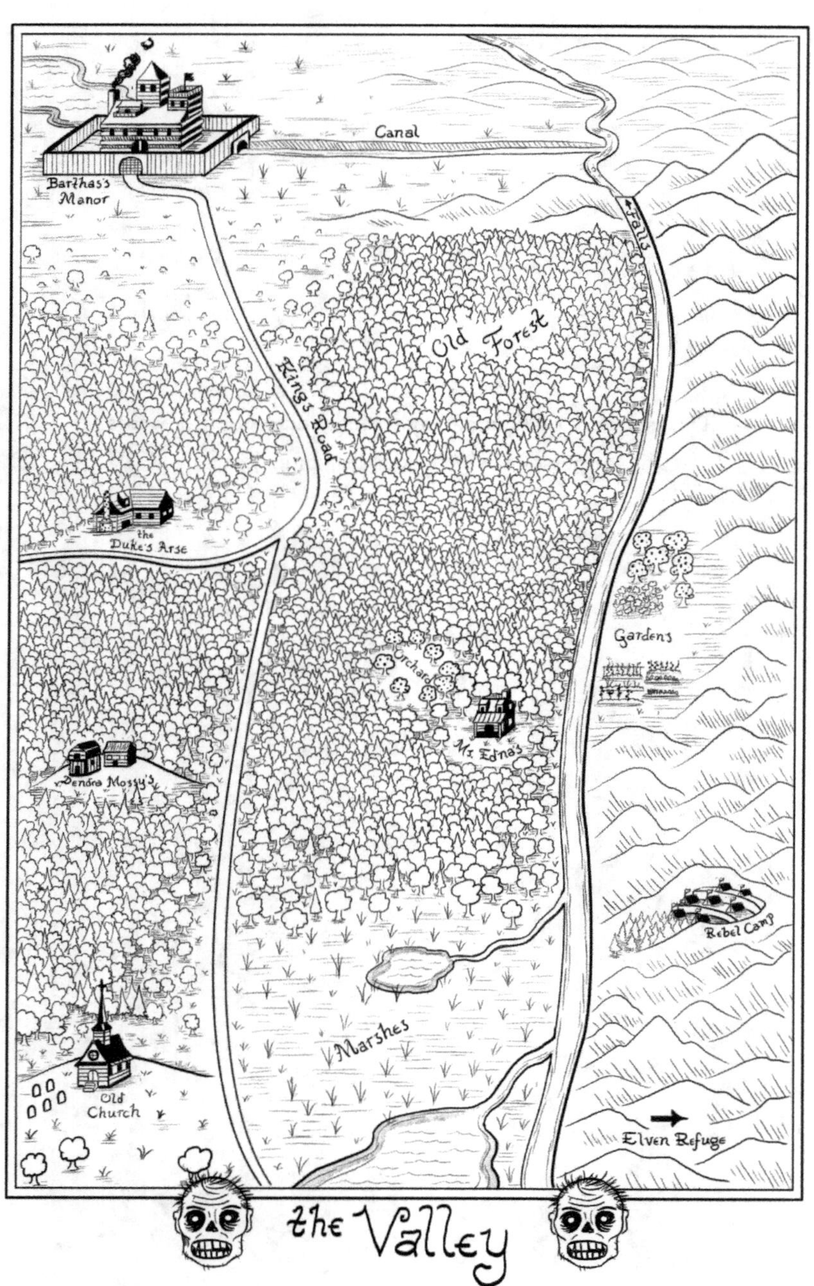

Canal
Barthas's Manor
Falls
King's Road
Old Forest
the Duke's Arse
Gardens
Orchard
Mr. Edna's
Dendra Mossy's
Rebel Camp
Old Church
Marshes
Elven Refuge
the Valley

MOMBIE
The *Zombie* Mom

by Barry A. Burgess

illustrated by Jake LaGory

For Jack William Burgess. May your life be filled with imagination and adventure. And for the memory of my cousin Patrice Nigro Andersen, whose gentle inquisitive soul inspired my Patty Pixie.

MOMBIE
The *ZOMBIE* Mom

List of Illustrations

Table of Contents

One

A Snowy Morning

It began on a Wednesday. It was the middle of the week, and hump day. I remember looking in the mirror that morning and worrying about the puffiness under my eyes, wondering if the stretched, swollen skin was adding to my wrinkles. I had turned forty-five that year and was perimenopausal as hell. My hair was now more than streaked with gray, and I was "Max and Patty's mom" to everyone who knew me. In spite of my dabbling in aerobics at the local Y, I knew that my principal duty in life was as chauffeur to my two kids: gymnastic classes, karate, band, birthday parties, even to Grandma and Grandpa's.

It was February, and at 6:00 a.m. the sky was still dark. But as I opened the yellow-and-green-striped curtain in our yellow-and-white-tiled bathroom, what was left of the moonlight showed that it had begun to flurry outside and the wind was beginning to blow.

I could hear Ben rustling the sheets inside. It took no great stretch of my imagination to envision him stretching and scratching and adjusting himself. He did this with his eyes still closed and it made me shudder some mornings. Twenty years of close association and seventeen years of marriage had taken their toll on our patience. We had met in college and sworn that we were the only ones for each other—based on what, I've never been sure. But we had two great kids: Max, thirteen-going-on-twenty, as rambunctious a redhead as they come, and Patty, my dark curly-haired pixie. Patty was eight and as sweet a child as still existed in the world these days. I was often humbled by her gentle views and considerate actions. In fact, I was often humbled by the simple pleasure of being a mother at all. But that was nothing compared to how I felt later.

I splashed some water on my face and began to brush my teeth. In the other room the alarm began to scream its electronic clarion call. I started to run out of the bathroom with my mouth still foam-filled, but Ben, like a somnambulistic orangutan, groped and smashed at the plastic alarm clock. I heard him grunt something but turned back to spit the thickening foam from my mouth.

"Honey? You up?"

I ran through a list of possible sarcastic replies but chose a polite reminder instead.

"You know that today is Patty's registration for Honey Bees, right?"

I heard a thump from the other room as he jumped out of bed.

"Crap! No, is that today? What time do I have to be there? Do I have a pair of clean khakis? What about my green shirt?"

"It's your shirt, Ben. I'm getting some coffee."

"Oh, for God's sake, Annie, why do you have to be that way?"

As I headed down to the kitchen I closed the door and pretended not to hear.

A blast of Black Eyed Peas blew down the hallway as Max flew by and beat me down the stairs.

"Max, I want you to get back up there and turn off that damned stereo if you're not going to be listening to it!"

"It's okay, Mom. Patty likes it," he yelled from the kitchen, already lightyears ahead of me. Patty and Max had adjoining rooms which shared a bathroom. I paused at the top of the stairs with my hand on the banister and decided to check on Patty. Her white door was covered in drawings and stickers. There was a drawing of her as an angel, Pikachu the Pokemon stickers, the "please knock" sign, the "do not disturb" sign (which alternated with "Please make up the room," which Ben and I had brought back from our trip to Montreal—the last time I remember us being happy with one another). I knocked gently.

"Pats? Patty, honey? You up?" Nothing. I turned the knob and pushed my way into what we liked to refer to as Patty's pink paradise. The room was painted Hostess Snowball pink and draped with white ruffled eyelet curtains, sheets, pillows, and bedspread. Tossed like a tiny doll on the full-sized four-poster bed lay a fragile figure half covered by a white duvet embroidered with daisies. She lay face down on the bed, snoring like a freight train. Patty's sinuses had been bothering her since the beginning of winter. I had bought vaporizers and even spent nearly $200 on one of those HEPA filters they sell on the Home Shopping Channel. Nothing seemed to work. She still snored—and snorted when she laughed. Thank goodness she was feminine in every other way and tended to be patient and a good listener.

The rhythm of her snoring suddenly changed as she began to roll over and rub her eyes. Her long curly auburn hair tumbled like a cloud over her shoulders and her eyes cracked open to peer out. It was clear she was not yet awake.

"Patty? Sweetheart?"

"Mmmmmm ... Mom?"

Her eyes opened a bit more.

"Punkin. It's time to wake up. Remember what today is?"

"Sure, Mom. Honey Bees."

"You hungry?"

A nod.

"Let's go. Dad is supposed to drive you and you know about that."

Patty rolled her eyes. Ben had been late or last-second for several of Patty's recent engagements and she had expressed her very righteous pre-teen outrage. We had discussed the concept of staying a step ahead of dear old Dad.

"So?" I asked.

Patty bounded out of bed and ran for the bathroom where she began furiously brushing her teeth and washing her face.

"I am NOT gonna be late, Mom. Not for Honey Bees! Cynthia McGowan's mother already signed her up early 'cause she works at the Y. Tell Dad we have to be there by eight o'clock, NO LATER!"

I was dismissed as my precocious beauty flew to her closet and rustled amongst the purple stripes, stars, and butterflies for a suitable outfit.

"Wear something comfortable," I heard myself say as I walked down the stairs to strains of Maroon Five. "You have gymnastics this afternoon."

The mother of Max and Patty, that was me. I remember in college I had seriously wanted to be a dancer. Those were the days when Cunningham was king, and I had studied with Viola Farber for a while down in Westbeth on the West Side of Manhattan, overlooking the river. Back when Ben and I were still exploring ourselves and we had a place on the Upper West Side. I wore berets and carried a dancer's bag. Ben wore a knapsack and rode a Motobecane 10-speed bicycle. We shopped at the Fairway and debated about whole-grain bread and the best herbs and our favorite cheeses over Nicaraguan coffee we ground in our German coffee grinder. We had walked through the apple blossoms in Riverside Park and debated whether we wanted the responsibility of a dog. Then I got pregnant with Max, and Eddie the dog came along once Max was toddling. After a year or so of managing the stroller up Broadway and wiping Eddie's feet off before we came inside during the winter, we decided to move. Two years later we found a loft in Williamsburg. Which was when we discovered Patty was on the way and it was off to a starter home in suburban Middleville where we are now, yellow ruffled curtains and all.

"Max, are you feeding that dog our bacon again?"

"Aw, Mom."

We both sighed big sighs, then laughed. We are all notorious spoilers of dogs in our family. Both Ben and I have encouraged the kids to be sensitive to animals, so we've had our share of birds with broken wings, nestlings, even a flying squirrel—and, once, a garter snake. Eddie (a Golden-Shepherd, or German-Retriever, mix) is almost twelve. He and Max have grown up together. Max learned how to stand by grasping handfuls of Eddie's fur to pull himself upright while Eddie stood stoically and winced. Before long they were rolling in mud and chasing squirrels together. Now Eddie still thinks the world begins and ends with Max, but Max is often late with Lacrosse. And now Patty will have Honey Bees. Poor, dear old Eddie: he had gone all gray on his muzzle, and recently it had reached his eyes. He tended to wheeze a bit as he winched up his arthritic hips from the floor after lying for a while. His ribs had begun to show and I understood intellectually that he couldn't live forever, but I couldn't bear the thought of losing "one of my kids," as I thought of him.

Ben came down the stairs smelling of Dr. Bronner's peppermint soap and with a spot of shaving cream behind his ear. His hair was slicked over like Alfalfa from the Little Rascals, and I couldn't help but laugh at his boyish gait in his schoolboy khakis with his honest green plaid shirt. Ben was enthusiastic about life. He was one of those people for whom belief was all—the details could be ironed out later. Benjamin J. Prockner (a Presbyterian from Stockton, Mass.) and Annie (née) DeLeon (a failed Catholic from Northport, Long Island) had been seen having their disagreements over such long-term commitments as a thirty- versus a fifteen-year mortgage and how much orthodontia we could reasonably afford for Max, and a host of other heady adult decisions. There were days when I wondered who those two star-crossed lovers from college were. *Where* they were, for that matter. Could they be the slightly graying middle-aged couple I saw reflected in the living room mirror? God, I looked tired this morning.

I skipped my reverie and held onto the facts of the day.

"There's a check on the table for the registration fee. If you take the parkway to the underpass you'll miss the tie-up at the elementary school and be able to circle back on Main. Drop her off at the front office to sign in since she won't be on her regular bus."

"Oh I was just going to pay in cash, don't worry."

"Be-en! I do worry! That is why we have no record of where our cash is going. Just take the check, okay? And Patty, take your Digi-mon out of your brother's cereal."

"He's digi-balling!" she whined. "He needs nourishment!"

"Fine. Ben?"

"Whatever you say, honey."

He winked conspiratorially at Patty, who smiled and looked down at her milk-sodden digi-monster.

"And no MCDONALD'S!!!"

They both froze and stared straight ahead.

I found myself smirking like a schoolmarm. Why did I always have to be the bad cop? Patty had had her father wrapped around her finger from the first moment she had fluttered those long curly lashes at him. Face it, Mrs. Prockner, your daughter was simply way more charming than you *ever* were. Prettier, too. And there is no one prouder of that fact than yourself, you dope.

"Max, get your La Crosse gear, and don't throw it in the car. That stuff's expensive. Ben, are you taking the Taurus or the minivan?"

"Either."

"Fine."

"Patty? Do I get a kiss?"

She was wearing her Sailor Moon top and her purple corduroy pants with the silver stars. Her hair was pulled back on the sides with rainbow clips and hung free and full to the back. Cynthia McGowan was going to get a run for her money.

Patty threw herself into my arms, gave me a peck on the cheek, and bounded up the stairs to get her knapsack. I heard the clatter of Max's La Crosse equipment slam into the back of the minivan and the whirr of the electric garage door opening.

"Damn, Honey, the snow is getting worse out there. Maybe you should turn on the radio?" Ben asked. He sounded surprised, honestly concerned. So I went out to the garage and felt the wind bite through the open door. Tiny flakes of snow blew past me into the kitchen.

I am not good with retreat. I go on with the plan for the day. Patty still had to get to the Y to register, and if they decided to close the schools, Ben could come straight back afterward. Max had a World History test this morning, and I knew he would be ready to jump at the excuse not to go to school, so I was determined to get him there. No. We had to go on. Ben and Patty to Honey Bees. And me and Max to the junior high. I would circle back, hit the cleaners, and Ben would continue to the office.

I explained this calmly and logically, and amidst much sighing and confusion about which boots fit whom, we sorted things out. I made Ben go back to get the funny red-and-white-striped knit hat we had bought in Stowe, Vermont. "You need a hat in this blowing snow!" I had insisted. We got into our respective cars—Max and I only decided to take Eddie in the minivan at the last minute—and off we drove.

Two

Separate Ways

"Daddy?"

"Yeah Punkin?"

"Are you mad at Mommy?"

"Why? Because she made me wear this hat?"

"Sorta'…. Other stuff, too, like the check for Honey Bees. Oh, and what about McDonald's? You promised me we could go!"

"Well, can you keep a secret?"

"Of course, Daddy. Honey Bee's honor."

"Well, you're not technically a Honey Bee just yet, but I suppose we can overlook that, for, say, as long as it takes to eat an Egg McMuffin?"

"Yay!"

The wind was blowing the fine powdery snow sideways across the windshield and there was ice on the wipers, which began to squeegee-squeak across the nearly dry glass. The heater on the Taurus's dashboard began to kick in, and Patty settled against her pink-and-purple knapsack in the back seat and listened to the rhythm of the wiper blades.

They passed the intersection for the parkway and continued on.

"Daddy, Mommy said to take the parkway…"

"I know, Punkin. This is a shortcut. We'll take the Old Farm Road up past the Haggerty house and then cut over past the pond. I wonder if anyone is skating? It sure is cold enough. Do those skates from last year still fit you?"

"I don't want to be late. Cynthia McGowan's—"

"I know all about Cynthia McGowan. She's a spoiled only child and her mother, Tammy, spends more time smoking those damned 'health food' cigarettes and getting her nails done than she does caring for that child."

"She has more Barbies than any other kid in school. She even has a vintage Malibu Stacey with the original box. Hey, Dad, look at that!"

A fragile, almost decrepit, wooden hay cart drawn by what looked to be a weathered old Clydesdale was clip-clopping along the shoulder of the road. A thin layer of fluffy snow covered the bales of hay in the back, and sitting in the buggy seat was a wizened woman wrapped in scarves and shawls, clutching the reins through a pair of fingerless gloves.

Ben slowed down and drew alongside the rickety cart and its delicate occupant. The crone turned to flash Ben a grin, which showed her teeth to be in the single digits. She licked her wrinkled lips and winked.

"Well, I'll be damned. Will you get a look at that old gal out in this weather? I didn't think any of the old farms in this area were still in operation."

"She looks older than Grandma," said Patty.

"She looks older than *God*," Ben muttered.

The headlights of an oncoming car glared around a curve and Ben concentrated on the road ahead. The swirling snow had begun to stick on the blacktop, and the wiper blades no longer squeaked. The windshield had warmed up and the snow melted as it hit the glass. Patty took out her Game Boy and settled into a rhythm of rocking and pressing in time to electronic beeps and trills as one of the Mario brothers fought for his life in a cyber-madhouse. The snow continued to fall as the Taurus hurtled on through the dim gray morning light.

After what seemed like too much time, Patty put her Game Boy down. Ben began to mutter to himself. "Is this it? No, that's not it. That's not the turn-off to town. What is that, an apple orchard? I don't remember an apple orchard out this way. Do you, honey?"

"What about McDonald's, Daddy? Are we still going? I'm getting hungry."

"Oh, your mother is going to kill me. Didn't you eat anything?"

"You said we were going to McDonald's."

Ben let out a deep sigh and reached for his hated cell phone.

"I better call Kadeem at the office and tell him I'm going to be late. Maybe he knows where the hell I am."

Ben fiddled with the phone again and again, pressing buttons and sighing in exasperation, before he finally pulled over.

"Great. Just great. Not a damned signal."

"Daddy, that's two curse words: 'hell' and 'damn.'"

"Well don't repeat them, Patrice." Ben always called her by her real name when he was annoyed.

For a full twenty seconds they just looked at each other, sitting in the car by the side of the road, snow swirling about the windows. The steady thrum of the heater was a comfortable interruption. Patty reached into her knapsack.

"Want a granola bar, Daddy? Mom puts them in our backpacks."

"Yes," was all he could muster; then, after a pause, "Thanks."

"You know Daddy..."

"Yes, Punkin?"

Her chocolate-colored eyes lit up with glee, and the corners crinkled with the thought. "They probably cancelled school by now."

Ben had to laugh. "You're probably right about that, Pats. Let's see what we can find out." He hit the radio "on" button and began fiddling with the digital control.

"Whoa, Daddy, turn it down!"

Squeals of uncontrolled frequency arcs and static blared from every channel he tried.

"Must be those microwave lines they were putting in out this way. Seems I heard talk of that some time ago. That's probably what's wrong with the cell phone signals, too. We just have so damned many..." he trailed off as Patty interrupted.

"Daddy!!! No swear words!"

"Sorry, Punkin. So many signals going every which way that they've begun to get all tangled up in each other. That's all there is to it. This was bound to happen sooner or later. Well, there's no point in worrying. That's what I always say. Now, your mother, she's a worrier. No point in it, I tell her. No point at all. Okay. So this is definitely the wrong way. Right? We agree about that?"

"Yup."

"Okay, so.... What do you say we head back the way we came from? We must have missed the turn somewhere after that cart with the old lady. The snow was coming down pretty heavily then and I probably just didn't see it. Think you can recognize the place?"

"I think so, Daddy."

"Well, keep your eyes peeled, scout. Apparently, I need all the help your mother thinks I do. If we can just get you to the Y and registered with Honey Bees, maybe we'll call our own snow day and go home and watch old movies."

"FrankenWeenie!" squealed Patty throwing her hair up over her shoulder.

"That's old?"

"DADDY!"

"Just teasing, Punkin."

"No, Daddy, look!" she leaned over the back seat and pointed beyond the dashboard.

There by the side of the road was a simple, generically simple, metal sign pointing to a turn-off. The sign read "Business District" in reflective white lettering on a standard green background. Another, pointing back the way they had come that morning, read "Town Limits."

"Well, will you look at that? I must have missed it this morning in all the snow, when we passed the cart and that other car swerved past us. There it was all the time, Punkin. I couldn't be any blinder if my eyes were painted on."

Patty began to giggle.

"Iz yo' eyes PAINTED on?" she demanded in a drawl, doing her version of Ben's impression of his parents' southern housemaid and nanny.

"Ya know ah tink dey iz!" answered Ben, imagining Annie's reaction at his being so un-PC, but still chuckling.

The snow seemed to let up a little, and they proceeded happily along the road as it cut through the old farmland and up a tree-covered hill. They drove up and over the crest and through another wooded area, passing what seemed to be a very primitive cottage among the trees. Surely it was just a summer cabin; there were still plenty of them up this way. But Ben could not see a single light on or an electric line leading to the house.

"More primitive than I like it. That's for sure."

"What's that, Daddy?"

"Oh, nothing, Punkin. Nothing at all..."

They drove on, neither of them saying a word about the increasingly unfamiliar territory. Soon, the snow started falling in earnest, and the sky took on a cold gray-blue hue. Patty did high-kicks, lying on her back across the back seat and humming the theme song to *Star Trek*.

"Honey, could you not do that for a minute?"

"What? Oh ... okay. Where are we, Daddy?"

Silence.

"Daddy?"

"I'm trying to think, Punkin. Hey look, over there in that field!"

"It's the old lady on the horse cart!"

"Yeah, but she's turning down that old dirt road. I can't follow her in the Taurus. We'll get stuck in the snow and mud. Let's just try to get her attention."

The cart had made its way halfway across a wide field filled with dead snow-covered milkweed stalks, toward what looked to be some sort of a farm or homestead in the distance. Ben pulled over and opened the car door, letting in a blast of arctic wind and causing Patty to squeal—a high C above shattered glass. Ben leaned on the horn and waved at the distant cart.

"Hey! Ho!" he hollered while waving, "TOWN?" He pointed down the road he had been following.

The old woman seemed to smile in the distance and nodded. Her horse whinnied at being stopped. Patty pushed him the rest of the way out the door and slammed it behind him. The old woman continued nodding and pointed down the road.

"TOWN?" he demanded again. But the wind blew the words straight away from him.

The crone nodded again.

Ben climbed back into the Taurus and shivered.

"Sorry, honey. Yeah, it looks like this is the way. I guess we had just gone farther than I realized. Look at that. It's past nine a.m. already. Well, time flies when you're having fun."

Patty snorted from the back seat.

"Your sinuses bothering you, honey?"

Another snort and, "Yes, Daddy."

Max was performing his own version of Chinese water torture on me in the minivan, bouncing a handball off the back of my seat and tossing his head to something that sounded violent escaping from the earphones of his portable CD player. He regularly begged us for an iPod, but Ben and I agreed: not yet—we wanted some control over what music he bought. His voice was beginning to crack, but he didn't seem to notice as he sang along tunelessly with the sounds only he could fully hear.

The snow was coming down furiously and I knew I had to stop at Citibank before cutting across town to the high school.

The handball flew between the seats, hit the dashboard and

bounced onto my lap.

"Ooomph," I said. "That is enough of that. Now take those headphones off for a few minutes. Sit up straight and talk to me." I heard my mother's voice coming out of my mouth.

"Honestly Max, you want to be treated like an adult and sometimes you behave just like a child. Now suppose that handball had hit my hand? Or had bounced in my face? You're lucky I'm driving so slow with all this snow. We could have had an accident."

I stared at him through the rearview mirror. He paused. I waited.

"Sorry Mom." In his favor, I must say he looked genuinely sorry.

Max was a good kid. He was just trying to manage a body that was growing too fast. He was already taller than me and threatened to top his father's modest five-eight within the year. I noticed that the peach fuzz on his upper lip had lengthened into a little white-blond moustache. I needed to mention to Ben, in our next lifetime, when we have privacy and a moment to ourselves, that Max was in need of a shaving lesson.

We came to a stoplight and I turned off the news radio.

"Max, how's Courtney? Have you seen her lately? I saw her mom in the Pathmark the other day. She's becoming quite the beauty."

"I thought you said you saw her mom."

At least I had his attention, for the moment, so I continued. "Yes, but Courtney was waiting in the car. I think she was wearing make-up."

"Yeah, she does that now." Max shrugged. "She hangs out with like all these older girls and they think they are like so cool. I mean she doesn't even get on the bus anymore." He shrugged again.

"I see. But you are still in the same classes together, aren't you?"

"Yeah, we have most of the same honors classes, except for math this year."

"You two were so close when you were younger. You were the only boy Courtney would allow to her pool parties, and the

Hannigans have such a lovely yard, and that in-ground pool."

"I like our pool just fine."

"Well, sure." And honestly, summer sounded pretty good right then. The wind was blowing hard, and the traffic light was swinging so hard you could hardly tell which direction it was facing. As I proceeded through the light, another minivan ran the intersection and crossed right in front of me. I swerved, skidded in the snow and narrowly veered around it.

"YOU SONOVABITCH!" I screamed.

Max's voice cracked as he muttered "wow" from the back seat.

I pulled over in front of the bakery. "Holy crap," I griped. My hands were shaking.

"No kidding," said Max.

"Let's just sit here for a minute, okay? Let me catch my breath."

"Sure Mom. You okay? I mean, like, you want me to drive?"

"Very funny."

"No I'm serious, Mom. Dad let me drive in the parking lot at his office lots of times. I mean I'll be ready for a permit in two years."

"Two-and-a-half. And the middle of a snowstorm is neither the time nor the place to be taking your first road lesson. Restrain yourself, Mario Andretti."

"Aw, he's old. Jimmie Johnson is cool now."

"Duly noted."

I carefully checked my side and rearview mirrors, pulled back onto East Pemburton Street and drove slowly north in the right lane. I noticed that there were very few cars on the road as the Citibank came into view. I angled the car into the drive-up window, did my thing with the ATM, and it spit out what I kept trying to refer to as our weekly budget. Ben had not yet grasped this concept and thought my efforts quaint. I placed the cash in my wallet and put it back in my bag. Then I carefully exited the bank parking lot and headed toward the high school.

We had gone no more than six blocks when I saw flashing lights and yellow roadblocks ahead. A policeman in a glistening yellow slicker and hood was waving cars off to the right with a matching yellow hooded flashlight.

"Oh, *no!*" I griped.

I rolled down my window part-way to avoid some of the blowing wind and snow, then took my turn pulling up to the officer.

"What seems to be the problem, officer? I need to get my son to school."

"Water main, lady. Whole series of them exploded all the way up Main Street. They're having a problem with freezing pipes in this cold. You're gonna have to follow these cars onto the Thruway and go all the way up to exit fourteen, then double back from the other end of town. Ask the cop on duty up there. They got one o' my buddies posted up there to help direct the cars we're detouring up that way."

I let out an exasperated breath and complained, "Oh, we are going to be *so* late! Oh, I could just spit!"

"Hey lady, that's how accidents happen. Now you just take your time, drive real careful-like up the Thruway. They say the snow is really starting to pile up. Stay in the right-hand lane, and when you get to the exit ask for Lenny. Tell him Joe sent you. He'll get you all straightened out and you'll be taking that test in no time, young man." He winked past me at Max.

"How'd you know that?" I laughed at him.

"Oh, call it officer's intuition. He looks a little green around the gills," he laughed back. He seemed to think that last part particularly witty, and sauntered off chuckling to himself.

Max's eyes narrowed in the rearview window, and his cheeks flamed red beneath his freckles. I drove up the ramp to the thruway entrance.

"That was weird."

"Oh, honey," I said. "These policemen train for years in reading faces. He could just tell you looked a little nervous."

"Well sure, we just almost got creamed by another minivan, for cripes sake!" Max sounded exasperated and embarrassed.

I turned the heater up another notch as I waited my turn to pull out. "You warm enough?"

"Fine."

We rode in silence for the fifteen minutes it took to get to Exit 14. It was a nerve-wracking drive. Only two of the three lanes were open, and no matter how I tried to avoid the big commercial rigs, the filthy, salt-riddled slush crested off their wheels like the wake behind a boat and onto my windshield. I was terrified that I would lose control of the minivan during one of these blind periods. Somehow we made it with no mishaps to the off-ramp, where a team of police stood in hooded yellow outfits identical to the one Joe had worn. I breathed a sigh of relief as I rolled down the window and asked for Lenny.

The policeman I spoke to flagged down another who had been warming his hands on a cup of coffee. "Joe sent this one," he hollered to Lenny. "They've got to get to the high school."

Lenny nodded, put his cup on his squad car and came over to the minivan. He had a pleasant, ordinary face under his hood and it was easy to put my trust in him. It was a relief to feel that we had almost attained our goal.

"Okay, here's what you want to do, Ma'am. You're going to make a left here, don't follow those other cars. They're not headed where you're going. Then, about a mile down the road, just past a billboard, you're going to see a detour sign. Follow that down the hill and just keep following the signs. You'll have this young man to his test before you both know it." He winked once. And I found myself smiling. "Joe called ahead to my intercom. Be careful now, if you don't mind my saying so, you look a bit frazzled, Ma'am."

Was it apparent to everyone?

The road was slippery and I drove slowly. We came to the detour and, as Lenny had described, it was nearly hidden behind a billboard for the local milk company, Blanc Brothers Dairy. I liked their cottage cheese but their yogurt had never been to my taste: too much cornstarch. Beyond the billboard was a road, scarcely an exit, which took a sharp turn to the left down a steep hill. No sooner had we crested the hill than we began to skid.

"Oh-Holy-Mother-of-God," I gasped as I realized I was losing control of the car. "Max, hold onto something, baby, please."

The car began to skid sideways, and the next thing I knew we were turning over, going down, and my head hit something hard. The steering wheel, I think.

Three

Ben and Patty

By 10 a.m. both Patty and Ben knew they were lost. Lost in a way they had never experienced before.

"I never knew there was so much undeveloped land out this way. This place is a developer's dream."

"What's that mean, Daddy?"

"Well, it just means that there are people who would love to build lots of houses and stores out this way."

"Well, I like it the way it is, Daddy. It's pretty. Look Daddy, a hawk!"

"Where, Punkin?"

"Up there, circling, see?" Patty stabbed her finger toward a distant dot, which was circling the fields on an upper thermal air current. "He's looking for mice."

"Yeah, and I think we're beginning to look tasty to him."

"Daddy, hawks don't eat people."

"Well, I'm starting to feel like a mouse who's being toyed with by a cat."

"A cat, Daddy?"

"A cat named Fate."

"Oh."

Patty was familiar with the concept of Fate. Ben was a big believer in the forces of the universe. He was always talking about "the gods." Being a non-denominational semi-Buddhist Jewish

Taoist, Ben borrowed freely from the concepts of other cultures. "Whatever works" was his motto. He was an egalitarian, a pantheist, and a lover of life. Fate one day, God the next, and by the end of the week he was beseeching the aid of the Bodhisattva Kwan Yin, the goddess of compassion and mercy. Ben believed in everything.

By noon, Patty had fallen asleep in the back seat, granola wrappers scattered about her. Ben checked the gas gauge and began to do a serious review of all safety measures he might take. There was a flare and a spare in the trunk. The cell phone still refused to respond. The radio did not work. And there was not a home or roadside snack shop in sight. The whole situation was getting just plain eerie.

Sometime later Ben noticed that the clock in the car had stopped and the read-out on his cell phone no longer seemed to register. The snow had ended and the wind had died down. Time was impossible to tell in the dim gray light, but Ben had the distinct impression that the sun was going down. That was when his headlights glanced across the wooden sign swinging in the wind: THE DUKE'S ARSE, and then in smaller letters, "ALE HOUSE & INN."

"Oh, thank you, Buddha!" he muttered under his breath so as not to wake Patty, who was still snoring quietly in the back seat.

He turned down the country lane and noticed that the snow seemed a little less here and had even begun to melt as the wind died and the air warmed. Ben said a silent prayer of thanks, drove the Taurus down the gravel road and pulled into a large open area in front of a low log-cabin structure. Light was coming out of the windows and smoke from the chimney. It was the most heartwarming sight Ben had seen in years. There was a horse barn off to the side and not a single car in the parking lot.

Must be one of those new-wave B&Bs, he thought as he turned off the engine, put his scarf back on, and adjusted the ridiculous red-and-white hat Annie had made him wear. It was pointed like an elf cap, but the point fell over to one side so that the red fringe tassel, which hung from the point, drooped over his left ear and swung back and forth like a horse's tail switching flies. Still, Ben had to admit that it was warm, and he was suddenly glad for Annie's persistent practicality. He supposed he deserved a silly-looking hat after all this.

Gods, what would Annie think of his getting lost in his own town? Had she been trying to reach him on his cell? Was she worried? What time was it? The clouds were beginning to clear and Ben could see stars in the deep blue-violet sky. How had it gotten so late, he wondered. The air felt warmer here. The sounds of laughter and music drifted through the damp air, muffled by the sturdy wooden logs of the cabin itself. He straightened his hair quickly with his fingers and replaced his foolish hat. He found a stale breath mint in the glove compartment and braced himself for a new environment. He had literally—somehow—been driving all day and his legs were stiff as he began to stretch. He buttoned up his old sheepskin coat and got out of the car. He shut the door as quietly as possible, glad that Patty was still asleep.

He locked the door with his key and made sure the dashboard lights were out. Patty would be safe enough while he went inside, found out where they were, and used the phone.

The gravel crunched under his feet and the wood smoke from the fire smelled delicious. Hints of roasting meats carried on the air. Ben suddenly realized just how hungry he was. All he'd eaten had been a stale granola bar.

There was a single window to the left of the entrance. Ben noticed that the glass was primitive and full of bubbles, and that the mullions had been made from split, unpeeled saplings. It reminded him of the rustic "twig chairs" sold at L. L. Bean and Smith and Hawken.

"Everything old is new again," he mused as he leaned against the split-log door.

The heavy wooden door creaked as he opened it. He realized the sound-insulating qualities of thick logs as a burst of light and sound flew out the door and the night air whooshed in behind him.

Before him was the oddest spectacle he had ever encountered—

even when living on the Upper West Side.

The room was larger than he had imagined from the outside. There was no second floor in this main entrance area, and the low, sloped roof went up to a peaked ceiling that was braced by some of the most beautiful natural pine logs he had ever seen. Wooden wagon wheels had been turned into chandeliers and hung by chains from the struts. Wax had built up beneath each of the plump golden candles. A fire blazed in an oversized hearth built of river rock, and an iron rack with three spits full of roasting meats was being tended by a funny-looking little fellow wearing a brown tunic and hose.

After the room itself, the first thing that caught Ben's eyes was an enormous man in the middle of the room who had lifted a wriggling Gnome. There was simply no other way to describe him. He was about four feet tall, spidery, with long limbs and eerily long fingers. He wore a tunic similar to the spitboy's but in a shade of green that was closer to gray. He had on the same sort of hose as the spitboy, but this fellow wore gray leather shoes that turned up at the toes and curled back. On the tip of each was a bell, ringing in time to his shaking by the Giant.

As the Gnome began to speak, Ben noticed that his nose looked just like the one Lucille Ball, in his favorite episode, had made from putty and lit on fire in front of Bill Holden. He almost laughed out loud, but was too close to feeling that he was losing his mind already.

"I said put me down, yah great fat lump o' lard! Before I curse you and your stinking kin for eternity."

There was laughter from the gathered crowd, and cries of "Hear, hear!" and "Atta boy, Ferny!"

Ben pushed the door closed behind him as the people nearest reacted to the blast of cold air from the outside. A burly fellow with red hair and a tangled beard lowered his tankard, glanced at Ben's hat, raised his eyebrows, and muttered something to the barmaid sitting on his lap. She was a voluptuous blonde with the pointiest ears Ben had ever seen sticking out from beneath her muffin-shaped white cotton hat. She got up suddenly, gave a hasty curtsy in Ben's direction and said, "Evening, your Worship, what can I get you?"

"Uhm, I just wanted to use your phone."

Blank stares.

The barmaid curtsied again, reached for her circular wooden tray, which she had left on the table, and tried again.

"We've got ale, mead, or barley wine, your Worship," and she hastily added the honorific "Sir."

"Okay. How about an ale?" Ben ventured.

"Right away, your Worship, Sir."

The nervous barmaid made yet another curtsy, which afforded Ben an ample view of her shapely physique. He was instantly mollified and smiled sheepishly.

"Thanks."

The redhead leaned to the fellow on his right and then jerked his head toward Ben, who was still standing by the door. For a moment their eyes locked on Ben's red-and-white-striped hat. Then the new fellow got up and walked over to another group standing in a circle talking, and soon most of the room seemed to be staring at Ben, or more accurately, his hat. Soon the Giant had put down the Gnome, who broke the silence with his reedy little voice.

"A Sorcerer, in these parts? Where?"

The Giant raised an enormous arm and pointed straight at Ben.

Silence filled the room.

"Me? Oh. That's funny!" Ben laughed. "What? Do you do that to every new guy in town? Dress up in these costumes and pull pranks. Pretty good, I've got to say. Pretty damned good! I went to that Renaissance Fair once. You guys are as good or better. Really. Listen, my little girl is out in the car and I just want to use your phone. Okay?"

There was more dead silence.

The bartender wiped his hands on his stained apron and started walking toward the end of the long polished bar. Now that he noticed, the bartender, who was smoking a cigar, had two small curved horns on his forehead, and as he came around from behind the bar Ben saw that beneath the apron were two hairy thighs which ended in what, for lack of a better explanation, were goat's hooves.

Ben felt himself go momentarily dizzy. The bartender was a Satyr?

The bartender removed the soggy, chewed-on cigar from his goateed mouth and wiped his lips on the back of his hairy hand.

"Listen, friend, this is a peaceful place. We don't need any trouble. There hasn't been a Sorcerer in these parts for a long time. Barthas ate the last one and we haven't felt the need for another since. You want ale? We got ale. Now, Twyla tells me you ordered yourself some ale. Isn't that right, sweetheart?" he pinched the barmaid's bottom for emphasis.

Ben swallowed. Something was going on here that he didn't understand.

"Great," he heard himself say. "I love ale."

This seemed to be an acceptable answer, as almost every one began to nod at once and the tension gradually eased.

Ben sat at the bar, and after a moment someone began playing the fiddle. The barmaid plopped herself down on the barstool next to his.

He sipped his ale. It was richer, frothier and warmer than he was used to.

"You new around here?" Twyla asked with a shake of her blond tresses.

"Very," he answered truthfully.

"We get a few, every now and then." Her foot touched his, and stayed there. "So what's your specialty?"

"Pardon?" Ben felt himself growing warm and was sure he was blushing.

"I mean lightning, or water? Fire?"

"Sorry?"

"I mean you're a Sorcerer, right?" Twyla uncrossed her legs and sat forward in her chair. "That's why you're wearing the hat, right?"

"Oh there seems to be some misunderstanding about that.

I just wore this hat because my wife picked it out for me this morning." Ben nodded and smiled and hoped that explained the misunderstanding.

"Well, listen, honey, people don't take to that kind of joke around here. I mean either you're a Sorcerer, or you're not. And if you're not, and you're going around wearing a hat like that, Barthas is going to be having you for breakfast, and not as a guest, if you know what I mean. If you don't mind me giving you a little friendly advice, I would take off the hat, if you're not."

"Listen, I have to check on my little girl. She's asleep in the car," Ben said to excuse himself, and quickly stood up.

"You got a little girl? I should have known, handsome fellow like you, powerful, Sorcerer and all. Sure. Sure. You go check on your girl. I'll be here when you get back." Twyla, too, slipped off the barstool, though with movements of her hips and torso that Ben couldn't help noticing.

"No, no, it's not like that. She's a real little girl, a child. My daughter," he nodded.

"Don't you mean your niece, your Worship, sir?" Twyla winked knowingly.

Ben despaired of making himself understood and felt a pressing need to get out of this place, back to the car to check on Patty. "Listen, you've all been very nice. But if you haven't got a phone, I really had better be on my way. If I could just pay for this ale?"

"Two and ha'pence, your Worship."

Ben fumbled in his pockets and brought out two twenties, three quarters, a dime, and four pennies. He opened his hands to the barmaid, she sorted through the pile, ignoring the paper and biting firmly into each coin. Twyla settled on the dime and threw it to the Satyr, who also bit the dime and nodded.

"Let him go. He seems harmless enough."

"Come back and see us when you're famous, your Worship." Twyla smiled, and again Ben felt himself blush.

"Er, uhm, okay. And thanks. Really. Thanks."

"You're welcome, I'm sure," she curtsied.

Ben shouldered his way through the crowd, and was overwhelmed by the aroma of unwashed, deodorant-free bodies, roasting meat, and stale ale. He felt desperate to get out into the fresh air and take a reality check.

He burst through the heavy wooden door and into the chill, still night, invigorated by the bracing air, the sparkling stars, and the strange experience he had just been through. The Taurus was where he had left it. Thank the gods. He stood motionless for a minute and listened to the stillness.

"Let's just get Patty, and get the hell out of here, old boy," he said aloud. "Don't think about this too much 'til you get home."

The gravel crunched beneath his feet as he pulled the keyless lock from his pocket and pressed the button. Nothing happened. No light. No beeping alarm. Nothing. *Oh God, don't let the battery be dead*, he prayed.

As he approached the car, a faint glow came from the front seat. *I turned off the dashboard lights*, he thought, quickening his pace. Aloud he added, in the voice he used to reassure the kids whenever he was least confident himself, "I know I did."

The windows were fogged up from the inside. He put the key in the door lock and opened the door.

There, dangling her legs back and forth over the edge of the open glove compartment door, perched a diminutive glowing form dressed in yellow-green chiffon. On her back was a set of iridescent dragonfly wings. She was licking a tic-tac.

Unable to contain his astonishment, Ben spluttered, "Who the——? What in hell?"

And the little creature said with a tilt of her head, "Daddy?"

Four

Mombie

I woke up stiffer than I have ever felt. Oh, I know. You've heard that before. But this was like something out of a horror movie. My back ached. My knees ached. My neck was stiff. The joints of my fingers, even the vertebrae in my back, felt swollen. My teeth ached.

The sun hurt my eyes, which stung and felt drier than the desert. Something was poking me. No, actually something was pecking me. There it was again. I tried to sit up. What was I lying across? It was some sort of splintery dried old plank. God, I could hardly feel my tongue in my mouth, I was so parched. How long had I been lying here? There was that pecking again.

I managed to slit my swollen eyes open enough to see a blurred black form waggling back in forth in front of me.

"Caw!"

My eyes struggled to blink open. I tried to recoil and all I succeeded in doing was locking all my muscles. What was wrong with me? I felt as if I'd had flu for a week and mono on top of it. What had happened to all my aerobic training? Was this it? Is this how it is? You finally wake up one day and realize this is the menopause?

No, you idiot! You've been in a car accident. Where was Max?

"Caw!" the bird pecked me again. I think it was a raven, a black one. It took a great deal of concentration and effort for me to lever myself up on my right elbow.

29

I managed to sit up and look around. It seemed I was lying on the front seat of some kind of old-fashioned buggy or cart. I felt like death on a cracker.

That's when I looked down and realized I was naked, though that was not the terrifying part.

I was ancient.

I was wizened, parched, dried up, slack, drooped, drawn. My entire body had fallen, caved, wrinkled, slid, and just plain deteriorated into a nightmare, my nightmare.

I tried to blink but my eyes were too dry to tell if I had succeeded.

Where was Max?

I slowly forced my torso to turn. My hips cracked and popped, and my shoulders froze, but I finally managed to look behind me.

Lying in the middle of the cart, quietly sleeping next to a wicked-looking pike and a travel sack, was the most hideous and fearsome creature I had ever seen. Its body was covered in green scales. Along the top of its cranium protruded a row of wicked razor-edged red spikes. As it slept I could see a multitude of spiky teeth, which overlapped its lower gums the way a dog's canines sometimes do. The hands, or paws, had sharp claws, long enough to be considered talons. Curled between the creature's hind legs and laid across its belly was a scaly tail, which terminated in more of the red spikes like the ones on its head. It looked like the result of an iguana mated with a human.

What's more, it appeared to be sentient. It was dressed in a leather harness and peplum of green studded leather, like a gladiator, and was wearing a pouch on its belt.

If this thing had come upon Max, it may have decided I was too bony to eat and eaten him first. It was probably sleeping off its meal. "I'm too late," I moaned. "I've failed." *Oh, God,* something started to well up in me.... I forced it back down, telling myself, *Look, there is no blood on the cart. Stay calm. You are in no shape to fight.*

I looked down and saw a black sheet or tarp lying near the cart.

Slowly, carefully, I crept down off the seat of the buggy and made my way to the tarp. I wrapped it around myself and tied off the two loose ends in the front, like a sarong.

Grandma Moses in a black sarong. I must look like a roll of petrified sushi.

I was considering leaving the scene of the crime, but it occurred to me that if the creature hadn't eaten Max, it might know what had happened to him. So I decided to get hold of the creature's pike to fend it off while I asked some questions.

Yes, I know it sounds crazy. But the whole situation was crazy.

So I crept up on the slumbering lizard or demon thing and took its pike.

Some warrior. Ha!

"Caw," the raven said, as it hopped over to join me.

I poked the sleeping demon thing. Nothing. It mumbled. I poked it harder, this time with the point of the pike. The creature mumbled again and muttered something in its sleep.

I poked one more time, hard. Its eyes sprang open. It sat upright and screamed.

Yes, I said screamed, like a little girl.

"Hey, jeez, don't hurt me lady! I didn't do anything," it whined.

I narrowed my eyes and the raven hopped onto my shoulder. Seemingly, I had a friend in all this madness.

"What have you done with my son, you monster!" I accused.

"What are you talking about lady? I didn't do anything to anybody. I don't know where your kid is."

"He was with me this morning. When I got here. Wherever we are. His name is Max. He's thirteen and has red hair."

"I'm almost fourteen. And, hey, you are *not* my mom!"

I found myself lowering the pike and narrowing my eyes again.

"So ... what? You're one of those brain-eating lizard-demons who assume the identity of their last victim?"

"Lady, you need to take a serious chill pill and stop doing

whatever drug you're doing." His shoulders slumped and he cocked his hips.

"So how do you explain this?" I used the pike to point to his general physique.

He looked down at himself and apparently was surprised by what he found. "Bitchin'!" he breathed in awe, "Look at these claws, dude. I could, like, take on Wolverine. Serious!"

"Max?" I whispered, horrified, fascinated, and almost relieved.

"Mom?" he croaked.

I nodded.

"Mom, you look awful," he said quietly. "Seriously."

"People have been telling me that all day. I'm beginning to believe it."

"Where's Eddie?" the Max-thing asked.

"Caw!"

We looked into one another's eyes and you could have cut the air between us with a knife.

"Where the hell are we?" I asked no one in particular, as Max hopped deftly off the cart and ran—slithered—up the hill.

That's when I took a good look around. We seemed to be in some sort of a low-lying swampland. The cart had been left at the edge of a lagoon of sorts, and a series of hummocks dotted the way through a low mist-covered marsh. There was a hill in the distance and the sun seemed to be coming up over it. The snow was gone, too; we must have been out for the better part of a day. I looked for evidence of the hill we had driven down in the minivan but nothing seemed to correspond, not exactly, anyway.

I was sure we weren't in Kansas anymore.

Was Max right? Was this all a hallucination of mine? No, he seemed to see himself the way I did. Or at least he saw himself that way in my dream.

Then I began to get nervous and wondered again about the brain-eating, identity-assuming demon theory. The Max-thing ran over to the back of the cart again.

"Mom, where did you get that pointy thing on a stick?"

"It's a pike, Max." Now I was calling the thing "Max." "I think it also may be called a halberd. I got it out of the back of the cart. It was lying next to you."

"Right. So if that was my lacrosse stick, this must be my knapsack." He pointed to the rough burlap day sack. "I had lunch and granola bars in it."

He rummaged through the sack and found two rolls of parchment. "These must be my world history textbooks. Ugh, and I guess this is what ... whatever I am now thinks of as a granola bar." He pulled what looked like five limp, dead salamanders from the sack.

Max sniffed the drooping reptiles, and before I had time to say another word, a long forked tongue snaked out of his mouth and wrapped around one. He sucked it into his maw of razor-sharp teeth, snapped it in half and began to chew, dripping saliva and blood down his chin.

"Mmm, good. Want one?"

My mouth fell open.

"Uhm, no, thanks. I just want some water."

I reminded myself to remain calm, but I found myself adding, "That was disgusting, Max."

"Kewl."

I rolled my eyes.

"Hey Mom."

"Yes?"

"Ya know what this reminds me of?"

"*The Twilight Zone?*"

"Nah, that's old. This reminds me of one of those online games. You know, the kind where you sign in as an alternate personality, a Sim."

"I never played one of those, Max, but I can tell you right now that this does not feel like a 'Sim'. Every bone in my body hurts, and just standing up is an effort. I feel like I'm a hundred and ten."

"Yeah, well, you look like you're a hundred and thirty, Mom."

"Thanks Max. I needed that."

"Just being honest."

"Let's see if we can find our way out of here, and maybe get some fresh water. There has to be fresh water coming into this marsh from somewhere."

"I'm on it, Mom." He scampered off like some long-armed scaly nightmare. His arms were so long that his hands hung past his knees when he stood up. It—he—had bandy short back legs, which tended to bow slightly like a chimpanzee's. He walked as often on four legs as on two, often placing his two arms on the ground and swinging the remainder of his body between them. His tail dragged slightly on the ground and swished from side to side as he wriggled and twisted his body back and forth, alternating left and right just like a real lizard. His long arms kept his chest and torso angled up, even when he was "running" at quite a fast pace. With his forward-jutting jaw and his upward-sloped—thorax?—he reminded me of the hyenas I had seen charging an impala on a trip to Hwange Park in Zimbabwe. It was terrifying. In my present fragile condition I shuddered to think how fast I would cease to exist if this thing turned on me. Then I reminded myself, this "thing" was my son, Max.

I was in some serious trouble here. And I was not looking my best, to say the least. The wind blew my hair in my face. It was stark white, thin, and wiry.

The Max-thing snuffled around near the edge of the lagoon, dropped down on all fours and slid into the water. I heard some splashing and a duck flew out of the swamp, quacking.

"Max," I managed to croak. "Max, are you okay?"

There was more splashing and then silence. Then Max's green form rose at the edge of the water and began waddle-walking toward me. He had a wriggling fish in his mouth and was giving me the thumbs up sign with one claw.

He approached, bent over, and dropped the wriggling fish on the ground before me. In his left hand he had some sort of plant cup, like a Jack-in-the-pulpit, which he handed to me. It was filled with a small bit of water. I drank like a dying woman. It tasted like swamp, but at least it was wet.

"Thanks." I couldn't quite manage to call him "Honey."

"Sure thing, Mom."

The intonations were Max's, but the voice and appearance were alien and horrific. This was doing a number on my "Mom-ness." I shook myself from my reverie and handed him the cup.

"More," I said. "Please?"

He scrambled down to the lagoon several more times until I felt a little less parched. I needed to rearrange my sushi blanket wrap, so I slipped behind a briar bush, unwound the cloth and handed it to Max.

"Use your claws, Max," I instructed. "Tear or cut a hole there, right in the middle, where I marked it with the dust. I need a neck-hole, then I can wear it over my head and cover these lovely girlish shoulders."

Max laughed a sort of hissing chortle. Then he cut a hole as neat as any Exacto-knife. I was impressed. I slipped the cloth over my head. It hung to my ankles and blew in the breeze, but with a little searching we found some sturdy vines, which served as a stylish belt.

Now I looked like one of those homeless bag ladies from the City, dressed in black plastic lawn-and-leaf bags.

Max neatly cut up the fish and removed the scales and skin for me. So we ate sashimi. It wasn't bad, and I had to have something.

We agreed that I would use the pike as a walking stick, since I needed something to lean on. Eddie seemed content on my shoulder. Max took the burlap sack, tucked it into his harness ("radical," he called it) and ran ahead to scout the way. He would scamper back to me and report on the terrain ahead as Eddie and I stumbled along behind. Little by little we made our way over the hummocks, splashing back down into the marsh, my feet sticking in the sucking mud and peat. There were strange-looking amphibious things in the water, and we heard some hoots and howls in the distance as we walked. When we reached the end of the marsh and I felt my bare feet on the dry ground, I said a silent prayer of thanks to no one in particular.

Now that I looked again at the structure in the distance, I could see that it had a steeple. It had to be some sort of a church, and that was a good sign. A church would mean civilization and people. People might begin to give me some answers. I began formulating a plan. I'm no good without a framework—as always I needed something to hang onto.

"Look Max," I said aloud. "That looks like a church up there. Let's head toward that."

"Okay with me. You okay, Mom? You look kind of winded."

"Yes. Yes. I'm fine. I wish you would stop telling me how awful I look." I didn't feel fine. I felt like last week's fish dinner.

Max just raised his eyebrows, or brow ridges, and I think he tried to whistle, but apparently the arrangement of his teeth and lips made that impossible. Only a hissing sound came out.

It took us another fifteen minutes or so to reach the church. About fifty yards from it I began hearing faint voices.

"Max, I hear people."

"Well, I don't, but okay..."

The church was an old country affair, mostly river rock and timber. It was quite charming, really. It had a small steeple that was also a bell tower. The roof was covered in slate tiles, many of which were cracked or broken. I couldn't help thinking of what such a roof would cost today. The heavy oaken door hung at an angle and weeds were growing in the cracks on the front steps.

Max scampered up the steps and ran inside. Eddie flapped once and sailed off my shoulder in a clean arc toward the church. He flapped a few more times, gained altitude, and swooped into the building behind Max.

Max came out a short time later. "Nobody inside. There's leaves and stuff all over."

I stumped over with my pikestaff and made my way up the stairs. Oh, it was beautiful! The floor was inlaid in circular patterns of natural stone mosaic. The beams were stout and strutted the sharply peaked roof on the inside. Many of the lintel posts were carved into gargoyles and angels. Above the altar was a broken stained-glass window depicting what seemed to be the Earth Goddess, surrounded by a nimbus or a halo. I was drawn to the altar and transfixed by the charm of this little country church.

"Wel-come," a hollow papery voice whispered.

"Who said that?" I gasped and whirled about. Well, actually, I creakingly turned my body around and slowly surveyed all areas of the church in sequence.

"Mom?" said Max. "What's going on? What did you hear?" He was standing in the doorway, illuminated from behind. He looked like one of the carved gargoyles with the backlight on his gangly crested form.

"Uhm, I don't know. I heard a voice. Thought it was talking to me."

Max looked around. In fact, he scampered around the perimeter of the church, sniffing loudly. Good lord, he was fast! He was back beside me before I could think.

"Nope. There's no one but us. I can smell only us."

"You can smell all that?"

"Yeah, Mom, it's amazing. I can smell things like they were painted on and glowing. I could smell you and Eddie from outside."

"Interesting," I said, deciding not to worry about what I might smell like to his lizard-nose. Still, I couldn't help wondering where this transformation was leading my son. "Let's go outside, Max. I want to see what's out in the churchyard. I heard voices before."

"I'm telling you, Mom, I've been all over this place. I even went up on the roof. These claws are amazing. I can go right up the walls. There's nobody around here except us, and Eddie. Nobody. Not for days. I can smell it."

"Well, I heard voices."

His brow ridges came up again. He shrugged and cocked his hips.

Fast is one thing I was not, in this decrepit body, but as I rounded the stone exterior of the church I distinctly heard voices drifting in from the churchyard. I hurried along as fast as I could manage with my arthritic hips and knees. Max ran ahead and I heard Eddie flutter past me.

"Nothing but gravestones," yelled Max.

I hobbled up to the graveyard and Eddie landed gently on my shoulder.

A clamor of voices assailed me as I arrived, none distinct.

"Help me…"

"Halloo…"

"Mistress…"

"Who is that? Where are you?" I called.

The graveyard looked still. Eddie cawed. Max just looked at me. Then, at once, I heard a chorus of voices whisper, "Welcome."

"Where are you?" I asked. "Please show yourselves."

"Mom?" Max whispered.

With that the ground in front of one of the graves began to shiver and shake. Max and I both stood frozen in place as little clods of earth began to shake themselves free from the mound followed by more from below. Tufts of grass were soon thrown sideways and a small mound of soil accumulated. A filthy gray hand burst up from the soil.

"Holy crap in a hat!" whispered Max.

More soil tumbled. A head emerged with sparse patches of hair interspersed across a raw skull. We saw two shoulders of what looked like a Civil War uniform. And then it pulled free from the grave.

"Stay back, Max! Don't let it touch you."

"Misstresss…" the thing muttered between lips more parched and cracked than my own. One ankle was raw bone and the blue pant leg hid whatever else lay beneath. Its withered fragile hands stuck out from the arms of the uniform. It pulled a battered Union cap out of a jacket pocket and placed it on its head as it fell to one knee.

"Mom, I think it's waiting for you to do something."

"Uhm, you may rise?" I tried tentatively.

It rose.

This was creepy.

"Can you speak?" I asked.

"Speak to me. Misstresss, you called," it moaned.

"I did?" I sputtered. Then more firmly I added, "I did!" I tried to look in control. I waved Max over. "What do I do now?" I whispered.

"I don't know," he said in his snarkiest thirteen-going-on-thirty voice. "I don't even have my learner's permit, remember? Looks like he thinks you're in charge."

Several more of the graves began to shake and I heard voices crying out.

"Stop that now, all of you. I want there to be no more of this rising up right now." What the hell was I saying? Was I doing this? Was this some strange psychotic hallucination? I was calling up zombies?

The graves began shaking again. I heard moaning from several of the graves. Two more forms erupted from the quaking mounds, one in a Victorian bonnet and shredded hoop skirt, another in a barbarian's furs and horned helmet.

Both fell to their knees, muttering, "Misstresss..."

"Max, Max, what the hell is going on here?"

"I don't know, Mom. But, if you want my opinion, It looks like you've become some sort of Zombie Queen or something." He began that hissing snicker again. "My Mom, the Zombie Queen. Mombie! That's it! Mombie the Zombie Queen!" He fell over in hysterical laughter, thirteen-going-on-three, barking like a hyena and waving his tail.

Eddie cawed, flew up and circled the creatures twice, and hopped back on my shoulder.

This was turning into a very long day.

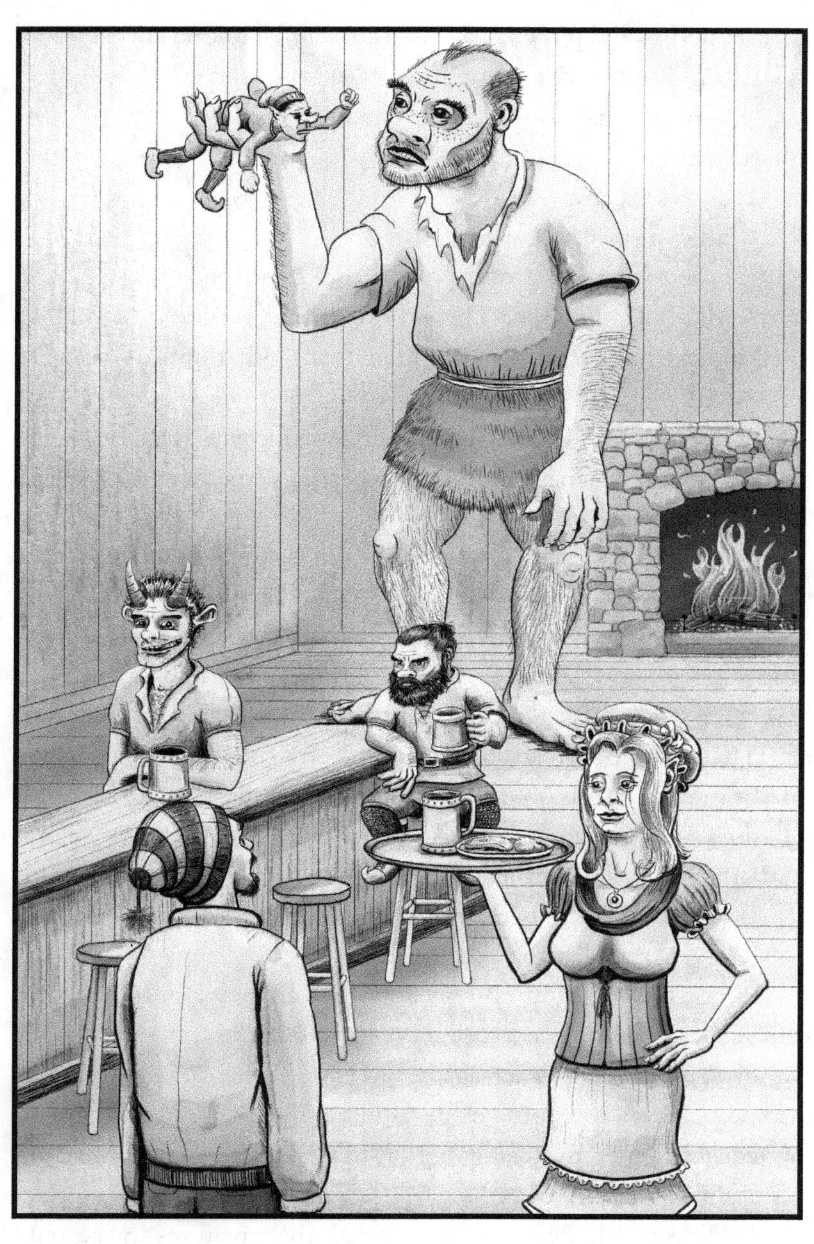

In the Duke's Arse

Five

The Duke's Arse

Ben sat down on the front seat of the Taurus and hung his head in his hands.

"Patty?" he asked. "Patty, what happened?"

"Well, gosh, Daddy, I don't know. I woke up in the back seat and everything looked big. Then I sat up and everything looked different. I mean I can see these colors now, and, and, and ... Daddy, you have all these colors coming out of you. Like a rainbow!

"And then I could feel my wings. Daddy, I have wings! I always wanted wings, Daddy. Really. I mean, I dream about it all the time. Only in my dream, I have wings like an angel, and these are more like a bug. But I'm not a bug, am I? I'm a Pixie, Daddy, a PIXIE!!" she screamed. Her wings started buzzing and she lifted into the air and flew around his head. "I am a Pixie!!!! Wheee!"

"This cannot be happening," Ben muttered. He took out the keys to the Taurus and tried them, knowing they would not work. He pounded on the dashboard. "NOoooo...!" he cried.

"Daddy? Are you freaking out?"

"Yes, Punkin. I am."

"Where have you been, Daddy?"

"I ... I went inside. It's an inn. I was looking for a phone."

"Did they have one?"

"Punkin, they don't even know what a phone is."

"Daddy, where are we?"

"Oh, Patrice, I only wish I knew. I'm a simple guy. This is all getting beyond my realm of experience."

"Can I see?"

"What? Oh, the inn? Hmmm.... Well, we will have to find somewhere to stay tonight, and it's getting late. I don't know, though. Maybe.... Well, I guess it would be okay."

"Daddy? Will you open the door? I want to try my wings."

"Patrice, listen to me. We're in a very strange place. There are some very strange people inside. I think I saw a Giant, and a Gnome at least, and—"

"A GIANT?!" she squealed. "Oh Daddy. This is so exciting! Can I talk to him?"

"Patty, I don't know who is our friend and who isn't. I need to contact your mother somehow. She must be terribly worried about us by now. I have no idea how long we've been gone. I want you to listen to me, and do as I tell you. Please, Patrice. Please?"

"Yes, Daddy. I promise."

"Patrice?"

"Yes, Daddy?"

"I love you very much."

"Me too you, Daddy." She whizzed through the air, then hovered like a hummingbird by the side of his face and gave him a peck on the cheek. "Oooh, look Daddy, I left a little glow spot, like when Mommy leaves a lipstick mark on your cheek."

He looked in the rearview mirror and there on his cheek was a tiny glowing dot.

"Cute. Okay, Punkin. You have a little fly around, but stay close to me. Then when we go inside, I want you to hide in my pocket and stay quiet no matter what happens. You understand?"

"Sure, Daddy."

She flew out the door and shot straight up into the night air, squealing and giggling with glee. "Wheeeee!" She turned loops, tried deadfalls, and flew slalom through the branches of a tree. "This is fun. Wait 'til Cynthia McGowan sees me! She's so jealous, she'll just die!"

She flew up to the peak of the roof and shouted. "Watch this, Daddy!" And she launched herself into an arc toward Ben, trailing a wake of sparkling colors that changed hue as she flew. "Wheee! Pixie Dust!"

Ben couldn't help smiling at her joy. Patty knew how to live in the moment. That had been her gift from the instant she had been born. He was so proud of her, even as a Pixie.

"Okay, Punkin. Into the pocket you go. We have to go inside and see if they'll give us a room for the night."

Without a word of complaint she flew straight for the pocket of his sheepskin coat, which he was holding open. Once inside he heard her muffled voice.

"Ooooph. It's smelly in here."

"Well, you won't have to stay in there long, sweetheart."

"Oh, Daddy, take the Tic Tacs. They tasted good."

Ben went back and grabbed the Tic Tacs from the glove compartment and the flare from the trunk. As he slammed the trunk shut, the front door fell off and all the tires wheezed and went flat. Something inside the car clunked and fell to the ground.

"Well, I guess that settles that."

"Yup," came a tiny voice from his pocket.

Ben threw back his shoulders and braced himself for the strange reality he knew he would find inside. The air had warmed and the stars looked bright and clear in the velvet night sky. He hadn't seen this many stars since he had been a child in the Massachusetts countryside.

The door to the Inn flew open and out came the burly redhead and his companions. They whistled shrilly and, in time, a sleepy, tousle-headed groom in a leather jerkin appeared with a lantern in the door of the horse barn.

"My gray stallion!" called the redhead.

"And our two bay geldings!" called the other two, who looked like brothers.

"Well, well, look here, brother. It's the Sorcerer. Out late tonight, your Worship? I think Twyla's looking for you."

"I've decided to stay the night," Ben replied, a bit stiffly. "And I need something to eat."

"The Duke's Arse is the best inn in the valley. Ask Twyla for something hearty, and mind they cut into a fresh loaf for you. Tell her Sylas said so."

"Uh, will do, Sylas, and thank you." He extended his hand, relaxing somewhat. "I'm Ben."

"Sir Ben, the Sorcerer, well, look at me, shaking hands with a Sorcerer. Fancy that."

"I ... uh ... yeah, fancy that!" Ben decided to drop the subject. "Well thanks again. Maybe I'll see you around, Sylas." He headed toward the door.

There was less of a crowd this time and Ben knew to head straight toward the bar. Twyla was wiping down tables and putting the stools on top so the floors could be mopped. A small group of Dwarves smoked long clay pipes by the fire, and the Giant seemed to be in deep discussion with the Gnome. The bartender was washing out some tankards while ashes fell from his cigar into the bucket of suds.

Twyla glanced up and smiled at Ben. "So are you famous, now, your Worship? You've come back."

"Well, no, honestly, but I was wondering if you might have a room for the night. My, car, uhm, wagon, seems to have broken, and I sure could use something to eat. Sylas said to tell you I need something hearty and to cut into a fresh loaf."

"Oh, did he? That old fox! We don't serve no stale bread here at the Arse. We're high-class, we are."

Ben paused. "I'd be more than willing to work for my room and board. I could chop wood or wash dishes or something."

Twyla laughed. "A Sorcerer? Washing dishes? Oh, go on with yourself!" She lifted the corner of her apron and wiped her wet hands on it, then walked toward the hearth, her hips swaying, shaking her head. She grabbed a large wooden platter., ripped a chunk of delicious-looking wholegrain bread from a large loaf, plopped it on the platter, and with a large carving knife sliced off several juicy hunks of fresh roasted pork.

"Set yourself down, your Worship. I'll bring you another ale. You hardly touched the last one so this one is on the house."

Ben sat at the rough-hewn table and she placed the platter before him. "Mmm, this looks delicious, thank you." Then he leaned over and whispered to his pocket. "Patty, you hungry?"

"Not for meat," came the tiny whispered reply.

"What have you there, your Worship? Some sort of magic talisman, I wager." Twyla sat herself down across from Ben, her ample bosom rosy from the heat of the fire. "You are a handsome and mysterious one, you are, with your dark eyes and that dashing goatee. I bet all the girls fall for you back in your village, they do. Now how about letting me have a look at what you've got in your pocket?" She leaned toward him and reached her hand toward his coat.

Ben leaned away, and said, "Really. It's nothing, its personal."

"Now which is it? Nothing or personal?" Twyla mocked him, and with a sudden quick move she tried to reach his pocket. Ben stood almost instantly to avoid her, but it was too late. Patty flew out fast as a dragonfly.

"I tried, Daddy. I really tried." She changed from pink to mauve and then rose again. "That lady tried to grab me, Daddy. Mommy wouldn't like that."

Ben stood still as stone. How could he undo this? How could he protect his little girl? She was so tiny and full of life. *Please*, he prayed, *let this resolve safely.*

He heard the Giant's voice rumble, "Oh, a pretty Pixie!"

The Dwarves all put down their pipes and stared at Patty. Just then the Cook came in from the kitchen, taking off her apron, and exclaimed, "Oh bless us all, it's a wee one!"

Patty flew to her father and landed on his shoulder and they all gathered around to stare.

"So that's your little girl," muttered Twyla sarcastically. "Huh."

The Cook, a tiny round figure about three-and-a-half feet high, seemed the most taken by Patty's presence. "Been a long time since we had a wee one in the Arse." Tears began to well up, and she pulled off her own cotton muffin cap and dabbed the corners of her eyes with it. "She's a beauty, she is. Come here, darling, Cook knows all about the wee folk. Cook grew up near the waterfall itself. Come and give your old Cook a cuddle, my little dear." She sat down at Ben's table and turned up her palms as an invitation to Patty.

Patty flew up from Ben's shoulder, once around the heads of the gathered crowd, and settled light as a feather in the upturned palm of the Cook's chubby hand.

"Ooooooo," murmured the various Dwarves, Giants, Gnomes, Humans, and Elves.

Patty took on a warm yellow glow and sat down cross-legged on the warm plump cushion of Cook's hand.

"Little darling," whispered Cook. "Twyla, go into the pantry and bring a crock of honey. Cook knows what Pixies eat, she does." She gently rocked her hand back and forth, cradling Patty like a baby bird fallen from a nest. "Oh, and look in my sewing kit. We'll need a thimble, and the salt spoon from the salt cellar." Then, turning back to Patty, she asked, "Now little Pixie, what is your name? You can call me Cook."

"I'm Patty. I'm going to be a Honey Bee. Only Daddy got lost, so we came here."

One of the Dwarves drew deep on his clay pipe and murmured gruffly, "That's some treasure you have there, your Worship. There are some folks around here as would pay a pretty price for such a rare jewel." He glanced at his fellow Dwarves.

Ben didn't like the way the Dwarf said that. There was something threatening about it. But just then, Twyla returned with the crock of honey, and set it with much aplomb on the table, affording Ben an ample view of her luscious curves. He coughed and looked down at Patty. From the pocket of her apron, Twyla drew a silver thimble and a tiny glass spoon. Cook took a healthy dollop of honey, plopped it into the thimble, and put the salt spoon next to it as she set it on the table next to Patty.

Patty walked over to the thimble, which was a large as a bucket to her now, dipped the spoon into it, and began eating sticky gobs of the golden syrup. At once she began to glow more brightly. It seemed to Ben that she was actually giving off pulses of light and color as she ate.

"Mmmmm!" Patty hummed.

The bartender took off his apron and came from behind the bar. He sauntered over to the group gathered around Ben and Patty's table.

The little Gnome piped in, "Blessed are the friends to the wee folk." He swept the gathering with his gaze, taking time to look deep into each of their eyes. "Not a word of this to anyone outside of the Arse. You hear me? Not a word. Or Barthas will be after the lass."

The bartender nodded, "Ferny's right. We're all agreed. Ain't we?" He pointed his soggy cigar at each of them until they nodded.

"Listen, mister, whatever your name is..."

"Ben, I'm Ben, Ben Prockner."

"Okay, Sir Ben of Prockner, you need to understand how things are here in the Valley." The gathered folk nodded.

The Giant began. "Barthas rules here now, along with his thugs. Says he was appointed by the Gods to lead. And, well, this little girl isn't safe in these parts anymore."

Cook nodded, wiping her eyes with her cap. "Poor little things. There used to be a time when the Valley was full of Pixies and Fairy Folk. Now Barthas has kidnapped so many of them, they rarely come out of the old wood. He and his thugs are cutting down more trees every day. Its bad times, I say, and I've been living in the Valley all my life."

Patty let out a tiny belch and curled up in the Cook's cap.

The Giant smiled at her.

A wind blew in as a cloaked figure slid out and pulled the door shut behind.

"Who was that, Porkchop?"

The Satyr answered, "That two-faced weasel, Pheek, the town clerk's toady. I forgot he was sitting in the other room. He must have been listening."

"Never mind him. This Sorcerer needs to eat, and this little Pixie needs to be put to bed. It's past her bedtime." Cook began cutting Ben's meat and feeding him.

"I can do that," Ben murmured and began feeding himself in earnest. "This really is delicious."

"Well, if you think that tastes good, wait till you get a bite of my pie for dessert." Cook thumped her ample breast for emphasis. "Twyla, upstairs, make up the front room for Sir Ben and his Pixie." And rising from the table, she added, "I'll get the pie."

Ben began to feel as if he were around friends, drawing in the warmth of the room and the company. The food was making him relax and feel stronger. He felt a surge of positive energy.

One of the Dwarves made a sudden grab for Patty and tossed her to his friends by the door. Patty screamed.

Ben jumped up from the table threw his arm forward and shouted, "NO!"

The beards of the three Dwarves burst into flames and they ran screaming out the door into the night, dropping Patty in the confusion. She flew to Ben.

"Daddy, you did it!"

"Patty, are you all right?"

"Sure Daddy, they just surprised me. I could have gotten away."

"Oh, Patty, I was so frightened for you."

"So you really are a Sorcerer, your Worship," said Twyla with some surprise, and her hands on her hips.

"I am?" asked Ben, finally ready—almost—to believe the barmaid. They all nodded.

"Those Dwarves won't be back anytime soon," added Ferny.

They all laughed and Ben began digging into his pie.

Six

A Visit to Miss Edna's

Pheek hurried along the lane back to town as fast as his little legs would carry him. He pulled his cloak tighter about him and stubbed his toe on a root. The moon was two-thirds full and high in the sky. He had time to get back to the Manor and tell Barthas that they were hiding a Pixie up at The Duke's Arse. There would be money in it for Pheek, and maybe a promotion. He rubbed his hands greedily. Barthas paid for Pixies with gold, and gold was a language that Pheek understood.

First he had to get to Barthas. At this time of the morning that would involve getting past his henchmen. The stockade fort they had built on the edge of the farm communities, ostensibly for "protection," was now referred to as "the Manor." Barthas was in the protection industry, and his deputies, not all of whom were men, were each more hideous and cruel than the next.

As Pheek arrived at the west gate of the stockade, he was brought to an office, which was actually an interrogation hut. Waiting for him was Barthas's right-hand woman, Blina Turdgirdle, a rough-hewn block of a woman who stood seven feet tall and was nearly as broad as she was high. Gossip said there was Troll blood in her veins, but she had a cruel intelligence that could only be Human.

"What would you be wanting at this time o' the morning, Freak?" she smirked, taking great pleasure in mispronouncing his name. Her hair was dyed a tawdry shade of red, and her expensive red silk robe had been hastily donned. A prominent hairy mole perched upon her mannish jaw, and a slash of ruby lipstick had been painted across her thin lips.

"I need to speak with Barthas about the location of a Pixie, Sir, er, Ma'am ... uhm, Lieutenant."

"And what would a little arse squirt like you know about a Pixie? Probably just had too much rum again and seeing lights in the night sky. Barthas has all the Pixies in the Valley!"

She glanced sideways at him and cinched her belt across her vast bulk.

"And an unregistered Sorce—"

He stopped. There was a hungry light in Blina's eyes at that. He had said too much.

"Tell me what you know, ink boy. You are just the clerk's toady. Tell Blina what you know ... and you will be rewarded," she added, trying to sound enticing.

Pheek stood his ground. "I bargain with no one but Barthas himself."

"Oh, so now you are bargaining, are you?" She smiled, and the effect was chilling. "Listen to me, you little weasel, I wipe my crack with lackeys like you. So if I bring you to Barthas and you make one wrong move, it's over for you. Understand?"

Pheek stood frozen where he was.

"Understand, arse squirt?"

Pheek nodded.

Blina picked him up by the scruff of his neck and carried him like a sack of potatoes across the dusty interior of the stockade to the largest building in the fort, a two-story affair with an upper balcony: "The Manor," Barthas's home.

Blina stopped briefly to speak to another of Barthas's lieutenants, Keivitch Krakower, a full-blooded Rock Troll who towered above Blina and wore heavily spiked leather armor. Keivitch carried a brutal morning star with an iron star the size of Pheek's head hanging from each of the chains. The spikes were the length of

Pheek's hands and sharpened to razor points. Keivitch spoke little of the common tongue and tended to lapse into the guttural grunts of Troll language.

While Blina spoke to Keivitch, she slung Pheek over her shoulder like a forgotten parcel. He hung there trying not to touch the hair on her neck.

Finally Keivitch grunted, "Phim too. Me Hogsha Tunk." He nodded at Blina and followed, poking at Pheek as Blina dragged him up the stairs behind her back, his feet bumping along the steps as he hung from Blina's grasp.

"Blunka Pheek!" Keivitch laughed as he poked Pheek. To demonstrate what he could do, he smashed his morning star into the log exterior of the Manor. It chewed a massive chunk from the solid wooden steps, leaving a mark like a giant beaver gnaw.

"Blunka Pheek!" He laughed again.

Pheek nodded and tried to smile to show that he understood the big man's joke. He tried to close his nostrils from the stench of unwashed body and rotten-meat breath.

At the top of the staircase Blina threw open the double doors to Barthas's "audience room." Barthas sat in the middle of the room like an enormous dollop of snoring lard, propped on a huge wooden throne constructed to support his bulk. A groaning buffet in front of the dais was covered with half-hacked carcasses of roasted fowl, pork, and what else Pheek cared not to know. Some of it had fingers.

Blina threw him onto the floor in front of the table.

"Talk, Freak!"

Pheek climbed onto his knees. "If you please, my Lord, I may have some information that will interest you."

"He knows where a Pixie is," Blina spat out.

Barthas looked directly at him. Now that Pheek's eyes were beginning to adjust to the light he could see that Barthas easily tipped the scales at a ton. Even lying down he was the biggest man or beast that Pheek had ever seen. Vast folds of greasy flesh rolled down his sides and dripped with oily sweat. Pheek felt himself growing nauseous in the close air of the room. Barthas stood up, and with a great, sucking, vacuum sound his flesh pulled free of the gargantuan throne and hung like suet pudding from his massive frame. Easily ten feet tall, he dwarfed his lieutenants. His face and back were covered in oily boils, and he wore a great bear-hide covering over one shoulder. Pheek noticed that the ground around him was littered with meat scraps and bones. Barthas had a Pixie in a cage hung by his throne. She was the most desolate little creature Pheek had ever seen, drained of her glow and sitting cross-legged in a corner of the birdcage they had used to imprison her.

Pheek gulped.

"I was hoping, your Lordship, that there might be some monetary recompense for my information."

"Monetary what?!" Barthas bellowed, spewing meat chunks all over Pheek. "Listen to me, little rat man, tell me where that Pixie is NOW, or I'll squash you like a flea!"

"In the Duke's Arse," he found himself blurting.

"And what else?" asked Barthas, leaning forward and towering over Pheek. "Sideous, get out here," he called. Barthas clapped his hands and an ordinary-looking mortal man, dressed in a long black robe and a cone-shaped red-and-white striped hat, stepped from behind the throne.

"Zap him," snapped Barthas.

Crackling bands of lightning arced out from the Sorcerer's hands and completed their circuit within Pheek's body. Pheek felt every muscle in his frame stiffen as his spine arched, and he howled for mercy.

"Again," Barthas demanded.

"NO! Please. That's enough. Have mercy on me, please. I'll tell you everything I know."

And he did.

By the time Pheek had finished spilling his guts about seeing Ben in the Duke's Arse, Barthas had called his other two lieutenants:

Shadow Stalker, a Swamp Demon, a creature with razor sharp claws and superhuman dexterity, and Irene, a blind seer. Irene was a frail middle-aged woman who had enormous precognitive ability. Barthas relied on her magic visions to safekeep his plans. Like many bullies, he was both superstitious and paranoid, and he kept Irene close to him at all times. He trusted her. She was his pet, his ace in the hole.

Barthas quickly told them that a new Pixie had been seen up at the old Inn in the company of a man claiming to be a Sorcerer. They were unguarded and seemingly untried in their abilities. Object: get the Pixie, and take the Sorcerer into custody, dead or alive. It was agreed that Blina would head the salvage mission and Shadow Stalker would second her, leading a battalion of thirty men on foot and five mounted.

Irene drew the curtains across the crude window in the audience hall and lit a fire in a bronze brazier. She placed a thin gauze veil over her head and began adding powders to the burning embers. A fragrance of musty roses and old blood filled the room. She rang a small brass bell three times and sat cross-legged on a woven carpet in front of the brazier. Fragrant smoke began to fill the room.

She moaned, then shivered all over as if with ague, and began to rock back and forth.

"I see the child creature. She is very bright. Her flame burns strong. The Sorcerer is tied to her by fate and blood. He is untried, unsure, and must be captured before he realizes his potential."

She paused and rocked back and forth. "There is more. A Swamp Demon who travels with someone shrouded in mist. There is great power in this unseen one, but she is closed to my vision. I feel death about her. There is the smell of the grave. She is..."

Irene slumped and slid unconscious to the floor.

"Itka venk?" asked Keivitch. He scratched his lumpy oversized head and looked puzzled.

"Get her up," snapped Barthas to no one in particular. "Where is this unseen one? This woman of power?"

Shadow Stalker delicately unsheathed one of his talons and

prodded Irene. She sat up with a start. "Danger," she mumbled.

"Danger? Where?" demanded Barthas.

Irene shook her head. "So much is unclear, my Lord. The woman is hidden from me, but I sense great danger in her. Danger for you, my Lord."

"Make it clear, seer. Make it clear," Barthas snarled.

"I must rest, my Lord."

"The rest of you. Out of here. I want that Pixie in my cages by sundown. It is already mid-morning. Now go!" Barthas leaned over his table of meats and began eating again. Pheek thought he was going to be sick.

"What about Freak?" Blina pointed to Pheek.

"Take him with you, and if any of this is a lie, bring him back to me, for dinner. Aha, ha, ha, ha!" Barthas's belly shook up and down in gelatinous laughter.

Pheek was beginning to think that he wasn't going to get any gold.

By noon, the salvage party had been organized, supplies had been gathered, and the horses had been saddled. Blina was wearing a shiny steel breastplate like a hideous, big-breasted, brawny Valkyrie. Her bullwhip hung on her hip, a broadsword was sheathed at her back, and her garish red hair hung in braids from beneath a horned steel helmet. A fresh coat of lipstick had been drawn across her lips. She sat astride an enormous gelding, also clad in armor. Five mounted riders joined her at the front of the entourage while a large covered wagon carried the thirty swordsmen behind.

Shadow Stalker wore a leather harness crisscrossed with throwing knives and hurling stars. A short sword nestled in an ankle sheath strapped to his leg. He ran ahead of the party like a scaly whisper of death.

Pheek hung trussed over the back of Blina's gelding as they set off on the road to the Inn.

Things were going from bad to worse.

Ben woke up feeling refreshed, recharged in fact, raring to go. Patty snored softly on the down-filled silk pillow Cook had placed on the bedside table. The bed was a rustic affair, a hay-filled sack mattress on a simple wooden frame strung with rope. Still, he had slept better than he had in years. The dinner had been superb and Cook's pie was better than his Grandmother Mabel's. Ben smiled. They seemed like nice people here. If only he could get some word to Annie, to let her know he and Patty were all right. He sighed and began to rise from the bed. Early dawn light came through the small dormer window in his room. There was a knock at the door.

"Come in," he said.

Twyla stepped in and curtsied. "Good morning, your Worship." She carried a tray loaded with sausages, bread, cheese, and a tankard of ale. "Cook sent up breakfast. She says you need to get ready. They are taking you to see Miss Edna today."

"Who is Miss Edna?"

"A Witch."

A nanosecond passed, then Ben caught his breath. "I see." He was learning to take things as they came and not ask too many questions.

There was a smaller tray within the first, filled with honey and a pot of homemade strawberry jam for Patty. Twyla set it on the table next to the pillow.

"That's some noise your Pixie makes," said Twyla.

"Yeah, she has a little problem with her sinuses. Has had, since the winter began. Her mother bought a vaporizer but I don't think it's done any good."

Twyla looked at Ben with complete incomprehension, gathered the empty tray and took her leave, adding from the doorway, "Hurry down as soon as you have eaten and dressed, your Worship. Ferny and Planks will take you to Miss Edna's cottage."

By the time Ben got downstairs the Inn was bustling with morning preparations. Their party gathered in the kitchen, and Ben sat on a bench before the fire, Patty perched on his shoulder. Ferny the Gnome was there, as was Planks the Giant. Porkchop, the Satyr, was shoveling down a plate of sausage and eggs and chugging some wine. He wiped his mouth on his sleeve and gestured for Ben to help himself.

"Thanks, no. Cook was kind enough to send up a tray. I ate. It was delicious. Thank you, Cook."

Cook nodded and winked at Ben.

Porkchop said, "Sylas is coming with his brothers. I figure we could use the extra guard. Safety in numbers and all that; no telling what is lurking in the wood these days."

Ben nodded. "Can you tell me more about this Miss Edna?"

"Local Hearth Witch," said Cook. "Quite talented really. A relative newcomer to the Valley like yourself, Sir Ben."

"I see," replied Ben, although, in truth, he did not.

"Do you ride?" asked Porkchop.

"Not well, I am afraid."

"We'll put you on the back of Ferny's pony. All right with you, Fern?"

"Sunshine can take the weight. She's a sturdy girl," Ferny replied in his reedy voice.

After breakfast they all gathered outside in what Ben had thought of as the parking lot when he had pulled in last night. What remained of the Taurus was an unfathomable pile of broken, twisted metal parts. Rust had already claimed most of the edges.

"My, uh, 'wagon'," he explained.

Porkchop nodded, and they followed him into the barn. The young groom, whose pointy ears made him look a bit like Twyla, had saddled Sunshine and brought her out of her stall. Porkchop, pointing to his goat legs and hooves, said he would feel more comfortable trotting along beside the party. Planks, whose long legs covered three of Ben's steps in a single stride, would walk as well. Twyla took a dappled mare, because she knew the way. And it was agreed that Ben would test his prowess with a gentle black mare by the name of Bella, who had big brown eyes and feathered fetlocks. If he had trouble he could ride back behind Ferny and they would use Bella as a packhorse.

Sylas and his brothers arrived. Willem and Jon were both solid-shouldered and full-bearded, armed with longbows and knives.

Cook waddled out with a basket for the trip. "Don't forget to leave the raisin cookies for Miss Edna, and tell her to stop by when she has time." She wiped her hands on her apron and added, "Now Patty dear, come and give old Cook a kiss. Mind you do as Miss Edna says and keep an eye on Sir Ben."

Patty, who had been unusually quiet until now, flew to kiss Cook's cheek. "Thank you for the honey this morning. Mom says its bad manners to forget to say thank you. Don't worry. I'll watch Daddy. These horses are beautiful. Daddy, when we get back can I have a horse? Or maybe a pony, like Ferny's?"

"Punkin, if we get back, when we get back, I'll buy you a stable-full."

"Daddy, now you're being silly."

Ben couldn't help but smile.

It took a while to adjust to the rhythm of the mare, but Bella was calm and seemed to know where she was going, so Ben allowed her to guide them while he simply sat astride. Patty flew back and forth between his shoulders and those of Planks: she liked the view she got from the Giant's shoulder. Ben had to admit that this was a beautiful place. They stopped by a stream to water the horses, and he dismounted to walk around a bit.

The Valley was further along in the seasons than home. It was early spring here, and while the leaves had not opened, the trees were beginning to show a haze of green and red buds. Fruit trees were starting to bloom, and the air was rich with pollen.

Patty flew to Ben and they walked amid the flowering apple trees. She hovered among the blossoms and leaned forward to taste the pollen on the stamens.

"Mmm, Daddy, it's sweet! I like it. Mommy said that Jeanie

Callow's mom takes bee pollen. Mom said she's a Health Freak." She flew from blossom to blossom until her tiny impish face was covered in yellow powder. "Yum, Daddy, look, I'm a Honey Bee!!"

"The best Honey Bee ever, Punkin."

Planks walked over and smiled down at the two of them. He carried a large wood-and-steel hammer on his belt. "Porkchop says it's time to go," he rumbled.

The journey was uneventful, and aside from his feelings of guilt toward Annie, Ben had to admit that he was truly enjoying himself. Dandelions were springing up in the meadows, and all manner of weed and flower had grown green and lush. Birdsong filled the air and squirrels chased one another through the trees, eating flower buds and moving like gymnasts in competition. Patty flew merrily along, chattering ceaselessly while Planks nodded and smiled in agreement.

Once they saw a hawk, and Ben reminded Patty that hawks eat small birds and flying things, so she hid in his pocket until the danger had passed. Before long they came to a quaint thatched cottage along a riverbank.

A picket fence surrounded a vegetable garden in the front where a scarecrow stood guard. A stout black woman with iron-gray hair wrapped in a red bandanna was tilling the soil with a three-fingered cultivating hoe on a long handle.

Planks yelled, "Ahoy, Miss Edna!"

The woman stood up and stretched, leaning on her hoe. She shielded her eyes from the sun with one hand and squinted toward them.

"I can see you, Planks Longshanks, but who's that you have with you?" she called.

"Porkchop and Ferny. And Twyla has come. She has cookies for you from Cook. Sylas FairHaven and his brothers are here, and some newcomers."

"Well, well," clucked Miss Edna. "Well. I guess we'd best go inside."

"Oh, don't let us interrupt you, Ma'am," said Ben as they approached. "We wouldn't want to stop your work."

"You won't stop me, mister, nothing stops Miss Edna from her chores." And with that, she let go of the hoe and it continued tilling carefully around the roots of the neatly planted onions and cabbages.

"Why don't we just step on inside?" Miss Edna gestured broadly and motioned them all in with a smile.

"Come on up here, honey child!" Miss Edna called, and Patty flew to her side. "Been a right long time since I had myself the pleasure of taking tea with a Pixie. Now you just make yourselves at home in Miss Edna's house."

They followed her up the steps to a wide porch covered with pots of every description sprouting fresh spring growth. The front door squeaked open on its own, and they entered a cozy living area with attached kitchen. There was a loft with a sturdy railing and a set of rough steps. An unattended broom was busily sweeping its way down the steps.

"That's enough for today, Jeeves." The broom danced over to a corner and stood still, leaning its head against a wall. A cupboard door flew open, and seven cups flew out and arrayed themselves neatly on the table. Kindling piled itself in a stone grate over a heap of dry tinder. Miss Edna turned to Ben and asked, "Would you do the honors?"

Ben understood, after the incident in the Inn last night, but replied, "I'm pretty new at this..."

"Oh, you ought to be pretty well charged up after this morning's ride. Give it a shot."

Ben concentrated. He tried to remember how it had felt last night when he had lit the Dwarves' beards on fire. Hot. Angry! And then he just let go and flung his emotions toward the pile of kindling. Instantly the flames roared up the wood.

"Whoa, there hotshot, we don't need a bonfire. I just want to make tea."

"Uh sorry. I need to work on that," Ben said with embarrassment.

Edna hung a large copper kettle on an iron swing rod over the fire. "So," she asked, "What can I do for you folks?"

Cook was in the kitchen, sliding the last of the day's meat pies into her large stone-and-mortar oven. She had just opened the iron grate below the oven and slid in a few more pieces of kindling when the small warning spell she had set on the front door went off.

She had just enough time to put her finger to her lips and send her kitchen girl running for the back orchard when Blina burst into the room.

"Where's that Pixie?" the mountain of woman bellowed as she cracked her whip, reducing Cook's best crockery to shards.

"What Pixie, uhm ... Ma'am?" asked Cook innocently.

"Don't play stupid with me, Stupid. I can play that game, too." Blina paused momentarily, not quite sure what she had just said.

"As you say, Ma'am," replied Cook with a curtsy.

A strange green scaly creature in a leather harness slid into the room. "Doess she have the Pixie?" it asked. "Why are you wasting time? Interrogate her. I will search the premisssesss."

"A Swamp Demon!" Cook muttered, making a sign against the evil eye.

"Mind your mouth and manners, Halfling, or we'll let Shadow Stalker sharpen his claws in your flesh," growled Blina.

"Oh, saints preserve us, Lady of the Heavens protect me!" Cook made the sign again.

The Swamp Demon came slithering down the stairs from the guest rooms. "He'sss been here. There isss Pixie Dust in the room but not fresh enough, maybe a day old. I can track them. Send me after them. I will catch the Pixie."

"Yah filthy beast, keep your hands off that precious child!" spat Cook.

Shadow backhanded her with the edge of one scaled claw, and a jagged scrape appeared on Cook's cheek. She fell to the ground.

"I curse you, demon spawn," she cried out defiantly, and as he passed she reached out for his ankle.

"Do not touch me, little woman. I despise you and your kind." Sullenly but urgently he indicated to Blina that it was time to track the Pixie.

Blina took a piece of parchment from inside her armor and tore off a bit. Her nails had been painted to match her lipstick. She raised the parchment to her lips and pressed a thin blood-red imprint, a kiss, into the vellum. Then she placed it on Cook's kitchen sideboard, took a vicious-looking dagger and pinned it deeply into the wood.

"You tell them Blina Turdgirdle was here. And I want that PIXIE!"

It was long after she'd heard the last horse's hooves leave the Inn that Cook actually began trembling. Her sobs began sometime after that.

Seven

Dendra Mossy

When Max stopped laughing, we determined that I could be nowhere near the graveyard without involuntarily raising Zombies. As it was, the mounds shook when I was within fifteen feet. The Zombies already raised (we had decided to call them Johnny, Klug and Bernice) showed me that I had their undying devotion. I couldn't get rid of them so I put them to work. It really wasn't all that different from having kids; some days it was either kill them or make them be useful.

We found a bucket and patched the holes in it, sent Johnny down to the marsh to get water, and set up a temporary camp of sorts in the old church. Bernice was good at gathering plants and herbs, when she wasn't breaking off bits of herself, and Max had no trouble catching rabbits and other small game. At first he was a little put off by killing the bunnies, but once he got down the techniques of skinning and boning I had my own gourmet grocery supply on demand. We even had pheasant one night (apparently they are quite slow, but they have lovely feathers and we saved some to adorn my sushi wrap). Bernice found some lovely roots, a sort of a wild parsnip, which we roasted to go with the pheasant. I had hunted up some flints, and with the aid of some dry grass I was generally able to spark up a fire.

All in all, things settled down to a somewhat domestic rhythm as we set up camp in the old church and swept out the leaves and debris with homemade brooms.

Living with Zombies was not as gruesome as you may imagine. This bunch were pretty old and most of the smell of rot had dissipated years ago. The worst of them was Klug, who smelled mostly of mildew. He was also strong, though he was pretty badly damaged by the passage of time, and he tended to walk into walls and trip over his own fur-clad feet. Mostly we made him just stay out of the way, unless we needed a strong arm.

Max tended to stay upwind from the Zombies. His sense of smell was far too keen for him to enjoy long periods of exposure to petrified flesh. I on the other hand had become less sensitive, as an elderly person. I think that both my hearing and my sense of smell had begun to fail. I had thought that menopause was the worst, but take it from me, old age is a whole other battle.

The least pleasant thing about being around Zombies was the way they tended to lose pieces of themselves. Small pieces of skin falling or tearing off was common. All of them had bare patches of bone and tendon showing. Less common but still frequent was the loss of teeth and articles of clothing. Klug even lost a hand once: he had been helping Johnny with the marsh bucket, and an entire hand had just come off. Max fashioned a pin out of a sharpened sapling and we awkwardly pinned it back in place. It took some stroking and concentration on my part to get it working again, but slowly I got a clear sense of the connective magic involved. I had also begun to realize that I had developed a telepathic relationship with each of the Zombies, and could control them even from a significant distance. It took only a thought to call them back to me or send them in a different direction. In a sense I felt myself infusing them with my needs or wants.

That, too, was not unlike being a mother. You had to be caring about someone else's actions all the time.

I mostly stayed in the church, to avoid the graveyard and to have some shelter when it rained or was cold at night. The worst part about staying in there was Sir Anthony. He was the fellow who had welcomed me the day we had arrived. He was buried in the crypt, under the main altar, and was constantly imploring me to let him out. It seemed that my mere presence woke the dead.

We never let poor Sir Anthony out, as that would have involved moving some extremely heavy stone slabs, and frankly I didn't know what to do with the three Zombies I already had.

Max kept telling me that being a Zombie Master, or Necromancer as he liked to call it, was incredibly good luck. All about how I could raise an army of the dead and how most Necromancers had to go through rituals involving incense, bells, candles and spell books, and even then they could raise only one Zombie at a time, which sometimes fell back into death soon thereafter.

Well, not only did I not need spells or rituals, I seemingly could not turn my necromancy off. What in the world I was going to do with an army of the dead, God only knew. Or as Ben would have said, "Goddess only knows."

I was more concerned with how to hold on to what was left of my family. I found myself thinking of Ben and Patty all the time. Safe at home, probably, wondering where in the world Max and I were. Patty would be registered at Honey Bees by now and Ben must have the police looking for me. I wondered if they had found the car. Then I wondered if that old wooden cart had been the minivan. Max believed in something he referred to as "translation of matter." Which is what he believed had happened to both of us, and his backpack.

Max said little about the "why" of it all, except to say that he missed Patty. He took to this new body all too easily, and began roaming further afield during the nights. His night vision was incredible and his slit pupils led me to believe that whatever he was tended to be nocturnal in its natural environment.

One morning, as I woke, Max told me all about the layout of the surrounding area. He said that there were several farms within a day's walking distance from the church. So we decided to risk exposure.

I went over the plan with Max again and again. "Remember," I said, "they may not be human. You aren't anymore." I paused, choking back tears that would not come. "But I look so old they may take pity on us. We'll just ask for a place to stay at first. Maybe request some odd jobs. Okay?"

Max nodded. I could tell my remark about him no longer being human had hit home.

"Mom ... Do you still love me?" Max was clearly shaken. "I mean even like this?"

"Maxwell Alexander Prockner, you will always be my son." I pressed his hand—claw—whatever—to my flattened chest, and kissed his scaly cheek. "Yes. I love you like this."

He nodded and we set out slowly down the road followed haltingly by the three Zombies.

It was a scene out of a cult film. All we needed was a petrified cowardly lion.

Still, in time we came to the first farmhouse. I had Max wait in the bushes with the Zombies, and Eddie and I went first as the parlay team.

The couple who answered the door looked pretty scared to have visitors, but I, as a hundred-and-ten-year-old gal (please don't let it be more), put up a pretty benign appearance. So they listened politely. I went through my spiel; I was travelling with my son and a few friends and we were looking for food and lodging in return for work. I had Max and the Zombies wave from the distant bushes.

Amazingly, at this point all I had to do was think toward the Zombies for them to wave.

The farm couple was nice, if rather small for Humans, at four-foot-six or so, but insisted that they were retired and no longer farmed their land, and they repeated again and again, "We PAID our taxes to Barthas and don't want no trouble!" I began to wonder who Barthas was. By the time a taller, more human-looking couple in the next farmhouse had repeated almost the identical words, I really began to get curious about this Barthas.

We decided to take a little break for lunch, as I had begged a bit of bread from the elderly hobbits, or whatever they were, and the idea of real rabbit-and-herb sandwiches sent a shiver of anticipation up my spine. So over sandwiches I told Max what the locals had said to me.

He chewed on his rabbit sandwich and said, "Mom, this sounds like one of those dictatorships we learned about. You know, like Cuba, or Zimbabwe, or one of them places you told me about."

"Those," I corrected.

"Those. Whatever," Max said.

"This bread tastes like heaven to me. It has been so long since I've had a piece of bread."

"Yeah," Max said, "I was thinking that it was going to taste great, but now that I've had it, it tastes dry and flowery."

"Floury?" I asked. "Like flour?"

"No, really, more like flowers. That's how vegetables taste to me, now, too. Anything that's not meat, and I'm getting to like the meat better before we cook it. I've been sneaking little bits before. When I cut it up for you, Mom."

"I see," was all I said. And then again, after a moment, "I see."

Really, I didn't see at all. My son was becoming more and more comfortable and in tune with his previously alien body. He had begun to move more like a reptile, to eat more like one, and now I had to wonder if he would begin to think like one, if I didn't do something soon. But what was I to do? How does one undo a transformation?

So I got myself up, and we wandered on to the next farmhouse where I found as pleasant a pair of Gnomes as I could have hoped for. They were stick-thin little figures with enormous stringbean noses and little shoes that turned up at the toes and had bells sewn on. They tinkled a bit as they showed me about the place.

I expounded the capabilities of my "adopted son" and companions and assured them that we would be up to the task of painting some barn walls, rounding up the goats from the hill and various other chores they bartered in return for a country home dinner and the right to sleep in their barn.

Of course it was another thing when the actual crew showed

up and turned out to be a swamp creature and three Zombies. But I managed to keep smiling, and Max did an amazing job of climbing the barn walls, hanging from the gutters and painting the entire side without a ladder, while I stood with Mrs. Mossy the Gnome and mentally directed Johnny, Bernice and Klug to run among the goats and corral them on the hillside. Oh, sure, there were limbs falling off and bits of Zombie flesh everywhere, but, by gum, I got them down the hill and into the barn and managed to chat up Mrs. Mossy, Dendra by first name, about the situation in the town with Barthas.

"Oh, that Barthas is an evil one," she began (once she had determined that I really and truly was not on Barthas's side—and was not in some way going to extract "taxes" from them again). "He took near all the magic folk from the Valley, and locked them up. Made them work for him, he did."

I smiled and concentrated on Bernice, who was about to take a fall over a small kid. (No use ruining our chance for a good, hearty, home-cooked dinner). "Now when you say magic folk you mean...."

She took my hint and nodded her pointy nose toward me. "You know, Elves, Centaurs, Pixies, Mermaids, Tree Nymphs...."

I nodded. It was my turn to be flabbergasted and try to keep a straight face.

"Right," I said, continuing to nod. And then, "Mermaids for sure," and I nodded again for emphasis.

She smiled sadly and shrugged, as much as if to say, "What can anyone do?"

So I asked, "And were there a lot of them? The magic folk, that is? Before, I mean?"

"Why, dear me, yes. That's what this Valley, the Painted Valley, has always been known for. Used to be that the rivers were full of the Merfolk and the woods just sparkled with Pixies." She paused a bit and sighed. Then she regained herself. She drew herself up and said, "You know, I'm sure that you must have heard rumors about us, the Gnomes, and the Elven Folk, but you know, I have personally never had a spot of trouble, and have always found them polite. Respectful even."

Sensing my cue, I dared the use of her first name and cut in with, "How do you mean, Dendra?"

She nodded and smiled. I knew I was on safe ground.

"Well," she began, "not three years back, before Barthas had come, we had trouble with our well pump. And there was a band of Elven Folk passing through, camping in our meadow. Stealthy as badgers, you know," she said winking at me. "Dressed in forest greens and browns, they were, and looking like the very shadows of the trees as they crossed my meadow in the morning light. They were armed with yew-wood bows and one was carrying a brace of coneys. I wouldn't have noticed 'cept that I was hanging the wash. Instead of walking they looked like they whispered across the earth, like their feet didn't touch the ground. While we poor slobs work the earth, as it were, stepping through goat crap and drinking from a murky well ... if you are taking my meaning..."

I stifled the thought that we had not had many an Elven band pass through suburban Middleville recently, but I nodded to show that I was listening.

"Well," she continued, "come morning one of them Forest Elves comes to the door, quiet as a churchmouse with his cap in his hand. He didn't say a word when I opened the door. He just looked at me with those big liquid brown eyes. Yanno?"

And though I didn't, I nodded to show that I did.

"And he says to me, 'Mistress Mossy, we thank you for the use of your meadow, and we wonder if we might borrow a cup of clean water from your well?'"

"'Me?' I said. "I sassed him for sure, I did. 'No cuppa clean has ever flowed from that murky old sump, and now the pump's broke as sure as your Forest Elven arse, ain't it?' I said!"

"And I pointed over that way toward the well, ya see. And as I looked the old windmill began to turn again lifting water from the pit we dug. And the water began to flow again sure as the Corn

Goddess comes in the spring. And I turned to him all quiet and mysterious as he was and asked, 'Did you do this?' and he winked at me sure as I am standing here and waved to me and said not a word more as he vanished round the corner of that very house. But to this day, as sure as the stars shine at night, that well flows pure and the pump ain't never broke again."

She paused and sighed and looked toward the well and said, "A blessing on it. That's what they gave me. A blessing on me well, just for the use of me meadow on a sweet June night. A blessing."

Dendra pointed me toward the well and the tears began to form in her eyes, as she whispered to me, "It's our blessings they want from us, Ma'am, sure as the grass grows green on the hill."

We walked toward the well, hand in hand, in silence, and I prayed. Yes, for the first time in years, I prayed. Not as a Catholic, but as a Human.

Dendra poured for me what I will always remember as my first drink of water.

Pure.

Alive.

Cold as the mountain it had flowed from.

And I felt reborn.

Power surged not only through me, but through Bernice, Johnny, and Klug, as well.

They were attached to me now.

I saw it all clearly.

I heard Dendra's voice.

"You've got to stop Barthas, Ma'am. You've got to. You and that swamp thing you call son. You have the power to stop him. I can see it plain as my well is pure."

"Why me? Why us?" I sputtered.

Then I stopped, after hearing her words, and said quietly, "He is my son."

"Sure he is," said Dendra. "It's clear to my eyes, my dear."

I smiled, and she added, "We are both giving each other some leeway here. To be honest, I have never met a Human as old as you are, certainly not one travelling with a swamp demon and three Zombies, and yet here I am about to feed you all a dinner from my very own table. Do the Zombies eat? Never mind, I don't think I want to know. Mr. Mossy," she called. "Set the table for four. Annie and I will be in in a minute."

And she reached for my hand so we could walk through the dusty courtyard. The house had a bedroom wing at a right angle to the original structure. Along with the barn, the homestead embraced the courtyard containing the well. We walked though and proceeded into a cozy kitchen painted in hues of sea green and sky blue. Even the dishes were sky-blue. Dendra held my hand and looked straight into my eyes.

I wasn't crazy.

I was an ancient telepathic crone in the charming country kitchen of a middle-aged Gnome named Dendra May Mossy.

I wasn't crazy.

She called me Annie.

At Miss Edna's house

Eight

Miss Edna Speaks

Patty was the first to speak up to Miss Edna.
"We want tea, please! With honey, please! For Honey Bees!"
she sparkled as she flew about.

Miss Edna slapped her thighs and guffawed.

"I should have known better than to get serious with a Pixie in my house. Come over here, sugar, your Auntie Edna has some raspberry jam for you." She held out her steady solid arm with a spoon cradled in her hand, and the spoon floated through the air like a hummingbird and held itself there for Patty to lick from: one little hummingbird to another.

"Now there," said Ben, "that's what I mean. How do you do that? That trick with the spoon, Miss Edna."

"That isn't a trick, Sonny. That there is magic."

"I didn't mean any disrespect, Miss Edna."

"Neither did I, son. What you're doing with the fire, now THAT is a trick, a parlor trick. I could counter that with a snap of my finger. You get me?"

"I'm not sure, Ma'am," he said, more respectfully.

The spoon containing the raspberry jam slowly drifted out the window and toward the back garden with Patty flying after it. Planks and Ferny looked at Miss Edna, who said, "Why don't you boys follow our little Pixie out into the garden and make sure she is safe? Mr. Prockner and I need to talk."

That was the first time that Ben remembered anyone in this crazy world referring to him as Mr. Prockner.

He called out the window, "Patty, you stay within the sound of my voice, sweetheart!" He could hear his voice beginning to shake.

Edna glanced over her shoulder at him and shot him a questioning look.

"You had better mean that, Mister."

"I'm not sure I understand you."

"Likewise, Mister. Come on. Set me on fire. Do your worst. Just imagine I'm trying to get past you and steal that Pixie."

Ben concentrated, and flames began to crawl up Miss Edna's overalls. But at that moment a spiral of wind whipped up and blew them out.

He focused again and the curtains caught fire, but they rolled themselves up in a ball and snuffed the flames out.

"Your Pixie, Sorcerer. Your little innocent friend Patty Pixie."

Ben began to freak out. Miss Edna had countered his every attempt. This time the effort hurt. Sweat began to form on his brow, and the tablecloth and three of the chairs burst into flame, but almost immediately the curtains un-balled themselves and busily smothered the little fire.

"Not bad, sonny, but checkmate, you lose."

And with that an enormous physical wall of force came smashing into Ben's chest and forced him to nearly crawl up the opposite wall on his back, as Miss Edna glared at him and said, "Ah ain't just whistling Dixie, darling. They call me a Hearth Witch 'cause most of what I do stems from the rhythms I set in my life—whipping eggs, sweeping stairs, hoeing gardens, stacking wood—peaceful things. I can now do all these things with my mind as easily as I can think. But I can do more than hoe, Mr. Prockner. In actuality, I am a high-level Telekinetic."

Ben found himself unable to move or even cry out, as if an invisible hand covered his mouth.

"So you think yourself a Sorcerer, eh? Some nitwit in your life happened to buy you a real-life analog of our Sorcerer's hat, you stumbled through the barrier and think you can just take the title of Sorcerer because a Giant called you that?"

The hand disappeared.

"I ... no. Not that. I ..." Ben stumbled. "My wife insisted that I wear this hat yesterday," he muttered lamely.

"What is your connection to that Pixie? Tell me now!"

Ben found himself tongue-tied. How much should he tell this woman he had just met? Suppose she was in league with those Dwarves who had tried to steal Patty? Suppose she was secretly aligned with this Barthas? Suppose she had her own agenda? What if she was a Power in and of herself? Everyone else had gone out and he was alone with Edna. What was a safe answer?

"We are related."

"Ah, ha, right. That's a cagey answer, Mr. Prockner. Okay, so you don't trust me, and I'm not ready to trust you. Let's talk."

"Okay," said Ben.

"You're a newcomer here, I can tell," began Miss Edna. "So was I, once. Where are you from? The U.S.?"

"Middleville, New York," Ben said quietly.

"Tampa, Florida. Originally from Decatur, Georgia, before I retired to Florida. I came through about five years ago. Trailer blew out in a hurricane and I wound up here in the Valley, like Dorothy Gale. Only I wasn't in a house, I was clinging to my toilet bowl. They tell you to do that in a hurricane 'cause it's heavy and bolted to the floor. But in a trailer not much stays where it was in a wind over a hundred-fifty miles an hour. One minute I was hurtling through the air, and the next thing I knew I came down here with a thump a half a mile from the Pixie's waterfall, still clinging to my toilet bowl. Some entrance, eh? Sure makes you wish for Glinda's magic bubble. The Pixies brought in a couple of Elves to tend to my broken leg and the rest is history. When I discovered what I could do, people began calling me a Witch, and I did nothing to discourage the idea."

"But you weren't always telekinetic, a 'hearth witch,' were you? Back in Florida?" asked Ben.

"Hell, no. I was a retired schoolteacher, living on Social Security and a pension that wouldn't provide dog food for a Chihuahua," Edna laughed.

The pressure eased on Ben's chest.

"You never know how or who you are going to be when you come through that barrier, sonny. People change. You still look like yourself?" Edna handed Ben a small hand mirror.

"Yeah. That's me. My goatee needs a trim and my neck needs a shave, but that's me."

"Okay. That's unusual, but it happens. One thing is for sure. You weren't travelling with a Pixie on the other side. People from back home rarely come through as magic folk. The magic folk are innocents, pure of thought and heart. Translations rarely pick a soul to become magic folk unless they are innocent. That's why Barthas tricks them. He cages them and drains their magic into batteries and sells the power back to the people of the Valley as electricity. There was never electricity before that fat bastard got here."

"Well, he is never getting Patty!" said Ben with conviction. "Not over my dead body."

"I hope you can put your money where your mouth is, Mister Prockner, because that is just what Barthas will do when he gets wind of a free Pixie in the Valley. Now who is she? Really?"

Ben looked into her eyes and decided to trust her. "Patrice Allison Prockner, my eight-year-old daughter, and the light of my life."

"Sweet Jesus!" whistled Edna. "A child."

"Yes," he whispered. "My child."

The teakettle began to whistle and flew off the grate to pour itself into a waiting teapot. Sylas poked his head through the window and asked if Miss Edna was ready for them yet.

"Give us another few minutes, Sylas. Let's let the tea steep while Ben and I talk a little more."

The window shut itself.

Edna turned back to Ben and said, "You can't stay here. You must know that. For one thing Barthas will find you and take Patty. For another, you will blow my cover. You are going to have to either join us and swear allegiance to the Rebels or get lost and try to keep her safe on your own. Now, you haven't seen what we are up against yet. It isn't pretty. Barthas was a gang member in L.A. He had committed murder before his twelfth birthday, as I understand it, and was translated here about three years ago at the age of fourteen."

Edna read Ben's face. "Yeah, it sounds pathetic, doesn't it? We are the victims of a megalomaniac seventeen-year-old. Only you haven't seen him. Barthas translated through as a two-thousand-pound Swamp Ogre. Nothing can stand up to him physically, and mentally he was trained in the discipline of the L.A. Crips. He understands how to raise an army and has done so by recruiting the Swamp Demons, the Trolls, the Ogres, and all the downtrodden losers of the Valley. They were the first to go online when he figured out the batteries. Now there are electric lights in the homes of all his cronies. Electric lights powered by the magical energies of our innocent Pixies and Wood Nymphs. He drains them dry without a care for their lives."

Ben found himself speechless.

Sylas and his brothers came in through the front door, followed by Planks and Ferny.

"Daddy, you should see Miss Edna's garden. She has tulips and daffodils in bloom!"

Planks held up a yellow King Alfred daffodil to prove her point.

"That's wonderful, Sweetheart. Now, have you been behaving yourself?"

"Yes, Daddy," she said, flitting over to watch the teapot pour out cups of tea.

"Help yourself. There's honey in the pot and fresh goat's milk, for those who like it. And there's more raspberry jam for you, little one."

Patty took the hint and flew down to the jam pot.

Just then they heard a cry from the garden, and Twyla, who had been standing guard, burst into the house.

"Barthas's men!" she cried. "They're on their way here. They broke the warning spell I placed on the pathway through the orchard. They're less than an hour from here. You have to flee."

"Flee? Flee where? Flee how?" gasped Ben. Things were moving too fast, and too much of it was beyond his realm of experience.

"We'll have to take them to the Eyrie," said Miss Edna. Then turning to Ben, she admonished, "You will have to train later. Right now I want to say this to you. Sorcerers can have power over fire, water, electricity, earth, or spirit. So far you have found some ability with fire. I want you to use every ounce of that ability to keep the party safe on the journey, and while you're traveling, practice any ability you can muster. I am going to have to stay behind and act naive. But that won't be easy if this house is covered in Pixie Dust. Everyone out into the garden and hold onto your hats."

A whirlwind began to blow through the house, clearing every counter and floor of dust or debris. It concentrated into a small tornado by the back door and blew out over the garden and into the river beyond. Buckets filled themselves from the river and splashed on the floors. Mops whirled out of closets and began swabbing each plank and stair. Bread flew out of a cupboard and knives from drawers. Sandwiches made themselves, and fruit from a basket climbed into a sack along with a plump wheel of goat cheese.

Edna handed the sack to Ben. "I'll try to meet up with you later. Right now you must flee this place. Go with Ferny, Planks, Twyla, and Sylas and his brothers. They know the way. The Eyrie is the only safe place for you. I'll hold them off and try to delay them any way that I can."

What was happening? Was this all a dream? Ben began to wonder.

Patty clapped her hands and flew about. "Oh, Daddy, it's an adventure!"

"Sure Punkin, an adventure."

What had he gotten himself into?

Barthas paced the floor of the lower Manor and the timbers shook with each footstep. A meniscus of water in a large goblet shivered with concentric rings from the vibrations. Sweat and grease dripped from the monstrous creature's bald head and beaded down his shoulders. A dark damp patch of the bear fur clung to the small of his pimply lower back.

"Put more wood on the fire!" he bellowed at the ratty-looking spit boy.

Something on the spit groaned for a last shuddering breath and lay slack.

"So listen to me, Irene. You gotta explain to me one more time why this dead grave bitch is such a threat to me and my posse. I ain't seeing this in my head the way you are, you crazy bitch."

"José, don't..."

"I told you to call me BARTHAS," he roared.

Irene covered her ears. "FINE. Barthas ... the thing is that I can't see it as clearly as the others. My ability to guess at the future has become real in this world and when I bring up thoughts of almost anyone I get visions of where they are and what they are doing right then, even scenes that I can tell are them doing things in the future. It is incredible. I feel like the Long Island Psychic, without the TV show."

She continued, "I used to convince people with hints based on astrological crap I learned about them. I mean, people tend to make stuff come true anyway, once they have a reason—and all the beads and crystal balls just set the stage. But this is like turning on a television into their lives and futures. Like having CNN of the psychic forecasting world, I just turn the channel. But all I see of that woman is that she is wearing black, she is a threat to you, and there is an air of death about her—almost as though she were dead herself, but that can't be. Beyond that, I see only smoke and clouds and that Swamp Demon darting through."

"But if this bitch is playing for the other gang, why is she hanging with one of our boys? Those Swamp Demons swore allegiance when I set up the first batteries in their crib. Like, he should be playing for our team. When I find out this Demon's name I am gonna put a hurt on him." The table shook when he smacked his hand on it. A dish fell off the far end and cut the air with the sound of its shattering.

"Barthas, calm down. Don't start breaking things again."

"Shut up, Irene. That's what the servants are for. Hey, you, spit boy. Come over here and clean up this crap for your LORD Barthas!"

The spit boy ran over to obey, and Barthas cuffed him on the back of the head, knocking him into a wall.

"Yeah, and that's what you get for not paying attention, ass-wipe."

"Barthas ... José ... look, I have told you before. I will do anything I have to do in order to get back to L.A. and out of this freaking nuthouse. I don't care whose side I'm on, I just want you to get enough energy in those batteries for a Sorcerer to open this damn barrier and get me *out!*" Irene looked desperate.

"Okay, okay, Irene. You know, man, it was a lucky day for me when I went into your tea parlor to have my palm read. Or else I would'n'a wound up here where these rubes are so ready for plucking. Like ripe fruit on a vine, that's what these pigeons are. This whole valley has just been waiting for someone like me to take charge. You might say I am doing them a service." He laughed grotesquely.

Irene looked disgusted. "Yeah ... whatever ... José."

Pretending he hadn't heard her he asked, "Where's Sideous?"

She replied innocently, "Oh, is he supposed to be here?"

"I told him to come by when he was finished checking on the

batteries. I don't like it down there. There's just too much damn moaning. You would think they were Humans the way they bitch and moan, not a bunch of freaking cartoon Fairies. God, I can't stand freaking Fairies, you know? Especially these cartoon ones here. I just can't."

"Whatever, José. I don't know what you mean by cartoon but, whatever...."

"Well, it's just girl stuff, those sissy Saturday morning cartoons. They're girl stuff. I mean I was down there one day and one of those cartoon mermaids says to me, "Oh wouldn't you like to see me comb my hair, my Lord Barthas?" and then she starts combing her hair and gets all silky with her hands through that freaky green hair she's got and her eyes get all big and soft, and I swear, it might have been my imagination, but those clamshells she's got on her tits seemed to be getting smaller and smaller, until I realized, I was getting dizzy and she was trying to pull some Magic crap on me, like she was gonna seduce me and we was gonna do it right there. Yanno?"

He paused and shook his head, "Girl stuff, sissy cartoon Fairy girl stuff, that's what that was. But us Swamp Ogres ain't too susceptible to that crap. I'm WAY tougher than that." He shifted his bulk upright.

Irene shook her head and sighed.

The door opened and Sideous entered. "The project goes well, my Lord Barthas." He draped himself and his long black robe over a high-backed upholstered chair.

"I didn't say you could sit, Sorcerer, but you MAY proceed with your report," growled Barthas. He needed to impress his control on Sideous, so he began rhythmically tapping his enormous blunt fingertips on the rough-hewn table.

Sideous stood and began pacing as he spoke. He was a man who loved hearing the sound of his own voice. "The batteries are nearly fully charged, my Lord Barthas. We have been harvesting the 'volunteers' nearly every day now. They are proud to be such an historic part of our new energy campaign. There are electric lights in all the swamps and hollows of our supporters' homes, and the barracks is also now electrified. And ... MUST you tap like that, Lord Barthas?" he snapped, a little louder than he had intended.

Barthas unfolded to his full height and rumbled over to the Sorcerer. His huge paw clutched the front of Sideous's robes, and he spat in his face. A gob of stringy phlegm ran down the side of the Sorcerer's nose. Sideous gritted his teeth and held his breath.

"Yeah, I MUST!" roared the Ogre. "Now get out. Everybody get the HELL OUT! NOW."

Then more quietly he mumbled, "I got stuff to do."

The room cleared and Barthas shuffled over to the roasting rack by the fire and its questionable contents. With his blubbery paws he ripped off fatty chunks of meat and began to eat and mumble to himself at the same time.

"Freaking Fairy bullcrap...."

Nine

Acquiring Skill

Tap left, tap right, tap down. One. Irene made her way down the rough-hewn stone steps to the dungeon, her cane feeling the way before her. Tap left, tap right, tap down. Two. Sounds drifted up from below, distorted by the echoes off the stone walls. Small puffs of fetid air wafted past her nostrils. The stink of unwashed bodies smothered the acrid crackle of electric discharge. Frightened voices condensed into a murmur like the sound of distant ocean waves. Down she went. Tap left, tap right, tap down. Thirty-five steps. Her left hand reached across her chest and skimmed the wall while her right controlled the familiar cane.

Irene had been blind since a virus had robbed her of sight in her teens. So much in life was unfair. But she had always been a fighter of life's battles; she had soon developed ways of coping with her handicap. Logic and organization were her weapons: diligence and memory organized the shapes and sounds of the external world into a kind of vision she could use.

Irene was desperate to get back into the Real World, where she had some control over her life. This place was unending madness. People transformed. Mermaids and Nymphs no more substantial than smoke. People flew on fairy wings. Magic spells created something out of nothing. Worse than all this, her clairvoyance, which she had feigned in the other world, was real here, and it was driving her mad. She had to get back home—and to accomplish that, she had to talk with Sideous.

Tap left, tap right, tap down. She had come down fifty-five steps. She was done. She had reached the bottom. The prisoners hushed as she turned the corner. She could hear Sideous fiddling with the knobs and dials on the batteries he had built. Arms and wings began reaching out for her.

"Help us, please..."

"Oooaaahhh...," moaned a toothless mouth beyond articulation.

"I BEG you. Help us. Take my child out of here."

These voices came mostly from the far corner of the room where the Fairy Folk cowered away from the iron bars. Iron not only held them prisoner, it was anathema to them. In time it could become their bane.

Irene did her best to shut her mind to their pleas. She had one job: get back to reality. "None of this is real," she told herself. "This is all a twisted dream. I must get out of this nightmare. They are not real."

"Sideous," she said quietly.

She could hear his robe swish against the stone floor as he turned to her.

"Irene, I almost didn't hear you. You are so quiet." She could tell he was smiling as he said this. Sideous was the world's greatest ass-kisser. "Did Barthas send you?"

"No. And listen, Sideous, don't pay any attention to his rages. He's still just a kid, and that Ogre's body has made his rages, his temper tantrums, *and* his hunger worse than ever. There are times when you just have to leave him alone. Let him eat until he falls asleep again. That's the way to stay safe around him."

"I shall try to remember that," Sideous said tersely. He did not like to be corrected.

"So, Sideous. How far along are you? Do you have the energy for this barrier spell? Are you up to it? And when?"

"Child's play, mere child's play. Once the batteries are full it is simply a matter of weaving the spell to direct the energies."

"So, *do it!* Sideous, I have to get out of this place. This may be home to you, but I hate it here!" Several of the prisoners moaned in agreement.

"Easy now, my eager Seer. The spell must be woven delicately under the proper conditions. It is a blend of all five of a Sorcerer's energies, fire, water, lightning, earth, and the most difficult of all, spirit. No amateur Sorcerer can weave such a spell. It is the spell of a Master." Here he paused for dramatic effect.

"And I suppose you are the only 'Master' in the Valley, is that it?" asked Irene.

"To the best of my knowledge," Sideous smirked.

"And the conditions?" hinted Irene.

"The full moon of either equinox and a volunteer willing to cross the barrier."

"I am the volunteer and the equinox is around the corner," said Irene eagerly.

"Three days after the equinox. The moon waxes full three days past the equinox."

"Promise me you will get me through whether Barthas is ready or not. I will foretell for you. I will do anything. Please, Sideous, get me through that barrier. Barthas doesn't have to know..." Irene begged.

"Oh? I wonder if he would approve of that attitude, my Lady." He gave her a nasty smile. "Tell me, honestly, what do you foresee for me? Eh?"

The same recurring image played inside Irene's mind. She absolutely could not tell him what she foresaw! So she shut her mind to it and lied. "Why, nothing but good fortune, Lord Sideous. You shall be Barthas's right hand. Long will be your days."

"Time will tell," he said.

"Six days from now, Sideous. I am counting on you. Where?" Irene turned and groped for the stairwell.

"Right there in front of you."

"Not the stairs. Where will you weave this spell of transference?"

"The courtyard, under the full moon."

"Until then. I am counting on you, Sideous." Her hand found

the cold stone of the stairway wall.

"Time will tell, my Lady Irene."

She imagined that he was smiling at her again.

She found the first step and began.

Tap right, tap left, tap up. One. Tap right, tap left, tap up. Two.

Back at Miss Edna's farm, Ben, along with Patty, Planks, Ferny, Twyla, Sylas, and both his brothers, had been hustled swiftly into waiting canoes. Before they had gone too far down the river, Ferny and Sylas drew their canoe alongside his and had some words with Planks, seated behind Ben.

Ferny threw Ben an apologetic glance. Sylas shrugged his shoulders and said, "Sorry, Sir Ben, but you are not really one of us yet," and slipped a blindfold over his eyes. "Now, we're trusting you not to remove that, on your honor, Sir Ben. Otherwise we shall have to tie your hands, and you wouldn't want that, now would'ya?"

"Patty?" Ben asked.

"Right here, Daddy. You look silly, Daddy."

"I thought you liked adventures, Punkin."

Peals of laughter warmed his heart. Patty was just fine. She had been perched on Planks's shoulder since they had gotten into the boats, only once flying up to visit Twyla.

Ben thought he might as well take advantage of the quiet to ask a few questions, explore a few options and listen. Time fell away as they travelled: hours passed in liquid silence. The smooth, sinuous sounds of the river were enhanced by the rhythmic dipping of the paddles into the water. Birds sang in riotous jubilation along the banks, and Ben could almost imagine the fish swimming below. He began to think on what Edna had told him, at the last minute, about his power as a Sorcerer: water was one of the things he should be able to control.

Maybe the blindfold was a good thing. It certainly helped his concentration. Pull the water, he told himself. Make it jump. Make it do something.

Splash! A spout of water responded to Ben's control.

"Looks like the fish are jumping," commented Planks from the back of the boat.

Ben smiled to himself and concentrated on the sound of voices.

"Twyla, are you there?" Ben sat up straight and listened as a voice sounded about ten feet forward of his right shoulder.

"Right here, Sir Ben!" Twyla called, and with that a spout of water spiraled out of the water and straight into Twyla's face. She sputtered, and coughed, "Why, you sneaky Sorcerer!"

Ben began to laugh. And spouts of water began to erupt all up and down the river. Everyone began shouting at him at once and he collapsed into heaps of laughter. Soon everyone was laughing and applauding.

"That will be about enough of that, thank you, *Sir*," said Twyla tartly, wiping herself off.

Ben continued to chuckle until he found that the chuckles had turn to gasps for air and he realized that he was crying, or maybe sobbing. Planks held his shoulders from behind.

"I know I seem a coward, but Gods! Planks, this whole thing is more than I can cope with. Patty is my daughter. That little Pixie is my flesh and blood. I would do *anything* for her. But how the hell do I learn my way around some crazy magical land, and how to be a Sorcerer, and everything else I need to know, before this Barthas can hurt either of us? How?" He pulled off the blindfold and blinked at Planks in the blinding noonday sun. They were at a bend in the river. Water birds flew overheard.

"You are going to have to put that back on, Sir. You gave your word," Planks said sternly.

"I know, but why? Is this all some sort of elaborate game?"

Planks's huge hands slid the blindfold gently back into place. "A deadly serious game for sure, then, Sir Ben. I cannot count how many of my dear friends have died trying to free us from Barthas's grip. I have lost relatives, a brother. I have given up the idea that my heart will ever be free of grief again. Count your blessings that you and your young Pixie are still alive. Do not look too far ahead. Take one step at a time. That is my advice."

He stopped paddling and let the canoe drift.

Ben found himself stupefied. Here he had been thinking of only his plight as real. He had never thought of these characters out of legend as having griefs or fears and worries. Died. Planks had said they died. It sank deeper into Ben's heart and understanding. They could all die; Patty, too.

"I ... I'm sorry. I just didn't realize," he confessed. "This has all been such a confusion of new information. All of it is ... strange, hard to believe. I didn't understand the severity of what you've all been dealing with." He heard a self-pitying whine come into his voice and suppressed it. "Look, I'm just a simple guy. My boring little life as a suburban dad just hasn't prepared me to be a ... a ... a Sorcerer with a Pixie for a daughter! I'm sorry I ignored your warnings of how dangerous this place has become under Barthas's rule."

He stopped for a moment, thinking hard, then spoke again. "I promised Miss Edna that I would work to develop my abilities and use them for the benefit of the alliance. So let me start now. Planks, just use your paddle to steer us, and let me propel the canoe." *If I can*, he added silently.

Ben concentrated hard on the water, and immediately a wave pushed them forward as Planks steered. He gave a sigh of satisfaction, or relief, and he could feel the others smiling with pleasure at his accomplishment. He kept the blindfold in place and listened closely to make sure they avoided the river banks.

They slid through the water in silence, and before long Patty fell asleep on Ben's lap. He found himself thinking of Annie. Where was she? How was she? She must have alerted the police by now. They would have an Amber Alert out, because Patty was involved. Ben wondered what Annie must be thinking. How was Max coping with the disappearance of his father and sister?

Max had taken the pike and was practicing martial arts moves in Dendra Mossy's moonlit courtyard while Dendra and I talked in the kitchen. She had killed a chicken in our honor and was also making biscuits from stone-ground flour. The beginnings of a gravy bubbled on the back of the enameled blue stove. I would have set the table but my crippled, arthritic knees and hips had pretty well given out for the night, and I sat in an old Windsor chair near the stove and literally warmed my bones by the fire.

I had offered to have Bernice or Johnny set the table, but Dendra had looked shocked by the suggestion. It was startling how much I had begun to rely on my Zombies. I had begun to think of them as functional extensions of my failing body. I even caught myself once wishing that I had brought more of them from that first graveyard. And it was not as though that were the only place it happened. Two ghosts had prostrated themselves before me in Dendra's house. I was not sure how much of it she could see. Even to me they looked insubstantial; whisper-thin outlines of the once-living. On the way in to Dendra's farm we had come across a series of isolated country graves by the roadside, surrounded by a broken picket fence, and it was all I could do to keep the six of them in their graves. Their voices had called to me for many yards down the road: we had gone nearly a mile before I felt them slip loose from my mind and let go. It seemed that Zombies just wanted to follow me. My very presence woke the dead.

After a delicious and truly satisfying meal, during which Mr. Mossy said very little, Dendra and I walked out into the courtyard to watch Max go through his karate and kendo moves.

It was impressive stuff, seeing him begin his routine by bowing solemnly to his imaginary opponent and placing his arms by his side. Mr. Kyuke had taught with a mixture of discipline and respect. Max threw chops in the air, feints, parries, back-flips, back kicks, front kicks and more. The discipline driven into this thirteen-year-old boy both impressed me as an observer and made me feel proud as a mother. Max admired Mr. Kyuke. He and his dojo had taken many local awards for their disciplined accomplishments. Watching Max practice in this new and powerful body brought a deeper understanding of how seriously my son had taken his studies.

Max threw his leg out far to the side and swooped around behind it, like a ballet dancer, to come to a halt facing the opposite direction.

"Okay, Mom. You saw that, right?"

I nodded to him.

He began again. "Now watch it this way." He did the move again, only this time his tail swooped out like a third leg and sliced through the air to stop at what we assumed was his opponent's neck, the spiky top spines pointing upward. "One ... then ... Two!" said Max with a firm punctuation.

"Whew," I managed to gasp out. "Well done." And then, "I see." I meant to clap but my wrists were so weak and my hands so delicate that I only managed a little patting sound.

"I've been working on my moves, to compensate for my longer torso and the tail. But I've figured out that the tail can be an awesome weapon, Mom! And these spikes are like natural plating. It's like being in Samurai armor. I need to practice my sword moves, but this pike is too long. We need to get me a sword, Mom. So I can protect you. I mean, look at you! You're frail as an eggshell. Aw, God, Mom, I can't let anything happen to you. I've got to protect you. I mean I've been thinking about this—like, about what would Dad do if he were here? He'd protect you. So I've got to protect you now."

"Thanks Max. But you just watch out for yourself. And while we're on the subject, if anything happens to me, your job is to run like hell."

"Fine, Mom." Spittle shot out from his fangs. It pissed him off suddenly to be treated like a kid again—he was a Ninja, or even better!

"Max, I am not downplaying your ability here, but you are just one person and things are looking bigger than that right now. Okay?

Just watch your own ass, okay, kid?"

"Okay, Mom." He paused.

"Max."

"It's okay, Mom. I hear you on this. I'm listening."

I sighed. "I love you, Maxwell Alexander Prockner."

"Ditto, Mom."

"Your monster is not only formidable, but obedient," murmured Dendra. She looked frightened.

Max and I had become a frightening pair.

Max stood on his hands. "Hey, Lady! I'm a NICE monster!" He clowned for her by skipping about the courtyard like an idiot, pirouetting on his tail, and finishing with a perfect back flip to land right in front of our hostess.

Dendra fainted dead away.

Ten

Button and Hook

By the time Blina and Shadow had caught up with their quarry's scent, Miss Edna had scoured the house and swept the garden of any remaining Pixie Dust. Ben and Patty were safely on their way down the river with her trustworthy Rebel friends and a good healthy lunch. Miss Edna had made a pot of ginger tea and was waiting patiently for Blina. She was preparing lunch for herself and the dogs when they arrived.

The troops came stumbling down the hill on foot and on their horses, eagerly following Shadow as he snuffled and crouched and dogged Patty's trail.

"She's at Miss Edna's house. I knew it," said Blina from her horse. "That Edna always plays so innocent, and this time we've caught her red-handed. I'll bet they're all there plotting their opposition to Barthas. Huh! His plans to modernize the Valley would benefit everyone. Some people just don't understand progress."

Blina stopped on the hillside above Miss Edna's. "Troops, you wait outside. Surround the house and stop anyone who attempts to escape. Don't be gentle with them—but take them alive. Shadow, you come in with me." As she dismounted she straightened her shining helm and breastplate and tested her grip on her sword hilt.

Shadow stood at the cheery stone fence, his hand on the wooden picket gate. "I tell you, Blina, the ssscent stops here. At the perimeter of her land," he hissed.

"They're in there hiding!" she screeched back. "I can feel it. I won't be fooled again. Irene predicted that they would head this way after the Duke's Arse. We should have been faster so they could not have left! Now, are you coming, or not?"

Blina stormed up the front porch of Miss Edna's house and threw open the screen door. Several potted petunias on the portico wall shook, rocked, and then righted themselves quietly.

Miss Edna sat in a wooden rocking chair by her kitchen table sipping tea from a cup without a handle.

"Tea, Blina? How nice to see you again. Come for anything in particular? Or is this just another social call?" Edna began calmly pouring cups of tea. "Will your monster take tea, or is he here strictly for dramatic effect? You can tell Barthas I was duly frightened."

"Where are they?" Blina demanded.

"Why, whoever do you mean, dear? You really ought to tell me if you have invited others to tea at my house. It is poor manners, otherwise." Miss Edna dusted imaginary crumbs from the table with her napkin.

"You know who: the Pixie, and that Sorcerer."

"Oh, Blina. Inviting imaginary Pixies to tea, isn't that just like you? You know Barthas has rounded up all the Pixies, along with every other sort of magical citizen. Why, you know that better than anyone, so how could you have invited a Pixie to tea? I wish I had known. I would have taken out the good china." Miss Edna continued to dust the table and smile at Blina.

Blina concentrated on hating Miss Edna with all her venomous spleen. She upended her sword and made ready to smash the oaken kitchen table to smithereens, but when she struck, the sword met a cushion of Miss Edna's invisible telekinetic shield. It bounced back up without disturbing a thing on the table.

"Temper, temper, Blina Eleanor Turdgirdle. I cannot have you breaking things in *my* house." Miss Edna stood up and adjusted the shawl over her overalls. "This is *my* house, Blina. And I have *paid* my taxes to Barthas and his dirty crew of mobsters."

"*Witch!*" spat Blina.

"So it has been said." A cleaver came off the rack of kitchen knives and began tapping on the cutting board. Six little knives lined up and began to do an intricate gavotte. A broom flew overhead.

"I hear witches ride brooms, Blina. Can they juggle knives too?" she asked with another smile before suddenly turning serious. "What is it you have come here for, Blina? I have no time for tomfoolery, and if you don't want tea I shall have to ask you to leave."

"The Pixie was here and you know it. The trail leads to this house."

"And yet there is not a trace of her in this house or garden. How do you explain that, Blina?"

"You are a witch." She spat again.

"That seems to explain a lot for you, Blina. However I know nothing about it and have little time for charming visitors such as yourself."

Shadow slipped in through the back door and announced. "I have their scent at the riverbank. They are gone. I cannot tell the direction yet."

Blina threw her helmet at the window. It stopped midway, just above a vase of dried hydrangeas, flew back, and climbed neatly atop her tightly wound braids. She stomped on the floor and snorted with frustration as she turned to exit the cottage.

"Do come back, dear," said Miss Edna, and poured herself another cup of tea.

The screen door pulled back and smacked Blina in the ass on her way out.

"WITCH!"

"Thank you! Come again," called Edna with a cheery wave.

Planks slowed the canoe and said, "You can stop pushing now, Sir Ben. We have arrived. This is as far as we are going along the river. The rest is uphill from here."

"What are we going to do about the canoes?" asked Ben. He

found himself concerned about being followed and discovered by followers of this Barthas. Much as he knew that these beings—he'd accepted that he couldn't use the term "Humans" to define this group—were an allied force, he was worried. What if they didn't think defensively? Ben had to protect Patty.

Sylas answered him this time. "Don't worry, Sir Ben, there's a cave along the riverbank, about half a mile from here. Willem and Jon and I will carry the canoes to hide them there. Twyla can follow us and sweep the ground with branches to cover our tracks."

"And I'll put a little warning spell along the way, to alert us to anyone who stumbles onto our path."

Ben knew he looked confused, and it was Planks who came to his aid. "Twyla is half-Elven, Sir Ben. She has some skill with simple magic spells."

"But I'm not magic enough to warrant Barthas's men taking me to the dungeons. That's why I hide my ears under my hat if they show up at the Duke's Arse." Ben could imagine her smiling through his blindfold; with or without Elven ears, she was charming and beautiful.

Planks was the soul of patient reliability as he explained the plan. "The rest of the way is rough terrain. We have to climb the mountain to get to the Eyrie. The way is uphill, rocky, and covered with brush and scrub growth. But once we get to camp you will have a rest. I warn you, Sir Ben, there is no path. We always come up a slightly different way so that we don't create a pathway and alert Barthas's soldiers. Now, we had better get moving. Hold onto my arm and I will steady you through the rough spots." Ben couldn't help but like this kindly Giant who had taken such a liking to his Patty.

Unfortunately, Planks's kindness did not make the climb any easier. It was steep and there were many rock outcroppings, most of which the blindfolded Ben managed to trip over. His hands were soon scraped from stumbling and catching himself on the rocks and branches of scrub growth. Planks warned him as obstacles approached, but all the same he kept managing to fall.

When Planks caught him from behind for the umpteenth time, Ben muttered, "Thanks. Are we anywhere near the camp yet?"

"Soon, little Sorcerer, soon..."

"Daddy, you sound like me now. Are we there yet? Are we there yet?" she chanted. Patty laughed and flew past his face. Ben could feel the breeze from her tiny wings.

"Well, Patrice, you're not wearing a blindfold and stubbing your toes."

"Daddy, Planks and Ferny explained that. The bad people have a magic mind-reader so you mustn't know the way to the Rebel base. You know, like in *Star Wars*, Daddy. It's a secret." She buzzed around his head.

"And I suppose you're Princess Leia?" he asked sarcastically.

"No Daddy, I'm a Pixie, and Cynthia McGowan is going to DIE of jealousy when she sees me."

Ben tripped again and Planks caught him.

The Giant's deep baritone voice said, "We are almost there. Once we get you settled in, I have someone I want you to meet, some old friends of mine, by the name of Button and Hook. You two have something in common."

"And what would that be?" asked Ben, taking the bait.

"A red striped hat," replied Planks quietly, "for starters."

Now they were travelling up steep slopes over loose hardscrabble rock. Ben slipped and fell more than once. His knees were scraped and his feet hurt. Patty continued to be upbeat and flew from Ben's shoulder to Planks's over the course of the long afternoon. It was already getting toward dusk when Planks pulled the blindfold off Ben's eyes.

"We're here, Sir Ben," piped up Ferny.

Ben blinked, rubbed his eyes, and squinted. It was dazzling having his sight restored after hours of darkness. He made out the towering form of Planks and located Ferny the Gnome by the sound of his voice. Sylas and his brothers stood stalwartly behind Ferny with their longbows in hand.

Being left in the dark for most of the journey, relying only on his ears and the sensation of the rocky ground beneath his feet, had heightened Ben's other senses in a way he'd never experienced. The blindfold had left Ben in his own world for most of the journey; now he was back in theirs.

He looked around at neat pathways laid with wooden planking between well-arranged gardens of vegetables and flowers. Along the plankways marched orderly battalions of Gnome and Elven archers. Every gate was manned with assorted Fairy Folk. Ben saw a group of Centaurs around a forge: it looked like they were making swords and plate armor.

The Rebel encampment was set on a natural bluff. Most of the soil had to be brought up, backload after backload, in slings that came up from the base camp. But, as Sylas explained, Miss Edna insisted that they produce. "Produce food for the People and the Peace will follow" was Miss Edna's philosophy. "Productive hands belong to Productive People."

"So," said Sylas, "when we are not raiding his weapons caches or causing problems for Barthas's troops, we make sure the gardens up here are weeded and fertilized. Whatever we cannot eat goes down the hill, for those whose farms Barthas has ruined by kidnapping their honest workers, either to be drained for their magical energies, or to be conscripted into his stinking army."

"Here's to Barthas!" yelled Ferny, as he dropped his jodhpurs and showed the crowd his skinny, bald, pink behind.

"Hear, hear!" yelled the assembled crowd.

Planks put his arm around Ben's shoulder and whispered, "Button and Hook are waiting for us."

"Let's go, Daddy," Patty buzzed in Ben's ear.

Ben nodded in agreement and followed the Giant down the narrow lane, toward what looked like a tavern or the local post office. It turned out to be both for this Rebel outpost, set back a little from the dirt road and with a wide front porch hung with brightly colored lanterns bearing local merchants' slogans. Ben read them as he approached the porch, each decorated with an appropriate image:

Sing Rite Harmony Potions

Calla Lily's Dew Drop Beauty Cream—it's Magic!

Fenwick's Enchanted Bread Fruits—
from our orchards to your breadbasket

POO-MORE'S REGULARITY PILLS
"YOU CAN'T GO WITHOUT THEM"

As they walked up the old wooden planks of the porch, a parrot on top of the doorway whistled seductively at them. Ben held open the rickety screen door and, with Patty on his shoulder, followed Planks, who had to bend over double inside.

The air was smoky with exotic tobacco and smelled of stale beer. A bar of dark wood wrapped the back wall, and behind it stood a pirate with a pegleg, a dagger, and an eye patch. He was introduced as Derrick, the bartender and postmaster. Planks purchased two large tankards of stout.

He led Ben and Patty to a table in the corner where sat a very thin older Human in navy silk pajamas and a red striped beret, wearing matching red silk slippers that curled up at the toes. Next to this gentleman sat a tiny, middle-aged Brownie, a Humanoid the size of a Yorkshire terrier. He was dressed in a brown tweed suit with a back belt, of the sort favored in dated British TV comedies that Ben liked to watch with his children back at home. On his feet were tiny brown Oxford lace-up shoes.

Ben shook the Human's hand and the fellow replied crisply, "I hear that Miss Edna sent you. I'm Hook, this is Button," indicating the Brownie.

"Resistance Espionage," explained Planks.

"Watch this," said Button. He jumped up and walked along a row of geraniums on the front windowsill. As he crossed from one side to the other his clothing began to take on the color and the texture of the leaves behind him. Another few steps and his face and hands wavered and blurred into the background. One more step and all that was visible, if you looked very carefully, were his eyes, looking back.

"Wow," said Patty.

Ben began to applaud.

"That's nothing!" Button said dismissively. "I can do plaid." His clothing and face almost instantly took on a loud orange-and-green tartan pattern.

Patty began to laugh in utter astonishment.

"Oh, that was so funny! Wasn't that funny, Daddy?"

"I got a million of 'em, kid."

Suddenly Button went stark white and erupted in red polka-dots.

Patty had to sit down, she was laughing and snorting so hard. "Ooh, hee, hee, hee, you are crazy! Do it again! Please?" She gripped her sides and rocked side to side.

"Okay, okay, I'll stop already," said Button, walking over to where Patty was heaving with laughter. He immediately turned purple with yellow stripes.

Patty screamed and shook all over. Tears ran down her cheeks, and Ben patted her on her tiny back with his pinkie finger to help her catch her breath.

"If you like that, you'll love my nephew, Squirt. He's just the same as me. We both work camouflage for the Espionage Unit of the Rebels," Button said, offering Patty his hand. As tiny as she was, Patty came up to his waist.

"Hello," she said, her wings fluttering with excitement.

"I work with Hook, and it looks like he's going to be teaching your Sorcerer. So we might as well get to know each other, eh?"

"Sure," said Patty.

Hook ordered more drinks and something sweet for Patty. "I

also heard that you and the young Pixie are newcomers to the Valley. Is that right?"

Ben nodded.

Hook faced Ben and said quietly, "Shall we all go for a stroll? I feel a storm brewing."

He stood and indicated the way for Ben. Button hopped down from the table and walked to the front door, emitting one shrill, piercing whistle while smiling at Patty.

Up came an immense bullfrog, as large as a Jack Russell terrier. It had a saddle on its back, and Button indicated to Patty that she should climb on.

"Hey, is that thing safe?" demanded Ben. "Patty, I'm not so sure you should be riding a frog. What would your mother think?"

A new voice came from the shrubbery outside the door. "He's a champion jumping bullfrog, he is, Sir. I raised him myself." Another Brownie in a brown tweed suit dismounted from his own speckled bullfrog and doffed his hat to Ben. "Squirt, here, my Lord Sorcerer," he said, and then knelt and kissed Patty's hand. "After you my Lady..." he said indicating the first Frog.

Patty climbed on and Button sat behind her; Squirt rode his bullfrog next to her. They each took off with a huge leap—at least six feet, thought Ben.

"Wheeeeeee!" squealed Patty.

"Watch this!" Squirt hollered from ahead. Ben began to follow the leaping frog, feeling a rush of panic as he watched Patty disappear.

"Button knows where we're going," Hook reassured him. "We needn't hurry. Your Pixie is in good hands. Button is head of our espionage unit. He has been right down into the very dungeons where Barthas is holding our people. He has seen the batteries that their Sorcerers built for the storing of energy. Not a single one of our men can match his camouflage ability, although he says he is training his nephew to follow in his invisible footsteps."

Hook held a stray branch aside for Ben and they continued along a hedge-lined path toward an area where Rebels trained with swords and staves.

Two Centaurs parried with a couple of Elves. The day was growing late, and in spite of the long, cooling shadows, both the Elves and the Centaurs were sweating from their workout. A sword clanged as it hit an Elf's upraised shield.

"That's one of the things I will need to teach you, Ben, to weave a shield for yourself. But first, you will need to master the five elements of energy. I understand that you have some experience with fire and water. Now it is time for your lesson in lightning, or electrical charges."

Clouds began to darken the sky and a breeze lifted the underside of the leaves overhanging the practice yard. The Elves threw back their hair and the Centaurs shook their manes, welcoming the updraft. A few water birds flew overhead and keened for the ocean.

"Looks like a storm is brewing, Hook," said Ben.

"Just what I was hoping for."

"Oh?"

"When a would-be Sorcerer first attempts to hold lightning, sometimes it helps to take hold of a charge that has already been started. So a moderate electrical storm can be a pair of training wheels for the novice. Now, for some reason Miss Edna thinks you have big potential, so I hope you are ready for some big failures, Ben. First let's see you catch one of mine."

Hook held his hands about two feet apart and a charge started to form in the air between them. Then he drew back one hand, like a baseball pitcher winding up, and with a huge crackling sound the bolt of lightning arced toward Ben. He held up his hands to catch it, but before Ben knew it the air around him crackled and his body went rigid with the shock of the electricity. He fell with a slump to the ground, smoking slightly.

"Oooof!" He waved his arm to show he was alive.

The evening sky came alive with a bright burst of lightning. Seconds later peals of thunder broke the silence. Rain began to patter softly on Ben's limp form.

"Again, please," called Hook. "This time I want you to try to catch one of those which the storm generates. Stand ready: you will feel the charge begin to build above you, and you must force it to obey you. Will-power this time, Mr. Prockner. The rebellion is counting on you." Hook opened a paper parasol he had been carrying to protect him from the rain.

Ben propped himself up and shook his head to clear his thoughts.

"And Patty?"

"... is safe. Don't use your worry about her as an excuse. A Sorcerer must be able to concentrate under *any* circumstances. Now come on. I want to see you hold one."

Another bolt cracked the sky nearly simultaneously with the rumble of thunder.

"Too late now, you missed that one. Now, heads up. Listen for the sky to tell you when it is ready. Then seize it."

Ben took a stance which seemed steadier. He reached his arms out in front of himself and called with the same internal voice he had used for the waterspouts. Then he began to feel the crackle of energy above him and reached out. The lightning began to arc toward him, then pulled away and crashed to earth near a rack of wooden practice swords.

The nearby Centaurs reared up and shouted, "Hey, we're getting out of here. You crazy Sorcs are dangerous."

"Better," murmured Hook, ignoring the Centaurs. "Again."

Ben pulled and twisted and yanked and pushed, got shocked time after time after time ... until finally he could not only pull a lightning bolt from the sky but could even create one himself, generating it between his hands. He even developed a little way of starting a friction from his palms, which he pushed from behind, like blowing on a spark to start a fire.

By the time he was ready to play catch with Hook by tossing an electrical charge back and forth, he was covered in mud and scorch marks. His fingers were bruised and his entire nervous system reverberated from being repeatedly shocked.

Hook, on the other hand, stood calm and pristine under his shellacked paper parasol, his navy blue pajamas and red silk shoes scarcely touched by the rain. He caught the electrical charge deftly and nonchalantly with his left hand.

"I think you've done enough for one evening, my friend. How about we get you cleaned up? And we get you some dinner. They should be serving in the Mess Hall about now, and we might be able to find your friends. Button will meet us there with your Pixie."

"But first we stop at my tent and get you cleaned up and into some fresh clothes. I will let you in on a little secret, Ben. You have to relax. You need to stay calm no matter what is going on around you. Everyone else will be counting on you staying calm enough to weave a spell or a shield. I came to this world when I was still in my twenties. So I took an apprenticeship to an older Sorcerer who taught me how to use my abilities—though not to control them. I had to learn that by myself. And like you, when I was an apprentice I also had trouble relaxing. So I began to analyze what part of the day I was most relaxed—and realized that it was in the evening, when I had washed up and changed into my pajamas."

"So that's why..."

Hook nodded. "I've worn them ever since. I bought them in good silk in every sensible color and consider them my uniform. Some Sorcerers, you will notice, wear shapeless or loose-fitting robes to keep them relaxed. Most reject binding clothes of any kind. I've just adopted pajamas as my trademark." Hook laughed and blushed at his own admission.

They stopped at Hook's red-and-white striped tent. "Nothing like trying to remain incognito," he sighed with a glance at the red stripes.

"I guess you give up anonymity when you put on the hat," observed Ben.

"Now you're getting it," Hook winked at him.

A diminutive serving woman in a white blouse and gray jumper brought a basin of warm water and some clean clothes, along with a pitcher filled with more hot water.

It felt wonderful. Ben had not stopped or taken a moment to himself since rising the morning before at the Duke's Arse. Hook provided him with a razor, some soap, and a hand mirror, and he took the time to shave carefully around his goatee and trim the scruffy parts.

He chose a pair of monotone striped pajamas in a gunmetal gray silk. And after combing his hair and shaving his stubble, he replaced his red striped hat on his head and felt better than he had in a while.

Sorcerer and apprentice, in their pajamas, walked arm in arm to the bustling mess hall, Hook sheltering them both from the light rain with his parasol. Ben felt oddly relaxed.

Planks and Ferny waved from a nearby table. The Mess Hall was one of the most solid buildings in the camp, constructed of logs from the surrounding forest. Great beams of pine braced the roof on the gable ends. Chandeliers of oak and hobnail hung from the crossbeams. The place could easily hold more than a hundred at a time. This, plus the well-stocked foundry Ben had seen on his way in, showed that these Rebels were more numerous and better prepared than he had realized. Maybe there was hope of defeating this Swamp Ogre Barthas.

Ben thought about what he had learned from Miss Edna. Barthas was a seventeen-year-old delinquent brought up in a gang environment. He sighed and took a moment to be grateful for Patty and Max. Ben and Annie had made mistakes, but they were both good kids.

Max and Mombie acquiring skill

Eleven

A Bad Habit

After Dendra came out of her faint, we convinced her that Max was completely safe and "under control." So she put us all to bed: Max in the stable with the horses, the Zombies in the pasture, the goats in their shed, and me in the front guest room. Oh, I must confess that the down featherbed and eyelet linens made me feel like a thousand-year-old princess. Gods, my joints were painful! It was maddening. And sleeping in this featherbed felt like a cloud of comfort for my old bones.

Dendra knocked on the door and brought a steeping cup of willow-bark tea with honey. "For your joints," she said. And then, more softly, "I had a mother once, too."

So this is what it was to be so old that everyone worried about you.

The tea eased my aches and the sheets were immaculate and luxurious. "My daughter has sheets like this," I murmured.

"Real Gnome work," replied Dendra. "I learned it as a child."

"It's beautiful."

I slept like a baby that night and awoke with a renewed sense of purpose. Max and I could not continue as we were. Dendra had sketched out the political situation for me, and if I had any hope of getting back to the real world, I was going to have to get to this evil overlord, Barthas, and the Sorcerers who supposedly controlled the barrier gate.

We couldn't live this way unless we wanted to become a travelling freak show, painting barn walls and corralling goats with Zombies for the locals. There was little future in that.

More than likely Barthas would find us anyway and try to make use of my talent for himself. It would be far worse to raise an army of the dead for the bad guys: it was better to do it for me—and my "side," whatever that was. At least then I would become a participant and not a pawn.

I had been set upon this chessboard with certain abilities and handicaps. Whether I chose to like it or not, Max was right: my greatest strength right now was my necromancy. I was a Zombie Mistress, a raiser of the dead. For better or worse, till death do us *not* part.

I was too frail to put up much of a fight by myself. Again Max was right: much as I did not want to see it, my only protection, aside from my brave and willing thirteen-year-old son, was the Zombies themselves. *That* was my ability. I was either going to use it to become a player, and get Max and myself home to Middleville, or we were going to be stuck here forever and wind up as pawns of Barthas.

So I did what I always do when under pressure: I began composing mental lists.

One: Gather more Zombies. Yes, much as I had fought it at first, if I was to make a show of myself, then I would have to amass at least an honor guard of Zombies to both impress and threaten Barthas. I began by sending a mental call to the six Zombies in the graves down the road from Dendra's farm.

Two: We needed transportation. My body was failing more each day, and I could not continue to walk. As if in answer to my prayer, Dendra offered us her old pony cart; when Max hitched himself to the old leather harness it made a fairly nifty pedi-cab. Our three battered Zombies could shuffle alongside.

Three: Max needed that sword. The pike would do for now, but if his training required a sword, then we needed to outfit him. I had to start thinking less like a parent and more like a leader.

Four: We needed to arm the Zombies. For now some of the Mossys' old farm equipment would do: a hoe, a rusty scythe, a metal rake, an iron bar, whatever we could find. But we would need more, I was sure.

Dendra sewed us some simple nondescript robes with detachable hoods. It was amazing to watch her fingers fly as she whip-stitched sections of black cloth with her Gnomish fingers. Even such simple skills could be full of magic. The robes made us look like travelling holy men. Mine covered some of my frailty. Max's was in three pieces, including pants so he could move freely. But the upper portion was long enough to cover most of his tail and thereby disguise his new non-Human self, just as the hood concealed his scaly face and fangs. We needed to look mysterious if I was going to convince Barthas that he needed to bargain with me.

I decided to luxuriate one more night between Dendra's inviting sheets. Max seemed happy enough bedding down in the barn for his brief snooze. Most of the night he roamed, so he knew the surrounding terrain like the best of scouts.

That night he sniffed out and dug up an old wolf skull, and we fashioned a sort of crown out of it for me. Mr. Mossy even joined in to help by carving me a gnarled wooden staff from a twisted oak sapling. I was beginning to look the part of a true Crone. My hastily wrought sushi wrap was history.

Lastly, we agreed that Max was no longer to call me "Mom" in public. He would refer to me as "Mombie," his Zombie Mistress. Max thought this was the best idea of all. It made him laugh no end.

Halloween was going to seem like a sham after this.

The additional Zombies arrived by noon. There were six of them: four decayed Gnomes, a Giant, and a Human. I set the Giant and the Human as point guards, front and rear, and had the Gnomes, along with Bernice, Johnny, and Klug, arrange themselves defensively about my cart.

Dendra had marked some local graveyards and family burial

plots on the simple map she had drawn for us. She also made note of a major battle site where Barthas and his Swamp Ogres had won a critical victory against the united forces of the Fairy Folk. There should be plenty of warrior Zombies to resurrect there. We intended to visit these sites first to gather recruits. Then we would hit some of the ransacked villages, after which perhaps we would head for the place Dendra referred to as the Manor—Barthas's fortress.

We were only a few miles from Dendra's when we met up with the first squadron of Barthas's forces, an assorted foot patrol of roughly twenty-five ruffians. They included Trolls, Ogres, Humans (both men and women), and a few vile-smelling Harpies, who flapped overhead and shook feathers and detritus on the unlucky troops below. The talons on their chicken feet looked sharp enough to gut a bear.

The company drew to a halt as it approached our cart. I formed a line with the Zombies. A murmur grew among the troops as they realized that these were zombies, not citizens. In fact, these were Zombies carrying metal implements.

"Stay where you are," I called, trying to sound as calm and threatening as I could.

"I am Sargent Troff Tunkerd, and I lead this company of Lord Barthas's army."

"You may tell your master that you have met Mombie, Zombie Mistress and Necromancer. I am on an important mission with my loyal bodyguard, Max of Dojo Kyuke."

Max drew back his hood and executed a karate kick. Murmurs arose from the motley troops.

"She travels with a Swamp Demon!" I heard someone whisper loudly.

"The Swamp Demons have sworn allegiance to Barthas," blustered Sargent Tunkerd. "How is it that you are travelling with one?"

"My business is my own. My companion is sworn to *me*, not your master. Stand aside and let us pass." The Zombies began brandishing their weapons and took a step forward. Klug moaned menacingly. Max whirled his pike in the air. One of the Harpies flung a clawful of dung toward the zombies.

The air was thick with tension. Finally I added, "We are on our way to a meeting with Barthas."

This last bit seemed to satisfy Sargent Troff Tunkerd. He made a motion with his hand and said, "Let them pass. We have no business with Necromancers. Barthas will know what to do with them. Heil Barthas!" He stuck out his right arm like a Nazi.

"Peace, Dude," replied Max with a similar salute, only his hand took the shape of a peace sign. I hid my face in my hood to avoid laughing, and we proceeded on down the road past the dumbfounded company of Barthas's "army."

Barthas himself was blissfully unaware of anything outside his own reality at that moment. A man's leather belt circled his blubbery bicep, and his other hand shook as he injected a solution of Pixie Dust into his vein with a crude homemade hypodermic. It was an eyedropper onto which a needle had been cobbled.

"Damn, that's the real stuff," Barthas sighed as he leaned back on his enormous wooden throne. "You should let me do you, Irene. You don' know what you're missing."

"That's one thrill I can do without, José. I watched my brother kill himself by mainlining drugs, remember?" Irene tried to catch Barthas's attention, but he was seeing things beyond the reality of his throne room.

"It's not drugs, Irene. It's magic. Pixie Dust."

"Look, José, you can tell yourself whatever you want, but you are addicted to that stuff. Look at the facts. You can't get through a day without it. You shoot up the minute you get up in the morning."

"So what? It don't mean nothing, Irene. I just like it. I can stop any time."

"That's what my brother always said. He used to tell my mother that he had quit, because it made her happy. He never quit. He couldn't. But in his mind he believed he could." Irene shook her head. "He would have broken my mother's heart, but sadly, she always believed his medicated lies."

"Well, I ain't your brother, Irene. And you ain't leaving. I told you before. I need you here."

They had had this argument a hundred times. "I have to go back. You know that. You swore you would let me. We've been through all this before. I have already foreseen for you. Bring the old woman to you, use her power, and you will defeat the Rebels."

Still in his drug haze, Barthas murmured, "So when is she gonna show up, Irene? See, that's why I need you here." His voice grew defensive, then arrogant. "You can't go back. I won't let Sideous open the gate for you." At last he whined, "Just stay a little longer until we beat the Rebels. Come on, Irene."

"José ... Barthas, we've been through this, over and over. First it was stay until the Manor was built, then it was until we had captured all the Fairy Folk, then until the batteries are built.... It will never end. I cannot stand it here any longer. If I don't get home soon I will lose my mind!"

Barthas snorted another line of Pixie Dust on the table and coughed as it flew up his nose. "I am telling you, Irene, this stuff is PURE."

"Oh God, of course it is PURE! Pure innocence. It's the very essence of innocent happiness, José. Some of the last drops of happiness for the sheer sake of happiness. That is what those Pixies and Fairies experience that we no longer can, because we've experienced too many painful things in our lives. We have too much pain. You and I cannot just experience this magnificent world that way any longer. We're too jaded to react with pure joy. But they are PURE. They are INNOCENT. They react with PURE JOY! Don't you see, Barthas? Don't you see what you're doing?" Irene clenched her fists as her voice rose to a shout.

"Relax, bitch," Barthas muttered, slumping sideways in his throne. "There's always more Pixie Dust. I leave those details to

Sideous." He started to drift away.

"That's just it, Barthas. There won't be any Pixie Dust left, because you're destroying all the Fairy Folk. There won't be any more pure joy in this tired old world. Because *you* are breaking their hearts the same way that my brother broke my mother's heart, with your lies, your talk of a bigger society, electricity for all. They don't need electricity, José. They need their hopes and dreams and joy back. You're destroying the very thing you seek."

The tears flowed down Irene's face.

Barthas spoke out of his growing stupor. "Relax, Irene. It's all gonna work out. You'll see. Take somma this, you'll feel better. Look at me—I feel HAPPY." He grinned in a pallid, empty ecstasy.

"No Barthas, what you feel is someone else's happiness, not happiness in your own life. You are living on borrowed happiness, and I can't stand watching it any longer." She slammed the door as she left.

When Ben reached the Mess Hall he headed straight to Ferny and Planks and asked, "Where is Patty?" They both pointed to a large table in the middle of the Hall, lush with flowers and melons and other fruits. When Ben looked closer he could see tiny figures moving amidst the foliage. He walked closer and could make out windows and doors cut into the melons, and vines which had been trained to arch around windows and form shutters of leaves and pediments of flowers. Roads and walkways wove between the structures, and Pixies and Brownies walked along quietly chatting with one another. Butterflies flew over their heads, and several birds sang sweetly from the rafters above the table.

The largest melon sat in the center of the table, and he could hear voices coming from the interior. He leaned down and squinted with one eye through one of the windows. There were rows and rows of tables packed with tiny laughing forms, all eating pollen and nectar, joking and calling out to one another.

It was another world, a world within a world.

Ben straightened up.

"The wee folk have their own ways of dealing with things, Sir Ben," said Planks. "Patty went in with Button and Squirt about an hour ago. They should be out soon. Let's see what we can do about getting you something to eat."

For the first time, Ben felt alone in this world. Patty was experiencing new things that he could only imagine. How will this affect her? Would this change her? Was she growing up—or finally becoming a child?

A Satyr, who reminded him immediatly of Porkchop, the bartender at the Duke's Arse, handed him a lathe-turned wooden cup of wine to place on his tray. There were fresh fruits and cooked grains; a creature with a bull's head stood by a rack of roasted fowl. From all appearances the Rebel forces were well fed. Ben took some roasted potatoes and roots and heaped his plate with steaming quinoa, finishing it off with a small piece of chicken. Even Annie would approve of this meal, he thought. After all, he was no longer taking his cholesterol medication. Ben had so little time to think of Annie and Max. Were they eating dinner back in Middleville?

They made their way back to a table near the Wee Folks' world and began to eat. The wine was good, and well earned after his efforts with Hook.

"Ben, today you held lightning," said Hook. "Tomorrow you will work spirit. Then we will begin to weave."

"Daddy!" came a familiar voice wafting on the air. "Oh, Daddy, it's all so beautiful here! Button and Squirt let me ride the bullfrog and we visited the Fairies and Pixies. Oh, and Daddy, I met a Mermaid, a real live Mermaid!"

"Hey, that's swell, Punkin Pie." Ben was so relieved to see her well and happy, truly happy. "Hey, won't that Cynthia McGowan be jealous?"

Patty squealed with gales of happy laughter.

"I see everyone arrived safely." Miss Edna's calm voice came from behind Ben. How had she gotten here so fast? Several of the men at the table stood up and clasped their fists to their chests and bowed when they saw Miss Edna. She motioned for them to sit down. There was a round of gentle applause.

Men and Women, Gnomes, Elves, and Folk of all descriptions began to gather at the four entrances to the Mess Hall. Quiet whispers sent others scurrying to find the stragglers. Soon the room was filled to overflowing. The room grew absolutely silent as Miss Edna looked out at them all.

"Thank you," she said.

Thunderous applause and rhythmic table-thumping was the reply.

"This applause is for each and every one of you. Take a bow," Miss Edna said, and her comment was met with nervous laughter. "Tonight marks a turning point. We welcome into our ranks an apprentice Sorcerer, Sir Benjamin Prockner of Middleville!"

There was wild whooping from the crowd.

Ben found himself blushing furiously, trying to hide beneath his hat as he was hoisted to his feet.

"Together with our experienced and loyal Sorcerer Hook, and each and every brave soldier among you, each Centaur (hoof stomping), Merman (tail- and fin-slapping), Elf, Gnome, Giant, Pixie, Brownie, and Man-jack among you ..." the roar grew thunderous ... "we shall storm the very heart of our enemy's dungeons and free our people!"

"HOORAY!" they cried in a single voice.

"Because this is OUR home, and this is OUR Valley, and we WILL LIVE FREE AGAIN, or die trying."

Ben wasn't so sure he liked that last part.

They carried Miss Edna on their shoulders out to dance before the bonfires. Ben found himself swept along with the crowd.

Later, when things had quieted down a bit and the camp got ready for bed, guards and scouts were appointed by a sturdy-looking Centaur clad in shining steel armor. The streets and pathways began to clear, and Ben found himself wandering toward Miss Edna's tent.

It was easy to find, as it was both the largest and the most centrally located in the entire camp. The exterior was bristling with armed guards. They crossed their spears and demanded, "Halt, who goes there?" as Ben approached.

Ben pointed to his hat, the very hat Annie had made him wear, but that felt like a lifetime ago. He managed to say, "Sir Ben, apprentice Sorcerer."

One of the guards dipped his head inside the tent and announced him. He heard a voice from within, "Come!" and the spears uncrossed as the guards nodded to him to enter.

Miss Edna was sitting at a large wooden table covered in maps and scrolls, illuminated by candles floating above the desk. Ben approached and, out of courtesy, began to remove his hat, but Edna stopped him. "Don't take that off. It's your badge of office. Wear it every waking moment. Hook does."

"Yes, Ma'am, er, General, uhm, Miss Edna."

"You can call me Edna, honey. Just Edna will do. You look like you have some questions on your mind."

"Yeah. Like for one, how in the world did you get here so fast?"

Miss Edna allowed herself a satisfied chuckle. "You noticed that, did you? Heh-heh. Well, that's a little trade secret, but I suppose that now that you are on our side… you ARE on our side, ain'tcha?" Edna squinted at Ben sideways.

"Absolutely! I want to protect Patty!"

"Okay, then. You are going to have to swear an oath with all the other new recruits in the morning, but I suppose I can let you in on my little secret." There was a silence as Miss Edna thought about it for a moment. And then she said, "I can fly on my broom." She nodded to a handmade broom propped in the corner.

Ben choked on a laugh. "You're serious?"

"Oh, it ain't easy. Lifting my own body weight takes the dickens out of me and gives me a beauty of a migraine afterwards, but yes, I get on the broom and propel it telekinetically. So while you were on the river and taking your sweet time climbing the pass, I gained elevation and headed for the mountain as the crow flies—or the Witch, if you will." Miss Edna winked at Ben.

Once again, Ben found himself dumbfounded. This world was getting stranger and stranger. Maybe he had hit his head, and this was all a dream. It made as much sense as anything he had just heard. He shook his head to try to clear it.

"Oh, you'll get over it," she continued. "You have to. We have too much to do to have you overwhelmed. We need every man we can get, and Sorcerers are not common. There are only about five in the valley, including you, and Barthas has two of them. The other one is reportedly in hiding and won't commit to either side. That's why we need you more than ever. Barthas is not counting on you to be strong or prepared. But you are inherently strong, and Hook will prepare you. It's just a matter of time. We have five days left."

Ben spluttered, "Five days? How can I ever be prepared in five days?"

"Well, that's the thing, honey. We have five days left until the equinox, and three days after that is the full moon. That's when Barthas will make his move to open the gate, which you need to get back to Middleville. You do want to go back, don'tcha?"

"More than anything! Edna, I have a wife and a thirteen-year-old son who must be worried out of their minds about me!"

"You so sure they didn't come through to the valley as well? It happens, you know."

"When we left, it was snowing and my wife took my son in the minivan to his school. That's the last time I saw them. It must be several days already."

"Well, time and seasons are different here, as you may have noticed. And you wouldn't be the first family or group of related acquaintances to be pulled through the gate. It happens. That's all I'm saying."

Ben had never considered this possibility. Could Annie be here, with Max? But where? And as what? His head was reeling.

Miss Edna motioned for Ben to come over to her side of the

table to look at the map she was studying.

"Okay, here is the Valley. We are up here, on the edge of the Valley in the mountains. Here is Barthas's Manor. That's where we must strike. But first we must pass through these villages and towns and gather reinforcements. There is a small base camp here, at the base of the mountain, where we will stop." Miss Edna pushed a stray lock of her grizzled hair back into her disheveled bun. "Flying blows the crap out of a girl's hairdo," she laughed. Ben smiled and she went on. "Here is the waterfall, where the last of our Fairy Folk are holed up, and I've diverted every soldier I can spare to guard them. They're the last of our precious resources. They are what we are fighting for."

"Wouldn't Patty be safer there?"

"Hard to say. Barthas has already attempted several assaults on our defenses, and we can't hold out forever. Barthas has numbers on his side. He has paid off the Ogres, the Swamp Demons, the Trolls, many of the Minotaur tribes, and three quarters of the teeming Goblin population, whereas we are leading a bunch of farmers and innocents. Oh, I give you that the Centaurs make fierce warriors and we have a few Giants and renegade Trolls. But overall, Barthas has the kind of strength we lack. That's why we have to surprise him with an attack."

"I'm not sure I am ready for all this," Ben mumbled.

"You had better get ready, man. It's your daughter that this monster is after. Let me tell you a little something about Barthas...."

Ben managed to find his tent through the darkened camp. His legs were shaking and he was crying. What Miss Edna had told him about Barthas had shaken him to the core. He opened the flap of the red-and-white striped tent and saw Hook sleeping quietly on his cot. Next to the other cot was a small stool, covered by a pillow, on which was a tiny, snoring Pixie. Ben managed to crawl under the blankets, but he couldn't stop crying, thinking about his family. Tomorrow would be a long day.

Twelve

Scyssa and Pheek

Sideous sat calmly as two Swamp Demons dragged a Mermaid toward the chair in front of the batteries. She struggled weakly, but with each twist of her beautiful form sad little whines escaped from her once-proud chest. Her iridescent green tail and fins scraped the stone floor.

"Please, just a few moments in the water, it would restore my magic no end. Just let me swim a little, please, Lord Sideous. Not yet. Let me wait a little longer. Please?"

"Now, now, stop your struggling. This does not hurt. Lord Barthas has need of your magic for the greater cause. Just sit still and stop your fussing."

Assistants clamped electrodes to her exquisite form and she writhed in anticipation. Somehow she looked all the more beautiful, and her haunting voice rang in their ears. Diodes glowed and electricity crackled between the terminals atop the batteries.

The mermaid slumped in the seat and the colors began to drain from her. Her face sagged and saddened. Her breasts drooped, and the clamshells became loose and ill fitting. Scales fell from her tail, and it seemed as though one could see the outline of human legs where once had been a glistening, shiny fishtail.

"Ohhhh..." she moaned weakly from the wheelchair.

The drab, drained, tired creature they rolled back out in the chair bore little resemblance to the alluring beauty they had brought in.

"Bring me another one," barked Sideous. He added silkily, "Barthas and the Empire thank you for your contributions. Generations yet to come will thank you for advancing the cause of the free people of the Valley. Your donation of magic helps build our tomorrow!"

The Mermaid heard none of this as she was rolled away like yesterday's cod dinner.

Barthas came down the stone steps to the dungeon. His bare feet slapped the steps as he descended, but his massive, gelatinous form barely squeezed through the opening of the stairwell. He oozed out, like sausage escaping from its casing, and his blubber continued to shiver for a few seconds before settling into place. The entire dungeon reverberated as he hammered his spiked iron club on the floor.

"Sideous."

"My Lord Barthas."

"You have enough?"

"Enough, my Lord?" he coughed. "I wasn't aware of such a concept. After all, what is enough to a man who desires power?"

"Just remember who rules this place, Sideous!" Barthas slammed his club on the floor again. Little chips of stone showered upwards. "I might look dumb in this body, Sideous. But I ain't! Where I come from a boy proves his cajones by killing a rival gang member. I offed my first culo when I was twelve." Barthas fingered a row of sharp steel knives that ran through a leather strap cinching his filthy bearskin tunic. "I know how to use these, and I will, if I get so much as a single vibe that you double-dipped on me, Bro."

"My Lord Barthas knows that I am his most loyal follower. Why, once I invented these batteries, was it not his plan to sell electricity as well as protection? Does my Lord Barthas not see the larger plan for the Valley? Was it not *he* who foretold the glittering beauty of electric lights sparkling on hill and dale? Is it not *he* who has led this glorious restructuring of our misguided and backward society? Did he not foresee the generous outpouring of donated magic, which is the very wellspring of our new world?" Sideous bowed obsequiously.

"Shut your hole, Toady." Barthas's voice was low and controlled this time. He hated Sideous with an ice-cold passion. "You think I give a pile of bat dung about all these freaking cartoon Fairies?!"

The prisoners began to moan and crowd into the corner. Barthas waved his spiked iron bludgeon about the room, eyeing an Elven male of indeterminate age. His elegant pointed ears began to quiver, but his eyes betrayed no fear. With an effortless swing around his head and then into the Elf's neck, Barthas took off the Elf's head. The body stood for a moment as its neck bubbled thick red blood, then it collapsed with a sickening crunch onto the stone floor. The rest of the assorted prisoners moaned softly in their cages and on the line for processing. A female Harpy fainted in a heap of filthy black feathers and oily dust.

"And get me more of that freaking Fairy Dust! I need it! I COMMAND it!" Barthas turned and began squeezing himself back through the opening of the stairwell.

After our encounter with Barthas's advance guard, things quieted down and I began calling up Zombies in earnest. We followed Dendra's map and visited both graveyards and battle sites. Battle sites yielded the freshest Zombies, but it began to unnerve me to see the carnage that Barthas and his army had wrought on tiny, peaceful, sleepy hamlets of the Valley. We skirted the few that had survived in order to avoid notice by the living. There daily life went on as it had for countless years: bakers baked, dogs barked, donkeys brayed, and children played.

But Dendra's map led us to the villages that had been ransacked. In those I raised Zombie after Zombie. Our army was growing. Their voices were a constant echo in my head, and I began to realize that I had a constant, pounding headache from trying to hold onto all of them. It was not unlike trying to herd a flock of chickens—or teenagers.

In a small town called Plunket, I had my breakdown. Children—no, babies, Zombie babies—began to answer my summons. Barthas's army had murdered innocent babies in their mothers' arms ... and I was awakening them. I started shaking all over and sobbing. My Zombies felt my mood and began pounding their various gathered weapons on the ground. Shovels, scythes, hoes, knives, and clubs set up a slow, thumping, funereal drumbeat. Several of those who still had a voice box began to howl a mournful cry like a wolfpack in winter. It was some kind of war chant, and I wanted to howl in agreement.

I sat in the pony cart and tried to get a grip on myself. Then I had to coax the babies and small children back to the long sleep of true death. Being a Necromancer, I was learning, wasn't all they portrayed it to be in the comic books and fantasy novels. So I calmed myself, and I sang them lullabies and rocked the smallest one in my arms. It was a battered little corpse of less than three months old, with the top of its head smashed in. I couldn't stop crying as I sang to it. I felt hot tears falling from my ancient, red-rimmed eyes. Max stood quietly in the corner with Eddie on his shoulder, and his head hung in desolation. We left the Zombie babe in a cradle we found in one of the cottages and tip-toed out, my army following in solemn, shuffling obedience.

This was no game. Some of those already following me were children's corpses. I needed every sword arm I could find. And we ransacked the village for rakes, shovels, anything that could be used as a weapon, and piled them onto the pony cart. I was intending to storm Barthas's Manor and hold him in siege until his food ran out. Zombies don't have to eat. We had all the time in the world, if I could just outnumber him. Every dead Giant, Troll, Centaur, Human, Gnome, Dwarf, and Ogre I raised was another strong soldier with which to ring Barthas like a gastric bypass.

The stakes had just gone up for me. Dendra had described the violence and carnage that Barthas had wrought, but those had been just words. Until now, I had thought of this world as one of those online games that Max played. No one dies; you just sign off when you are bored or tired. But there was no signing off here: this was a deadly game of death and destruction, and I was taking Max right into the heart of this darkness.

Was I right? Did I know what I was doing? Did I have a choice? We had to get home. I had to change him back. Didn't I?

That night we made camp near a small lake. There was a well-constructed dam at the outlet of the stream, and we watched the beavers cutting down a sapling to add to it. It was certainly harder work than I was capable of in my aging body. Setting up camp was easier. I slept in the pony cart and the Zombies settled downwind of wherever Max lay. Little bits of everything sloughed off them during the night and the smell was probably awful, but my old nose couldn't smell much of it any more. Before we settled in, Max slipped off to hunt, and I sent Bernice and a small party of newer recruits to gather herbs around the lake. I still had a chunk of Dendra's delicious whole grain bread, and I gnawed on it with what was left of my teeth.

Bernice got back before Max and I set about sorting through the herbs and greens. Zombies are not meticulous about most things, and there were plenty of weeds, bugs and stray branches in the basket. Still, it was easier than trying to do it myself in this aching old body. I found myself relying on my Zombies more and more. Dendra had given us a few of her old pots and pans. I began stewing the herbs and greens with a dash of the precious salt that she had spared us.

It seemed that Max had been gone a long time when he finally reappeared out of the woods holding the hand of another Swamp Demon. Or perhaps I should say Demoness, because, clearly, it was a female of the species. She was bandy-legged and long-armed, and wore a leather corset to afford modesty, and a matching pleated leather peplum miniskirt. All I could think of was Xena, Warrior Princess, who was clearly far too mature for my scarcely teenaged son. Two short swords hung from her belt. Her forked tongue snaked out to taste the air. The scent of the Zombies had her ready to bolt.

I was gobsmacked.

"Mombie," Max winked at me, "This is Scyssa. I found her drinking from the inlet stream on the north side of the lake. She's running away from her family because they want her to marry some guy who's a hit man for Barthas. I told her we were going to take him down, and she agreed to join us."

Scyssa did some sort of a body wiggle which worked its way down to the tip of her tail, and she extended her scaly green-taloned hand toward me, palm up. I took this as a formal greeting and bowed slightly as I said, "Hello, Scyssa." I took a deep inward breath. "Max? May I speak with you?"

"Mom!"

I gave him a look.

"I mean, Mombie!"

I started walking toward the woods with Eddie on my shoulder and motioned for him to follow. "Caw!" said Eddie.

"What do you think you are doing?" I began. "You can't just invite her to join us like we're the Boy Scouts! We're alone in a dangerous place, your father must be out of his mind with worry about us, we have to find a way to get out of here!" I sputtered in a furious whisper.

Max was calmer than I expected. "Mom, she's all alone. Scyssa has been cast out of her tribe. You saw what Barthas's soldiers do to wanderers and stragglers on the roads around here. They either take everything for Barthas, or kill you, or both. We can't just leave her out here on her own. Besides, she's a trained warrior. She can help us defend ourselves once we're on the main roads."

Maybe Max was better apprised of our dilemma than I gave him credit for. My baby was growing up. Maybe I had better do some myself. "Can we trust her?"

"As much as anyone else, Mom. As far as I'm concerned, anyone against Barthas is with us. You trusted Dendra. She could have tipped off a spy, but so far she hasn't; at least not that we know of. Besides, I think Scyssa is kind of pretty..."

You could have knocked me down with a feather. Pretty? That bandy-legged half-iguana? Oh my God! Is that how the Gods will punish me? Am I looking at my future daughter-in-law? I thought I had prepared myself for anything when Max had hit thirteen. I had imagined Goth Valkyries and Valley Girl cheerleaders, but one thing I had *not* prepared myself for was a a Swamp Demoness. But I calmed myself, swallowed, breathed, and asked, "What did you find for dinner?"

"A wandering lamb. The soldiers must have scattered the villager's flocks. I am telling you, Mom, this place is falling to pieces politically and socially."

We went back to the camp, where Max fashioned a spit over the fire I had built. He had become expert at skinning with his claws and a knife from his bandoliers. I stuffed the lamb with herbs and wild onion grass, then we tied its legs to its body with some sturdy vines to roast it. The smell was delicious. We passed around the bread, although it was not to Scyssa's taste. Conversation was slowed by her small command of the common speech. Max could, somehow, understand some of her native tongue, which included many sibilant esses and frequent showing of those prominent incisors in a sort of a smile.

Scyssa was the daughter of the tribal chief. Some fellow named Shadow Stalker had brought great glory and wealth for the tribe by working for Barthas. So they had sought a marriage between him and the chief's daughter. But Scyssa had other plans. For one, she felt she was too young to marry. But more than that, she hated Barthas and what he was doing to the Valley. She even claimed to have connections to what she called the "Rebels." Scyssa had been brought up according to her traditional father's rules, but she had a liberated mother who bent them regularly. Her father had expected her to sacrifice to the old gods and obey her elders; her mother had encouraged her to learn to hunt and defend herself like a male. But now that Barthas had taken over, her father saw only the wealth that Barthas brought to their previously humble lives. So when the marriage had been proposed, Scyssa had fled her tribe.

So here we were. Two Swamp Demons, a Crone, and an army of putrid Zombies, sitting around a campfire like the Hardy Boys on a springtime camp-out. And yet that morning my "ability" had raised a Zombie babe, a horror out of a nightmare. I was glad when the lamb was done and I could suck on delicious greasy bites of roasted lamb. Even Scyssa liked the lamb. And as Scarlet O'Hara always said, "I'll think about that tomorrow."

Pheek lolled on the back of Blina's warhorse like a sack of luggage. Everyone else had dismounted as they led their horses along the rocky riverbed while Shadow Stalker sniffed ahead for any trace of the Rebels. Pheek's hands were tied to the saddle, but he could see and hear. He certainly knew where they were, several miles north of Miss Edna's place. Shadow kept insisting that he could find their trail, but it was clear that they had stayed to the river and maybe taken to the hills. Pheek was half the size of his captors, and he struggled stealthily to free his hands from the knot, hoping no one would notice.

"Here," whispered Shadow Stalker. "Here isss where they left the river to go through the brush up the mountain."

"I don't like it," complained Blina. "There are Rebel camps in this area. We are no more than twenty in this company. They could surround us."

Pheek had freed his right hand and began moving it slowly toward the knot that tied him to Blina's rear saddle pommel.

"Do you wish to lose them? I have their scent now. We cannot waste this chance to take out the Sorcerer while he is untrained. And what about the Pixie? Are you willing to lose the chance to catch a last Pixie for Sideous?"

"I still don't like it," grumbled Blina. "We have to split up. Pick six of the best assassins from the men and go forward. If you can catch them, kill the Sorcerer and take the Pixie. If you are too late, as I fear, scout what you can, assess their numbers, and return to the Manor."

Pheek had loosened his bonds and was lowering himself from Blina's horse while her back was to him. As long as she was distracted by her argument with Shadow Stalker he had a chance to inch his way into the bushes before anyone noticed.

"Now, I don't like it. But we are wasssting time. I am losing their ssscent. I will take Blenem, Derrick, Fillip, Jackson, Schaler, and Blunt. Be quick about it. Leave your horses and take only what you need for a few days. We have to move quickly."

There was some shuffling around as horse bridles were handed off to comrades, and Pheek used the confusion to hide his slow crawl into the bushes. Blina's attention was on the exchange, and her horse was handed off in a group of other soldiers. No one noticed that the parcel of wriggling weasel was missing. So Pheek crept further up the hill under cover of the dense scrub growth.

Blina was on her horse and heading back while calling out orders to the remaining troops when she blurted out, "Where's that sneaking ass squirt!? Who the hell let the weasel get away?" She glared at the soldiers while they shrugged their shoulders and feigned innocence. "Search the bushes!"

But Pheek was a stealthy weasel, and he easily remained hidden for the short while that the soldiers pretended to search.

"Aw, to hell with him!" Blina roared. "Let's get back to the Manor!"

Pheek waited a long time after their hooves had thundered off before he started climbing after the Swamp Demon and his six men. The way was steep and rocky, covered by laurel shrubs, scrub oak, and pine. The evening was drawing on and it was hard to pick out the prints of the soldiers' boots. But Pheek was patient, and after some intense climbing he heard Shadow Stalker and his men ahead of him on the incline.

The Swamp Demon was whispering orders to his men in soft words that Pheek could not make out. But when he saw Shadow Stalker move ahead alone, he could surmise the plan. Pheek crept low through the brush and tailed him at a safe distance.

Pheek saw them before Shadow did. A sentry unit of Miss Edna's guard was lazily traversing the far perimeters; there were two Centaurs with bows and a collection of Dwarves and Gnomes, all backed up by a hulking Hill Ogre. Shadow Stalker smelled them before he saw them and crouched down in the bushes, but it was too late. One of the Dwarves heard a twig snap and turned suddenly toward Shadow's hiding place.

"What's that?" asked the Dwarf, and he held up his hand to silence the others. He motioned them forward toward the sound when a dagger flew from the shrubs and took a Centaur in the throat. He died with a gurgled cry of surprise. The other notched his arrow and aimed toward the spot where the dagger had come from. But the Swamp Demon was already ten feet away when the arrow whizzed past him. He blasted out a shrill wail through his pointed canines, and the six assassins came running from their hiding place downhill. Within seconds the Dwarves and Gnomes had engaged with the trackers in sword-on-sword combat. Shadow's soldiers were outnumbered, but they fought like men possessed. The remaining Centaur abandoned his bow and began fencing with Shadow Stalker. But the Swamp Demon was a killing machine: he not only fought with his sword, but used his claws and spiked tail. Things were going badly when the Hill Ogre stumbled over something in the brush, and pulled up a wriggling Pheek.

"What this? A thief? A sneak? A traitor?"

The distraction was the opening the Centaur needed. With his foe's concentration broken, he landed a glancing blow to Shadow Stalker's arm. Three of the assassins were dead, along with four Dwarves and two Gnomes. Shadow hooted sharply again and the remaining three began to back up and disengage. Another hoot and they were running madly down the slope to escape, Shadow Stalker far ahead of his Humans.

The Centaur took the wriggling Pheek and sent the Ogre crashing through the low wood after the intruders. It was an idle threat. Ogres were slow and stupid, but they could break a man in half with one blow; few Humans would dare take one on alone. The sentries' main mission was to keep the Rebel camp from being discovered, and the Ogre would ensure that the intruders, who had scattered down the hill in different directions, did not come back.

Aeolys, the Centaur, regrouped his remaining men and imitated a birdcall, which brought a back-up group of sentries to join him and his prisoner.

"Let's bring this weasel to Miss Edna," he said. "He looks like he'll sing."

Pheek began to struggle, then immediately stopped when Aeolys gripped him more tightly. He looked sidewise at his captor and whined, "I know nothing. I was their prisoner. I am on your side."

"You can tell all that to Miss Edna, thief."

"I am no thief!" protested Pheek. It was only technically true: people lost things; was it Pheek's fault that he was good at finding them?

The remaining three Dwarves and two Gnomes snorted at him with derision, bound his hands behind his back, put a sack over his head and shoved him forward roughly through the brush and back toward camp.

"Miss Edna will decide that, thief." Aeolys's voice was low and controlled. He had just lost seven good soldiers in what should have been a simple skirmish. His arm had a gash in it from one of Shadow Stalker's daggers, and both the remaining Gnomes were limping. Someone had to pay for this.

Ben was in the practice yard with Hook, learning the secrets of working with earth, causing landslides and creating sinkholes, when they heard the commotion. A crowd was forming, and above the mingled bodies crushing the sentries and their captive, Ben could see Planks Longshanks standing head and shoulders above the crowd.

"That's him! The one who tipped off Barthas! He was in the Duke's Arse the night Sir Ben arrived!" The crowd turned toward Planks when Ferny stepped forward and corroborated Planks's statement. "Aye. That's the sneak. Weasel that he is."

The crowd began to jeer and heckle. "Hang him!"

"Gut the weasel!"

"Kill the traitor!"

"Justice for the people!"

Fortunately Miss Edna arrived before anything rash happened. She was accompanied by an Elvish male of indeterminate age, who began examining the wounds on the Centaur and the Gnomes.

"Bring the traitor to my tent. You three go to the healing tent and wait on Doctor Rosenblatt. Mr. Prockner, Sir Hook, may I have a word with you?" All this Miss Edna said with perfect calm, as if teaching a class of elementary school kids.

Ben and Hook walked over to Miss Edna and the quiet Elf.

"Ben, I would like you to meet Doctor Rosenblatt, our healer."

Ben was surprised by the name, but before he could ask, the Elf took his hand and said, "Moishe Rosenblatt, Williamsburg, Brooklyn. I was an OB-GYN to the Hasidic community before this. One Shabbat I was in temple and stepped out to use the men's room. When I opened the door I stepped through into the Elven glade, northwest of here, not far from the Mermaids' waterfall, and the rest is history. Imagine my surprise when I finally looked in a mirror and saw this goyshe face!" Doctor Rosenblatt laughed heartily when he said this, and Ben found himself liking the doctor immediately.

"And now that the introductions are over, we have work to do," Edna said impatiently to Hook and Ben. "That traitor needs to spill his guts, and I will need your help to do that."

Doctor Rosenblatt stepped forward and cleared his throat. "Miss Edna, if I may? Mightn't I show Sir Ben some of the healing work we do here at the camp, before the ugly business begins?"

Ben wasn't too sure what Rosenblatt was referring to, but if following him meant a reprieve then he was all for it.

"Very well, Moishe. But I want him in my tent within the hour."

Doctor Rosenblatt took Ben's arm and led him to a tent set off to the side of the main tactical tent, which was filled with Miss

Edna's maps and notes about the movement of Barthas's men. This smaller tent was crammed with cots and manned by Elves and Gnomes dressed in crisp white linens. For the first time Ben noticed that Doctor Rosenblatt wore similar white linens, although his tunic had a green leaf embroidered on it. A Centaur stood in a corner nursing a large gash in his bicep that had been bandaged with clean gauze. Blood was seeping through the bandage.

Doctor Rosenblatt walked slowly toward the Centaur. "Aeolys, that looks bad. What was fast enough to give you that? I've seen you use a sword, and few men can best you."

Aeolys spoke under his breath but with quiet respect, "A Swamp Demon."

"Ah, that explains it. So Barthas has lured the swamp folk to his cause?"

"They were one of the first communities to get electricity."

"Of course. Let me see what I can do for that wound." The doctor unwound the bandage and began singing in a queer high Elven tenor voice what sounded like a Hebrew prayer. The entire tent went quiet and all eyes turned toward the doctor. Slowly the bicep began to pull together and the wound healed over, leaving nothing but a slight scab.

He turned to Ben and explained, "I was the assistant cantor for the temple. So when I came over here my talents seemed to blend into one. Over there I was a doctor who sang, here I am a singer who heals. Oh, sure, some of the simpler stuff can be treated with willow-bark teas and some sterile sutures, but when I use my gift, for truly it is a gift, I feel a certain satisfaction in doing something I couldn't do back home. Magic, of course has its price, and the healing takes something out of you each time. But the price of magic is something I assume you are learning with Hook."

Ben nodded. He couldn't think of anything to say after witnessing a small miracle. But he knew that he was exhausted after a day of Hook's tutoring. Magic had a price indeed.

"But the time has come for you to be at Miss Edna's tent and assist in the interrogation of the prisoner."

Ben's eyes bugged out. Him? Assist an interrogation?

The Doctor continued. "I have no stomach for such work and will stay here. I assume you know the way?" He gently waved Ben toward the tent flaps.

Ben took the hint and bowed, saying, "Very nice to meet you, Doctor. I am sure we will see much of each other."

"You arrive as the crisis draws to a head. There will be hard days ahead if we are to take back this world. Gut Mazel, Sir Ben."

Ben stepped out into the chilly night air and made his way through the planked paths toward the light radiating from Miss Edna's tent. He could see Hook's striped beret through the flap.

"Evening, Miss Edna."

She wore the grimmest face he had ever seen. "He is in a separate tent. Set away from the family tents. I'll try to muffle his screams, but we may have to make some noise and draw some blood tonight. Follow me and do exactly as I say."

Ben didn't like the sound of this. He hadn't heard from Patty in hours and now he was involved in some kind of "enhanced interrogation." This just seemed to be going from bad to worse.

When they got to the tent where Pheek was being held, Edna burst in and with her telekinesis grabbed the little weasel by his bound ankles and hung him upside down in mid-air. She shook him until pocket watches, silver spoons, and coins began to drop from his waistcoat pockets.

"Help! Murder! Rape!" the little weasel cried.

"You'll wish for all of those things before I am done with you, you little traitor. Town Clerk is it? You record taxes and entries for Barthas? Then you ought to know quite a bit, you sneaking rodent. Now how did you get here and why did you leave the Duke's Arse the other night?"

Edna nodded to Hook and an arc of lightning flew from his hand into the prisoner. Pheek shuddered and stiffened in a seizure. Ben knew how that felt.

"I'm sorry, I couldn't hear you," smiled Miss Edna.

Pheek began to sputter, "I'll talk. I'll talk."

"Oh, is the weasel speaking? Funny you were so quiet that night you fled the Duke's Arse. Where did you go? And what did you tell them?"

"Just the local news, my Lady. Only that the Smigels had a new pup, and old Lady Landbury's goose had gotten out again. Nothing more."

Edna nodded to Hook and eyed Ben. "I need a little help here, Mr. Prockner," she said in a stage whisper. But her demanding eyes were serious. Ben did what came naturally after a day of working earth: he opened a yawning sinkhole beneath the suspended and inverted Pheek. Everyone in the tent stepped back from the edge. Pheek sighed a greedy sigh as the gold watch and the silverware plummeted into the nothingness below. But he also began to sweat, and a sad frightened keening escaped his trembling lips. "Don't drop me, please," he whispered.

"Then cut the crap, you two-faced little weasel. You went to Barthas, didn't you?"

"Yes."

"And?"

"And I told him about the Sorcerer and the Pixie," Pheek blurted out.

"And what did you get for your troubles, little rat?" queried Miss Edna.

"I got beat up and tied onto the back of Blina Turdgirdle's horse all day."

"And you still believe you've chosen the right side, scum?"

Pheek remained silent and looked down into the gaping, bottomless hole beneath him. A tear escaped his eye.

Edna looked at Hook and Ben, then hooked her head toward the tent flap. "Don't worry," she said. "I can hold him from this distance. I won't drop him accidentally."

All three—the Witch and two Sorcerers—walked away from the

tent. Edna whispered, "I'm thinking we can use this stooge if we fill him with misinformation and send him back. But my problem is, how do we trust him? What hold do we have on such a two-face?"

Ben surprised himself. Before he even thought it through he asked, "He has a mother, right? Everyone has a mother."

Edna smiled in spite of herself and said, "I like your thinking, Mr. Prockner. Get me someone to find his mother. More than likely she's in the refugee camps. Most of the first evacuees were from the cities."

She went back into the tent. Moving a table over onto the side and ignoring the upside-down Pheek, she called for a servant. "Gentlemen, shall we have tea while we wait?"

Thirteen

Bad Decisions

Ben waited patiently with Miss Edna and Hook, taking tea while Edna dangled the weasel over the pit with her powerful telekinesis. "Aren't you getting tired?" Ben asked her.

"Comme ci, comme ça. Fortunately, he's not heavy. And more than that, Mr. Prockner, it's good practice. Haven't you noticed the men in the yard practicing with their swords? Well, each to his chosen weapon, I say. You ought to be practicing every moment you can. A war is coming. You're about to meet some of the refugees. Twyla has gone to fetch them."

Just then Twyla drew up to the interrogation tent with two of the saddest-looking wet weasels and a slew of raggedy pups. The older weasel was wrapped in sodden knitted shawls clutched at her breast, the younger had deep circles under her eyes. The pups ran about the room until Ben heard himself comment, "Careful near the edge." The sinkhole still yawned wide and deep. Twyla made a little dip of respect toward Ben, coincidentally showing off her ample bosom. She winked.

The elder weasel came forward weeping.

"You shame me, Pheek. I don't know what we ever did that caused you to go so rotten. You're working for a Demon, Pheek. Have you sold your soul, or don't you recognize your old mother and your wife? She's the wife you left to escape barefoot into the hills with your rotten pups"—which were now running under the tea table—"and if it weren't for Miss Edna's kindness, well, I don't think we would be here to tell the tale. They're teaching the young ones to use swords, just in case. It's *that* serious, it is."

"Ma, I'm in an awful way," whined Pheek. "Barthas is cruel and demanding. I *had* to do what I did. I thought he would pay me and then I could have helped you and the kids. I thought there was gold in it."

"Gold, always gold. And was there any gold for you?"

"No, he beat me up and took me prisoner."

"You *are* a fool, Pheek. You're a true weasel, just like your father. The glitter of gold wins your heart every time. From now on you do as Miss Edna tells you."

Edna interrupted. "And you, Stupid Pheek, remember we have your mother, your wife and your kids."

A knife calmly floated through the air to hover at Pheek's neck. "The knife will be at their throats if you mess up. Do you understand? I've killed before and I will do it again if it means bringing peace to this Valley."

"I understand. I swear it."

"You had better."

Miss Edna concentrated her thoughts, and the weasel swung upright and floated over to the more solid ground beyond the sinkhole. She let go, and he fell to the ground, his hands still bound behind his back. Edna barked, "Blindfold him, stuff his ears with wax, and lock him in the brig. I plan to have a conversation with him in the morning."

The guards took Pheek to the brig, and Ben turned to Edna. "Do we trust him?"

She smiled coldly. "It doesn't matter. He's a little rat in a big war. If we feed him with misinformation about our numbers and our facilities and drop him blindfolded on the edge of the old forest, he'll return to Barthas with lies. It's his mother and wife I pity."

"You wouldn't really…"

"I'm a pacifist, Mr. Prockner, but in a war, people get hurt."

Her comment made Ben feel even more uncomfortable.

"And Mr. Prockner," she added with a real smile, "see if you can fill in that sinkhole for me. I don't want someone stumbling in during the night."

Patty was as happy as she had been in her whole life, cavorting with Fairy Folk and Pixies, even visiting a Mermaid. And best of all, she had become what she had always dreamed of: a Pixie.

When morning dawned she couldn't wait to get to the Wee Folks' Mess Hall to see the rest of the little folk. Each day she met someone new. One Fairy had taught her to heal flowers, another to make vines grow and flowers bloom. And Button and Squirt had become her fast friends, taking her everywhere and introducing her to everyone. Soon they were supposed to ride the bullfrogs near the waterfall and meet a Unicorn. A real live Unicorn!

Patty couldn't wait. She was sprinkling Pixie Dust everywhere in her excitement. She got off her pillow on the bedside table, flew over to her father's bed and settled on his ear. "Daddy, I'm going to breakfast."

Ben mumbled something and sat bolt upright on his cot. Patty took to the air. Her heart felt more alive and innocent than ever. She saw the beauty in all things and could see people's auras. The world looked full of joy and harmony. Oh, Button and Squirt had explained that there were bad people out there who were out to hurt her, just like Daddy. But while the old Patty understood and remembered learning about "stranger danger," the Pixie in her believed that such people just needed to be loved. Even Patty recognized that this change might be dangerous ... but it felt so good! Maybe it was all the Pixie Dust.

Ben focused his eyes on her and said, "Morning, Punkin."

"Daddy? Can I go with Button and Squirt to see a Unicorn? They say it's safe and we'll ride their bullfrogs and I can be back in time for dinner. Can I? Please? It may be my only chance. I promise we'll be careful. I know about the bad man."

"Sweetheart." Ben rubbed his eyes and thought about today's lesson with Hook. He would start weaving together the elements he was learning to control. Hook had called him a natural, but Ben wondered if that wasn't just fluff to get him committed to an impossible suicide mission. He tried to focus on the darting Pixie in front of him and remember that this was his eight-year-old daughter.

"It isn't that simple. Barthas has spies everywhere." His mind flashed back to hanging a terrified weasel over a gaping chasm the night before. "I want to talk to Button and Squirt. You all come out of that crazy magical melon you eat in and meet me at breakfast. Then we'll discuss it."

"Aw, Daddy!"

"I said we will discuss it."

"I'm going to breakfast."

"Patrice, don't be that way. Please. Even if you are a Pixie, I am still your father. I need to look after your safety. This is a dangerous world. You don't know half the things that I know about what's going on. There is a war coming and I have to learn from Sir Hook how to be part of it."

"I know Daddy, but you're a powerful Sorcerer now. Everyone tells me so."

"Well, I don't know about the powerful part. I'm still a student."

"I understand, Daddy. It's like you're back in school now, like Althea Jackson's Mom. She's studying to be a nurse."

Ben had to laugh. "I guess that explains it as much as anything else, Punkin."

"See you at breakfast!" and Patty flew off. She slalomed between the tents, above the heads of the big people, leaving a trail of Pixie Dust as she flew. Mushrooms and flowers sprang up wherever it landed. People looked up and smiled as it sprinkled on their shoulders or fell on their upturned faces. Patty had met some Fairy Folk, one of them a Dryad who was sick from being away from her tree and worried that Barthas's men would hew it down. Then she would die, and the Fairy Folk die forever; for them, there was no resurrection of the dead. Ben had explained to her that some people believed in that concept. She had lately heard whispers in the camp of a powerful Necromancer in the Valley who was raising an army of the dead. Like in those Zombie movies. So apparently, in this world, it was true.

Eww. Really? she had thought. *Like that's so gross.* Like that series her mom wouldn't let her watch, *The Walking Dead.* And no one knew whom the Necromancer was working for, so everyone was worried about it. Someone had used the term "wild card" about her, because apparently the Necromancer was an old woman.

Patty knew her dad thought she was still a child. But she knew what was going on. She heard the talk in the Mess Hall. And Button and Squirt were planning an espionage trip to the dungeons again, to see if they could free any of the Fairy Folk imprisoned by Barthas. They had succeeded in an earlier raid by using their camouflage abilities. They were brave fighters for the Rebel cause, just like in *Star Wars* where the Ewoks joined up with the rebels on the Moon of Endor. Only here it was Fairy Folk. And one thing Patty knew for sure: the good guys always win.

Patty flew into the magical melon Mess Hall, past the garlands of flowers over the doors and what her dad called the pediments, and settled at an empty table to wait for Button and Squirt. When they arrived they were wearing their usual tweed jackets and knee breeches, the kind people wore in those old-fashioned newsreels when the men were golfing. Patty thought they were funny, but Button and Squirt were very sensitive about their wardrobe, particularly their bow ties. Squirt could make his twirl like a circus clown. Patty laughed every time he did that. Sometimes he made her snort-laugh.

Button was in a serious mood that morning. Apparently a spy had been captured, and the enemy knew about her dad and about Patty herself. It seemed he was collecting Pixies and Fairies especially out of all the Fairy Folk. He did something with the Pixie and Fairy Dust. Something mean. Patty wasn't sure she understood that part. But she knew that she and her dad had to fight for the rebels under Miss

Edna. Patty liked Miss Edna. She always offered Patty some honeyed tea and listened to what she said. She was kind of like a mom, but Patty still missed her real one. She hadn't wanted to mention it to her dad because he seemed so worried about fighting the war and getting them home to Mom and Max. She wondered about Max. She almost missed his teasing. But she tried to concentrate on what Button and Squirt were saying about the trip to the Unicorn.

"Still damned dangerous," growled Button. "He has advance scouts all over the place. His pet Swamp Demon was with that group that attacked the base yesterday before the spy was caught. It's only a matter of time before Barthas realizes that we're up here in the mountains, and how many vulnerable refugees are sheltered here. If he attacked en masse, it could be a slaughter, with Fairy Folk taken prisoners to run those accursed batteries he sells electricity from. I'd rather die. I mean it, Squirt. You're my nephew and I love you, but you're young and you haven't seen what I have seen."

Squirt waited a moment out of respect for his uncle's passion and commitment, then began to speak. "I know the cost of this war, Uncle. I lost both my parents to Barthas's batteries, and I've sworn to be part of the force that takes him down. But Patty is new to this world and just experiencing the joy of the Fairy life for the first time. We've sent messages and confirmed that they're going to bring the Unicorn out of the old forest where He hides, and they'll meet us before dawn at the river's edge. I've borrowed a boat from a pea-pod Pixie. We can be there and back up the mountain by early tomorrow morning."

"It still means leaving the refuge," replied Button with his arms folded. "I won't support you in this in front of Sir Ben."

"Uncle, Patty is the only Pixie who has never met the Unicorn. I only want her dreams to come true."

"And I only want you both to stay alive! Now come on, or we'll be late for our meeting with Sir Ben."

Patty was devastated. She had posters of unicorns in her room at home and there was always a rainbow in the picture. Unicorns meant purity and goodness. She just *had* to meet one.

Ben was waiting for them on the outskirts of the Wee Folks' table, standing near a corner and admiring the way the flowers and vines grew into arches over the walkways. Button and Squirt wandered down the tiny walkway to stand beneath him on the edge of the table. Patty trailed along behind the Brownies, looking as sullen as a Pixie could.

Button looked stern while Squirt pleaded his case, and her father looked the way he always did before he said "No" to something she wanted. Patty couldn't even hear what they said. All she could think of was that poster on the wall, of the unicorn with the rainbow behind him. This was her dream.

"I absolutely forbid it!" She heard her father say. And then she heard Button turn to Squirt and say, "And don't you be getting any wild ideas. I know you young ones. Listen to Sir Ben. He is a Sorcerer and part of the alliance. He knows best."

So it was over. No rainbows. No Unicorn. Patty flew to her tent to sulk.

Barthas gnawed on a juicy roasted leg bone in his throne room. The spit-boy, Nutkin, stood patiently by the roasting rack and never commented on the questionable carcasses that the cooks hung before the fire. He was a Gnome, long-armed and long-fingered, and he wore the amusing Gnome shoes that turned up at the tips. But the amusement stopped there. Nutkin's face was grim; he knew his life hung by a thread. One misstep and his carcass would be turning on that monstrous rack, just another piece of meat to feed Barthas's endless hunger. Nutkin had been conscripted into Barthas's army before he could flee into the mountains with his family. He could only hope they were well and that he would find an opportunity to escape this nightmare.

"Bring me my kit," demanded Barthas. "I need a hit."

Another Gnome ran to a cabinet and pulled out Barthas's "kit": surgical tubing to tie off a tourniquet and the needle big enough to pierce his Swamp Ogre veins. Barthas wound the tubing tightly about his arm until the veins stuck out. Then he took the powdery Pixie Dust and made a solution with water in a spoon. His hands trembled and he began cursing and spilling the precious sparkling solution as he attempted to draw it into the needle.

"Bag this crap. Somebody help me." Barthas handed the eyedropper to Nutkin, who began drawing the solution into the needle. When it was full he handed it back to Barthas, who took it with his shaky but enormous hand, plunged the needle into his bulging vein and squeezed the rubber bulb. "Ahhh, yeah, that's the stuff." His corpulent form seemed to melt into his gigantic throne.

"Now I can think clearly. Fetch me Irene. I want to talk to her."

Irene walked slowly from the adjoining room and said, "I am here, José. Where else am I going, back to Los Angeles? I could only wish. It would be an end to these nightmares."

"Yeah, well, I want to hear about those nightmares. That's why you're here. What can you tell me about the rebels and that Dead Woman who you say is gathering an army of Zombies? That ain't good, Irene. It could mess up my plans. And now we have a new Sorcerer and his Pixie who are missing, thanks to Blina and Shadow's bungling. What the hell is going on? You're supposed to be my secret weapon and warn me of all this stuff ahead of time. Get with it, Irene. Predict something!"

"The Sorcerer and his Pixie have joined the Rebels, but you knew that when Shadow lost them in the mountains."

"Yeah, so what do I need you for?"

"But here is something I have foreseen. The Pixie will be on the riverbank, alone and unattended."

"When? Where along the riverbank? Is this in the future or in the past?"

"It is in the future, but I cannot tell how far. The Woman of Death gathers power in the South. There is a forest between us and she remains undecided in her alliance. There is a chance to win her over and draw her to our side. Stay open to negotiation. But the child Pixie will be alone on the riverbank. I can't tell if it is dawn or dusk but the sun is on the horizon. I have seen it."

"You hear that, Blina? Get your ass to the riverbank and get me that Pixie. And Sideous, what's the story on our supply of Dust?"

The Sorcerer emerged like smoke from the shadows by the open door and bowed low to Barthas. He wiped the corners of his mouth with his sleeve and began to speak. "The Fairy Folk do not do well in captivity, my Lord. There is less and less Dust the longer we keep them in cages."

"So what do they want? The freaking Hilton Hotel? Make them happy. I don't care how you do it. I want more Dust."

Irene broke in. "Free them, José. They need to be free to be happy."

"Well, ain't that a news flash, Irene? Which side are you working for?"

Irene gripped her white cane and pointed it at Barthas. It shook with her anger. "I have no sides in this, José. I just want to get home, and you should come with me."

"And leave this set-up? I'm a king here! People bow to me. Now mind your own business and dream me up some info on those Rebels. Half the villages we reach these days are empty. Those Rebels are taking in refugees. I can't have that. Sideous, how many Trolls do we have and how many Ogres?"

"Most of the Hill Troll tribes have come over to our cause, and the Swamp Ogres have been joining the army ever since you gave them electricity. We have a strong Dwarven troop and plenty of Men. The Swamp Demons are on our side. And since we have taken most of the horses in the valley our mounted cavalry is unbeatable. Come to the practice grounds within the main stockade and you can see them drill. Keivitch is a disciplinarian with the troops. They have been trained to take orders in his native Hill Troll language, as he speaks little else. But that lethal morning star he carries keeps the troops in line. As long as we feed them and house them in the barracks they will remain loyal. There is little food anywhere else in the Valley. Their hunger binds them to us."

"Irene, what do you see about the full moon past the equinox. Will the gate open?"

"The gate will open." Irene tried to shut out of her mind the vision of Sideous's violent death and the chaos which would follow. She tried to keep her face still and impassive. She had dreamt it too many times to hope that it was a false vision. Something was going to happen when that gate opened and the moon drew full. Something terrible for Barthas and Sideous and perhaps for Irene, but the gate was her only hope: she had to get Sideous to open it for her, even if it meant his death.

"You're not saying nothing, Irene. I don't like it when you get quiet with me. What do you see that you are not saying?"

Irene spoke quickly but quietly. "The Death Witch, José. Everything depends on your negotiations with the Death Witch. If she joins us, we win. Without her on our side I see chaos and danger."

"So when the hell is she going to show up?"

"Soon. She is moving north and building an army that rivals our own. Perhaps you should send an emissary to invite her to the Manor to talk."

Barthas sat up in his throne. "You hear that, Blina? I want forty armed and mounted Men sent south to find the Death Witch. Bring her a present. Woo her. Offer her a peace treaty. But bring her to me! Now, I've had enough of government. You all have your assignments. Don't come back here until you succeed."

Irene heard the others rushing out to their assigned duties. She waited until she was alone with Barthas.

"José, I want to move my room from the Manor to the Gatehouse Cottage. Do I have your permission?"

"What about when I need you? I need you close to me, Irene. You are my lucky charm."

"I will be at the Manor every day. But the cottage is quieter and better suited to my visions," she lied.

"Okay, okay. Damn it all. Move if you want. Get one of the

servants to help you."

"I have very little to move. Just my clothes and a few trinkets I use to foretell, my cards, my crystal ball, and my brazier. I can be moved into the empty corner room tonight."

The corner room opened out onto the plains approaching the Manor. It had been built as a guardhouse when the stockade wall went up. Irene would need to know when the Death Witch approached. She *had* to talk to her first or her plan would fail. She had foreseen their meeting, and how important it would be. And Barthas must not know.

Late that night in the rebel camp, Patty slept soundly on her pillow, snoring like a tiny glowing sailor. A shadowy form crept soundlessly into her room and climbed up the table leg to where she was sleeping. Patty could feel something shaking her, but when she opened her eyes she could see nothing but the shadows from her pillow and the glass of water her father kept on the bedside table with her.

"It's me, Squirt." He had used his camouflage ability to blend into the shadows.

Even in her sleep Patty knew he shouldn't be here. What was up?

"Don't you want to see the Unicorn?" he asked.

Patty gasped. It was past midnight. She was too young to be allowed out past midnight, and her father had absolutely forbidden her to risk the visit.

"I have everything ready. We can ride my bullfrog down the mountain, and the boat is waiting for us by the riverbank. Don't be a scaredy-cat. Come on. The Dryads are bringing him to the riverbank at dawn. We can see him and be back by early morning."

"We-ell, I'm not supposed to, Squirt. You heard what Daddy and Uncle Button said."

"Shhh, you'll wake him up. Come on. Follow me and see the Unicorn."

Patty was waking up now, and she thought about her unicorn

poster. It was her dream, after all. "Okay, but you promise we'll be back by breakfast?"

"I promise."

The Unicorn danced before her eyes, white, multicolored, *alive*. Ben's warnings grew softer, more distant, until ... the deal was done.

Patty took to the air and followed Squirt quietly out of the tent to where his bullfrog waited with a double saddle. They mounted him silently, and he bounded off toward the cliffs down from the bluff leading to the river. They flew down the incline in silence and Squirt put his arm on Patty's tiny shoulder.

"It will be okay. Relax."

It took quite a while to get down all the stepped cliffs and outcroppings, but Squirt seemed to know where he was going, and sure enough, when they got down to the river there was the boat. It was little more than some bark laced together to form a canoe, but there was more than enough room for both the Brownie and the Pixie. Patty sat on Squirt's lap as he began paddling across the river.

"Look at the moon, Patty. It's nearly full. See the way it reflects on the water?"

She scarcely glanced at the moonlit water. "Tell me about the Unicorn."

"It's one of a pair, older than time. They were the first Fairy Folk to come to this Valley. In a way, it's their magic that makes all our magic possible."

"So they're like ..." She thought for a moment and then remembered a favorite story book. "They're like the godfathers to all the Fairy Folk."

Squirt nodded. "That's right. Godfathers."

They rowed for what seemed like hours until they finally hit the far shore. The forest came right up to the shoreline of the river. It was dense with tall pines and ancient, mighty oaks. Vines and moss hung from the branches.

"Stay in the boat. We'll be able to see them coming."

Patty waited and held her breath until she saw a faint, distant light approaching. It wound its way slowly through the shadows of the old trees. She could see that the Unicorn was accompanied by the translucent forms of Dryads, or Tree Fairies.

Patty had expected something like the drawing on her poster, but the Unicorn was bigger than the largest stallion Patty had ever seen. Its skin was a luminescent ivory white, and the single spiral, rainbow-colored horn that sprouted from its forehead glowed even in the predawn light. It was glorious, proud, and majestic in a way that Patty never could have imagined. She lifted up out of the canoe on her Pixie wings and began to fly up to the height of the Unicorn's face. The beautiful shining beast approached slowly as Patty flew to meet it.

The Unicorn's face was right in front of her. She could feel his sweet breath, like morning dew, or fresh-baked bread. She could see the light pulsing down the spiral horn in a myriad of colors. But his eyes drew her the most. They were soft and brown and ancient with understanding. This was it. He was a real Unicorn, and he was full of rainbows. It was *way* better than her silly poster. Wait till Cynthia McGowan heard about this!

Just then a twig snapped in the bushes. An instant later a butterfly net came down over Patty, knocking her to the ground and trapping her. When she looked up through the net, all she could see was the hideous, lipstick-coated lips of Blina Turdgirdle curled over her craggy teeth in a triumphant grin.

"Gotcha!"

The Dryads disappeared like smoke and the Unicorn bolted for the forest at the speed of light. Patty saw Blina kick Squirt into the river as if he were a football. And then all she could hear was Blina's hideous, gloating laughter.

"I got myself a Pixie. Barthas will reward me for this. Ah, ha, ha, ha, HA!"

Patty could hear Squirt splashing in the river. "Patty…<glug>…. Patty…<gulp>"

It was too late to do anything. She was a prisoner. Blina Turdgirdle's prisoner, the one Miss Edna said was the B-word.

Barthas berates Irene

Fourteen

False Bravado

Scyssa made an honest comrade. She worked hard. She and Max stood guard over the camp and scouted the lands forward. We were moving north from Dendra's and the church, still picking up Zombies on the way. I was thrilled to have found the dead of many Ogres, Trolls, and Swamp Demons, along with a few Giants. I had begun organizing them by race and assigning weapons. Gnomes who were not too decayed got small bows, Dwarves got axes and stood behind the bigger, stronger races, who carried pike arms and hoes as a front guard.

We had named some of the more corporeal Zombies. Klunk, an Ogre. Shuffle had broken legs, Smiley no jaw. Stretch was a Giant. It helped me keep them organized and form them into fighting units. In fact, I felt like a kid playing with toy soldiers. But I had to take strategy into account. At each village we reached, survivors came out to tell us that Barthas's men had beaten them and burnt their homes, demanding "taxes." Many had fled. We weren't sure where, but Scyssa insisted it was into the mountains. Richer villages gave up their gold and survived, but the poorest villages had been burnt to the ground and many innocent people murdered in cold blood. The villagers made the sign against evil when they saw my Zombies, but they didn't ask too many questions as long as we didn't bother them.

Every strong arm I raised could be used to fight. The more Trolls and Ogres I acquired, the better. The question remained, however, for whom was I going to fight? If Barthas really had the key to this gate back to MY world, then I had to negotiate access for Max and myself. It really might be a case of signing a pact with the devil. Max was dead set against it: he was all for joining the Rebels and assaulting Barthas. We had both seen too much carnage to think of Barthas as anything but a monster.

Meanwhile the strain of holding what had become thousands of Zombies was giving me pause. Every now and then one would wander off like a lost sheep, but once they got far enough out of range they collapsed like puppets. And it wasn't only my head that hurt. Everything ached. I had what seemed to be advanced osteoporosis, and my spine had collapsed into a dowager's hump; my knees creaked like old hinges and every finger joint was swollen with arthritis. Lately I needed help dressing and feeding myself. Darling Max kept telling me I looked like the "crypt keeper." It was great for a girl's vanity. I not only felt like crap, I knew I looked like it, too.

Late one afternoon, I was wending my way north on the pony cart, which now had a Zombie pony, with my army flowing behind and almost surrounding me. Max and Scyssa came back at a run from scouting, loping across the fields toward our caravan. I repressed the thought that they looked like a pair of baboons, swinging forward on their long forearms. I reminded myself that they were sentient beings, one of them my very own child. What I couldn't help noticing was how they did everything together these last few days. I had hardly spoken with Max, who constantly huddled with Scyssa talking in their indecipherable lizard-ese. A mother could begin to worry: everything told me that Scyssa was a "nice" girl, but they were both thirteen—or the Swamp Demon equivalent, in Scyssa's case.

I had to stop worrying, though, as they raced up to the cart and both began to talk at once.

"Forty armed men on horseback carrying Barthas's banner."

"Coming down King's Road."

We were travelling north on King's Road toward the Manor, passing along the outskirts of what was called the Old Forest. I had to stay calm.

"How long do I have?"

"Maybe an hour, maybe two."

"That's plenty of time."

We were at a bend in the road just east of the Inn, which the locals called the Duke's Arse, and there was plenty of time to prepare. I had some of the larger Zombies pull dead trees and limbs across the road to make a barricade. I arranged some troops in ranks and rows along the road leading up to it, and behind me I placed the main bulk of the army. Let them get a real taste of Zombie soldiers before they arrived, and then force them to meet me on *my* terms.

I didn't have long to wait.

"Let me do the talking." I gave Max my most piercing mother-stare. He nodded and covered my back with Scyssa as Barthas's men arrived.

After riding slowly down a lane lined with armed Zombies who clearly outnumbered them, they looked ill at ease, threatened. Individual Zombies are pretty scary at any time, and even more so in great numbers, standing still with weapons in their hands.

The head honcho dismounted from his horse and got on one knee. He looked shaky, and no wonder, with Scyssa and Max flanking me and brandishing their swords.

In the robes that Dendra had sewn for me, wearing the wolf-skull crown, now redesigned with pheasant feathers, Max had said I looked "creepy." Good. Let them take it all in.

"Great Lady of Death, I humbly kneel before you as an emissary of Barthas the Magnificent. I bring gifts and treaties of peace."

I knew instinctively it was protocol to tell the emissary to rise, but this was serious business. Intimidation was the name of the game, and I fixed him and his men with the same stare I'd given Max many a time—usually over doing homework or cleaning his room.

"What need have I of gifts or treaties? I control life and death! Tremble before Mombie the Zombie Queen! Run back to your

Master and tell him that his doom is approaching. I am the rightful ruler of this land and he is the weakling who pretends to the throne. You have seen my armies. They will swell further before I approach his gates. As we pass the graveyards and battlegrounds north of here, I will raise every corpse and grow my army until we shall overwhelm you. And if Barthas should be foolish enough to fight me, I will raise your own dead to my side. Consider fighting your dead friends. Now run to your Master and tell him what you have seen and heard."

The emissary remounted and his men galloped north, forgetting both gifts and treaties. I made the Zombies rattle their weapons and moan, and they galloped even faster.

"Mom, that was *awesome*!

"Yeah, and you were always disappointed that I didn't join the PTA."

Scyssa looked baffled, but impressed.

I might have talked big, but I was shaking in my rickety old bones. I had no real idea of Barthas's numbers, except what I had gathered from talking to villagers. But I had a fair concept, and I also knew that most of his army had been "conscripted" if not outright kidnapped and forced to fight. The villagers had also told me that Barthas was relatively new to the Valley but had wrought a lot of damage in a short time. I knew my Zombies would literally fight past death for me—after all, death was one thing that didn't scare them.

Perhaps it was even possible that Barthas was from our world, swept in by a random gate such as Max and I had found. People had described him as a massive Swamp Ogre, but with the cunning of a Man. The question was how to get close enough to talk without endangering myself. I was a 110-(okay, maybe 130-)year-old crone. There would need to be a hostage exchange to ensure my safety, but who? I sure as hell wasn't giving up Max. That would be tricky, but time would tell. At least those guards looked truly scared when they fled back up the King's Road. Barthas would have something to chew on before we met.

I felt proud of myself.

Ben had just gotten up, washed, and put on the fresh pajamas Hook had ordered for him. They were a deep midnight blue with a woven stripe, pure silk like the others. Apparently imports from the Far East (east of the mountains) were still available. They felt great, he thought as he finished shaving around his goatee and trimmed the scraggly hairs with a scissors. Then he donned the red striped hat and looked at himself in the oval mirror above the washstand. What would Annie think? Where were Annie and Max? Middleville seemed a million miles away. It probably was.

It had rained during the night, and mud was squishing through the plank pathways. Ben had given up Hook's slippers in favor of his sturdy hiking boots. He headed for the Mess Hall, but before he got there he saw people crowding the entrance and talking low and concernedly. He pushed his way through.

"Sorcerer coming through," he said, falsely assertive. He strode to the Wee Folks' table where Button awaited him with a glum face.

"They've done it."

"What?" muttered Ben. He knew, but he had to ask.

"Gone to see the Unicorn. And something's gone wrong or else they would have been back by now. I am sorry, Sir Ben. I warned Squirt not to go, and he disobeyed."

"So did Patty." Ben felt his legs going weak and sat down abruptly on the muddy floor of the tent. "Oh, gods, I think I'm going to faint. Patty's eight years old! When will we know something for sure?"

"I've sent scouts down the outcroppings and hills toward the river to look for signs of them. But it's steep and they don't have jumping bullfrogs. It may be some hours."

Edna came in wearing a printed cotton nightgown and robe. She looked weary. "I heard," she said.

Ben nodded.

They all remained silent.

Edna called for tea and Hook insisted that Ben practice weaving a shield out of the five elements. But Ben's heart was not in it, and he kept fumbling the weave.

Hook tried to cheer him up, or at least convince him to keep practicing. "Look Ben, I know you don't want to hear this, but Barthas killed my partner. Yes, that's right. I was married. Before Barthas arrived, I lived the simple life of a Hedge Wizard. Moving a recalcitrant cow with a jolt of lightning. Disappearing a stubborn hummock by moving earth, rerouting a disputed riverbank with water flow. The villagers gave me gold. I gave the gold to Alan and he stayed home and tended the garden and the horses, chickens, and goats. Oh, I know that doesn't sound like much to a city slicker like you, but we thought it was heaven. We loved one another, too."

"This is my daughter!" Tears were pouring down Ben's face. "What are you saying? Are you telling me Patty's dead?!"

This wasn't the reaction Hook had hoped for. "All I am saying is that no matter what, you must keep fighting."

Ben wove a shield larger and more solid than he ever had before, and with it he hit Hook across the practice yard, where he landed in a heap.

Hook slowly got up and pretended to brush the mud from his immaculate pajamas. "THAT is what I am talking about Mr. Prockner! Well done. Take a break."

To himself he muttered, "That could have gone better."

Ben stormed off without looking back. He headed to the outskirts of the lower garden terrace, where the scouts would first come over the hilltop. For one time in his life, he wished he smoked so he would have something to do while he waited. He took out the Bowie knife Miss Edna had given him and began to whittle a stick. Time passed. He whittled another stick, and then another.

Finally, a contingent of Dwarf scouts dragged a very bedraggled Squirt up behind them through the dense mountain laurel and brush. He was wet and covered in duckweed. His bow tie was missing, as was one brown wingtip. His head hung dejectedly when he saw Ben.

"Where's Patty?"

"I've lost her," Squirt sobbed. "We met the Unicorn, but Blina was there waiting. I was a fool, Sir Ben. I'm going to get her back. I swear it." He groveled at the cuffs of Ben's pajamas.

Ben shook him off and ran back up the hill to find Miss Edna.

Blina held the butterfly net up to the light of the lantern she had hung from her horse's pommel. She glared in at Patty like a bug in a trap.

"You had better let me go. My father's a powerful Sorcerer and he will fix you good."

"Shut up, prisoner. No one is coming for you. You're my pet now." She grabbed Patty through the net and shoved her into a cage. The iron bars were painful to Patty, so she moved to the middle of the cage, where she sat still and tried to think.

Maybe Squirt could rescue her. Maybe her dad had learned enough to rescue her. But she didn't even know where Blina was taking her. All she knew was that Miss Edna had called Blina the B-word, and that meant she didn't like her. Blina tied the cage to the pommel and covered it with a horse blanket. Patty could no longer see out. After a while she heard other horses and voices: a company of cavalry that had been hiding in the woods with Blina. Patty heard the name Irene several times and gathered that she was the mind-reader who had told Blina where to look for Patty.

So *that* was how they had known to wait along the riverbank for her and Squirt. Patty thought it was kind of like cheating for a test, when you know the answers ahead of time, but what she really wondered, what kept worrying her, was what they were going to do to her.

When the company began to ride, Patty got jostled around in the cage until she couldn't avoid bumping into the iron bars. They felt cold and burned all at the same time.

The ride was painful and long and they only stopped twice to water the horses. It was late in the day when they arrived at Barthas's house. The Manor, they kept calling it. Blina pulled the blanket off the cage and Patty blinked in the strong sunlight. She could see a large wooden structure, its terraces crowded with Trolls, Gnomes, Men, Giants, Dwarves, and more, all calling out and heckling.

"Blina's got herself a Pixie!"

"Gonna feed it to Barthas?"

"Hey, Blina, How'd you get so PRETTY?"

"How about a kiss?"

Blina whirled about, eyed the crowd above her, and spat a thick gob of mucus on the ground. "Sure," she retorted. "Who wanted that kiss?"

The soldiers seemed to shrink back from this comment, and a murmur and a hush fell over the men. Many of them blushed and looked sickened.

Patty had to admit that Blina was undoubtedly the ugliest woman she had ever seen, with the large hairy mole sprouting from her chin. She had covered her face in powder, which clung to the long dark hairs over her upper lip, and her red lipstick and dyed hair made the sallow, pock-marked skin look that much grayer. But more than all that was the dreadful scowl which pulled her mouth down in a scarlet frown. And Blina was enormous, close to seven feet tall and covered in shining steel armor. Patty felt smaller than ever to be in her hands.

"Oh yes," Blina crooned, "you are the pretty one. Barthas needs a new Pixie and you will do nicely."

"Where are you taking me?" Patty asked in her tiniest voice.

"Oh to a lovely place where you will be with all your fellow Pixies and Fairies."

"I don't believe you." This was definitely a case of stranger danger, and Patty had ignored all the warnings. Her father had forbidden her to visit the Unicorn—and look what happened. She had been trapped and kidnapped by a bad person.

But the meeting with Barthas was far worse.

Blina carried the tiny cage up the steps to the front door of the Manor and swung the door open. Immediately inside was a vast hall, and sitting on a log throne covered in cushions Patty saw the huge Swamp Ogre, snorting Pixie Dust off a mirror with a rolled-up tube of paper. Patty knew all about drug use from the film they had watched in health class.

If Blina was ugly, Barthas was beyond repulsive. His misshapen face was like a melting wax sculpture of a monster. Hairs sprouted from his ears and back like bristles on a boar, and the heat from the constant fire roasting strange meats made him sweat a thick oily residue in which were stuck scraps and droppings of flesh from his continual gluttony. Patty couldn't believe that this stupid-looking creature was the cause of all the Valley's troubles.

Blina presented the cage triumphantly. "Irene was right. I set troops all along the riverbank to watch at dawn and dusk. I took the stretch of river closest to the old forest, and sure as clockwork our spies heard the boat approaching before dawn so we all crept back into the woods to wait."

Patty thought it had to be the worst thing in the world to have to hear how easily she and Squirt had been fooled. It was worse than being scolded by *both* Mom and Dad together. It was worse than the principal's office. This whole thing was the worst thing that had ever happened to her. She felt like crying, but Pixies don't—can't—cry. So she did what Pixies do: she straightened her tutu and her wings and fluttered them experimentally to make sure they still worked.

"Oh, she's a lively one. Put her with the others," smiled Barthas cunningly.

Blina carried the cage to the interior of the Manor and opened a door into darkness, where stairs led down into a cold, uninviting cellar. There were electric lights here, the first Patty had seen since they had come to the Valley. Most people here used candles and oil lamps.

The lights illuminated an area below one of the main beams from which hung a row of small birdcages of various size and design, each holding a Pixie or a Fairy. The cages hung over a table with raised sloped edges, perfectly positioned to collect the Dust that was produced by the imprisoned Fairy Folk. And Patty was about to become one of them—she'd be providing Fairy Dust for a monster! She couldn't. She wouldn't!

"Here's a nice hook where your cage will fit, just between the pink one and the green one." Blina flashed her a horrible gloating smile as she hung Patty's cage in the line of entrapment.

"Bye-bye, now. Sideous will take care of you from now on. I'm sure you will get along. Sideous is very good to our girls."

Patty waited in silence as Blina's heavy feet trod up the stairs. Then she tried the door to her cage, but it had been wired shut by Blina herself, and Patty's tiny muscles couldn't budge it.

"Don't bother, honey. We've all tried. There is no way out but death. And you wouldn't be the first to pick that escape," said the pink Pixie.

Death? Patty wasn't about to die for those awful monsters. She was going to get out ... somehow.

"Take it easy on her. She's new. I've never seen her before. What's your name, honey?"

"I'm Patty Prockner. I came here from another world and my father is a powerful Sorcerer who will free us all."

"That explains it. She's a transfer, like Dr. Rosenblatt."

"I know Dr. Rosenblatt," smiled Patty. "Daddy and I met him. He's nice. He helps the wounded who come in from the villages that Barthas burns. I just came from Miss Edna's camp in the mountains."

"Shh, honey. The walls have ears, if you know what I mean." The tiny Pixie looked around the dank basement room and shook her head while placing a finger to her lips to indicate silence. "The less said about Miss Edna's plans, the better."

"Okay. I get it," replied Patty. "Mum's the word." She had heard Max use that expression from an old movie he'd seen. Daddy had said she was too young to watch all that violence.

She suddenly realized—not exactly by thinking, but just sort of knowing, absolutely and for sure—that although she actually knew a lot about Miss Edna's plans, because she was "only" a Pixie Barthas was unlikely to interrogate her. Unless she messed up and said too much. So "mum's the word" it would be.

"I'm Pink, and this is Tweet, Minxie, Dahlia, Rose, Wixy, Bart, Blue, Kiki, Ivy, Coco, Periwinkle, and Elissa. Though lately Elissa prefers to be called Dido. Welcome to our nightmare, Patty Prockner."

"Uhm, thanks?"

Ben found Edna leaving the brig where Pheek had been kept. She looked tired and put her arm around him. "I'm sorry."

"That's it? You're sorry? What the hell are we waiting for? We have to go after her! Patty is an eight-year-old girl!"

Edna turned to Ben and said. "Look, Ben. Patty is a Pixie now. She is just one of many more Fairy Folk who have been captured and tortured by these monsters. We have to free all or none, and our plans are coming down to the wire. We have to pack up and leave here tomorrow for the long march down to the Rebel camps below the mountain where we will pick up more soldiers. I even have women willing to fight who have been training in the practice yards. They are willing to give their lives for this cause, and in fact we are ready to go except for one thing: this Necromancer who the people say is roaming the south lands and heading north. She could put all our plans in jeopardy."

"Screw her! I say we leave now and free Patty before this Necro-whatever arrives."

"Necromancer, Ben, a raiser of the dead. She's raising a Zombie army. Did you ever fight a Zombie, Ben? They fight hard—and they're already dead. Piercing does little harm to a Zombie. You have to take off their heads, as a rule. We had a small-time Necromancer in the Valley a few years ago. Raised a few Zombies, caused some trouble and the villagers eventually hanged her. *This* woman has raised an army. Do you understand? There are reportedly thousands of Zombies of every race, impossible to kill, and fighting for this one Necromancer. Do you understand what kind of pure power that takes? Whoever the hell she is, she is now a major player in the game—and honestly, I have to admire her guts and strength."

Ben changed the subject. "What did you tell Pheek?"

"The very thing they won't believe: the truth. I told him that we now number in the thousands, are well armed, and plan to storm the Manor. Barthas will suspect a trap and think we're exaggerating. And while he waits, we will march on him. I hope you're ready for a long hike, Ben. We begin tomorrow. There are few horses to spare. And the way down through these mountains is rocky and rough. The troops are building a pontoon bridge to get us across the river. But it's a long march through the old forest. We're near the equinox, and the moon draws full three days after that. We have to be there when his Sorcerer opens the gate to our world. And you and Patty have to get through. But this Necromancer could ruin everything if she joins Barthas."

Barthas was getting his own news about the Necromancer in the South.

"What the hell do you mean she said she was the rightful ruler?!" Barthas bellowed at his emissary to the Death Witch. The soldier knelt as gobbets of half-chewed meat spattered his clean uniform and left grease stains on the floor.

"My Lord Barthas, she refused our gifts and treaties and told us to take news of her numbers to you."

"And those numbers?

"Our best estimate? I would say several thousand..."

"Jeebus Christmas on a cracker!"

"And they were of every race, even Ogres, and Trolls," the commander finished.

"The Ogres and Trolls swore allegiance to us, Goddamn it!"

"Sir, these Ogres and Trolls were dead. They obey none but the Death Witch. She is very powerful, my Lord. Their numbers are great."

"Get me Irene. She moved out to the guardhouse cottage. Someone go get her for me!" Barthas was boiling to a rage and he threw a gnawed leg bone at the commander still kneeling before him. "Damned monkey house this is turning into."

Barthas began pacing the floor, shaking the room with every heavy step, and the spit-boy slipped into the shadows of the great roaring fireplace. Better hot than dead for Nutkin. He always hid in the shadows when Barthas was in a rage. "Get me Sideous and Blina and Keivitch! I want to see everybody. Here! Now!" Barthas seethed.

Irene was the first to arrive, tapping hesitantly into the room with her white cane. "What is it, Lord Barthas? The servant told me you were displeased. Maybe more of your medicine, José?"

Irene had begun referring to his drug use as his medicine, as it seemed to upset José less. He was so irritable. But then José had such delusions of grandeur. He couldn't imagine himself as a player on life's stage: he had to be the boss. He had been this way even as a child growing up in the slums of Los Angeles. When he joined the Crips he had been eager to make his first kill. He was a killer, that José. Still, Irene had a soft spot for him. He had grown up under her eyes and always came into her fortune-telling shop to drop a few bucks when he had the cash. So she had stuck with him when they arrived here. But she wouldn't stay much longer. The clock was ticking, and with each passing tick Irene began to hate José more.

Still, she waited calmly for his orders.

"Listen, Irene, I want to talk to you about the gate. You're too important. I been thinking about it more and more, and I want Sideous to concentrate on opening the gate in L.A. so we can pull in my friends from the Crips. I need help here, I need Hector, Malik, and Umberto. I need officer material, and I can't trust none of these cartoon Fairies with any real responsibility."

Irene felt a rising sense of panic and apprehension, but she kept her voice steady. "What does all that have to do with me, José? I don't care if you bring in every Crip in L.A., as long as I get out and back there myself!"

Barthas slurped loudly from his wooden goblet of wine. "That's the thing, Irene. I need you. I need my lucky charm. I need you to predict for me. I can't let you go."

"*WHAT!?*" Irene's voice rose to a shriek as she tapped herself close and stared up at him. "What about your promise to me, José? You promised that if I foretold for you, you would let me go! Get another Seer. The Valley is full of people who claim to see the future."

Barthas looked away into the fire to avoid Irene's eyes, unseeing yet still accusing. "Yeah, but none of them is the real thing, Irene. We couldn't have caught that Pixie without you, Irene. Shadow and Blina were bungling the whole thing, until you told them where and when to look for it."

"And I never should have told you how to find her. The poor little thing is miserable. I've just ruined another life."

"Hey, hey, that ain't no attitude to take. We're fixing this Valley. Giving them electricity brings these savages into the modern age. We're real heroes!"

Irene gripped Barthas's goblet of wine and angrily threw it into the roaring fire. "That's what you are doing, José. Putting out the flames of life that have burned in this Valley for centuries. You are destroying the natural order of things. Mark my words, José, you are destroying the very thing you seek. You are a monster, José, both physically and mentally. You are not taking the only thing I care about away from me. I won't let you. I am getting through that gate and out of this madhouse. You just try to stop me."

"Well that's just the thing, Sweets," Barthas smirked. "In case you ain't noticed. You're blind, and you ain't real strong, and it will be real easy to have a few soldiers hold you under house arrest until after I get my old friends through. I don't need you at the ceremony. I only need Sideous."

Irene remained defiant. "You do need me at the ceremony, José. Like it or not, you need me to guide Sideous so he can find your friends." She let that sink in and then added with ice in her voice, "You promised me my freedom, José!"

Barthas picked up a piece of roasted meat and waved it in Irene's direction. "Well, the thing is that circumstances have changed. Our priorities have changed."

"You mean *your* priorities have changed, don't you, José?" She didn't even bother hiding her sarcasm now: Barthas was too superstitious to kill her. He might have her roughed up a little, but in the long run, he needed her far more than she needed him—and they both knew it. But if he was going to renege on his deal, then all bets were off. Madre de Dios, at that instant Irene hated him with all her soul. She would gladly kill him, if only she could.

"All our priorities have changed now that this Necromancer arrived. We have to regroup and figure out how to deal with her."

Irene gritted her teeth. "I told you. You have to negotiate. Begin a dialogue with her."

"Well that's the thing about that damned Death Witch. She's making threats. I can't have people making threats to me! What do you see? Can she make good on them?" Barthas was in a sweat from the drugs, alcohol, and nervous fear. He reeked even more than usual.

"I warned you, José. She is an outside force of great power. Her Zombies number in the thousands. There has never been a Necromancer of such power. You have to negotiate with her."

"Damn it all! I don't want to share!" Barthas began slamming his cudgel into the floor of the Manor.

"Careful, José, you'll break something." Irene stepped back from his anger. "Go to her. Meet with her and form an alliance and you will crush the rebels if they attack. With her power alongside your strength you would be invincible."

"Invincible, eh? I like the sound of that. Okay, I will meet with her, we can make a deal."

Not before I do, thought Irene. *Not before me.*

The door opened and Blina, Keivitch, and Sideous hurried in, none of them wishing to be the last to arrive. Barthas told the soldier, now covered in greasy spittle, to fill them in on the situation with the Death Witch.

Irene slipped out unnoticed, to return to her cottage room and wait for a sign. Her room was strictly organized, like that of the blind everywhere. She went straight for her Braille Tarot Cards, then sat on her modest bed and, without any surprise, dealt out the Empress, Death, and the Moon.

Tonight was the night. Irene called for her servant, Paulette, a smiling, round little woman who ignored the politics of military life, and had her arrange for two ponies just after midnight. Irene would take Paulette with her. What could be less threatening than two women on ponies, one of them blind?

Fifteen

Meetings, Secret and Public

I was in a dead sleep when Max woke me. The pounding headache was still there as I felt the Zombies wake up with me. Everything ached, but I focused my attention on Max.

"Shh, Mom, it's me. Scyssa and I found a couple of women headed this way. They're riding ponies, and they say they have to talk with you. It's important. No, actually, the blind one said it was imperative!" Max took a breath.

"There's a blind woman on a pony who wants to talk to me in the middle of the night?"

"Yup."

I sat up and tried to arrange my hair into a bun. My arthritic hands fumbled it and I finally asked Max to help me. His dexterous claws swept the hair back from my face and twisted it into a neat bun, which he skewered with a sharpened stick.

"Thanks, honey. You've been a big help. I mean it. And Scyssa is a nice girl, for a Swamp Demon. I don't know what I would have done without the two of you. If things go wrong, just remember, your job is to get back through to our world and find your father and sister. Don't worry about me. I can't live too much longer in this body anyway. It's just too old."

"Mom, don't talk like that. We're both gonna make it out of here."

"We'll see, dear. Shhh, now. Here comes Scyssa with the ponies."

The two women dismounted and cautiously walked toward me. The taller woman, the blind one, held on to her companion's arm and swept her white cane back and forth looking for rocks and rubble. *Well, I'll be damned,* I thought to myself. *She's not only blind. She's from our world. That white cane proves it.*

"That's far enough," I heard myself say. Instinctively I brought several of the Rock Troll Zombies forward to surround me. The blind woman recoiled when she heard them approach. She must have smelled them as well. Her nostrils flared in revulsion.

"We mean no harm," she said. "I am Irene. I have come to talk with you."

"I thought Barthas was in charge. I only want to talk with those in charge."

"Please, Madame, I come on my own. I may have information which could prove valuable."

"Talk."

"My name is Irene Sanchez. I am from Los Angeles, and I know you are from that world, too."

"How do you know that? No one here knows me. How could you know that?"

"I know many things. I see things. Some of what I see has yet to happen. Some of it never will. I am a Seer. I am the Seer to Lord Barthas."

"Then what the hell are you doing out here in the middle of the night without a guard? A blind woman like you could easily get killed in these parts."

"Barthas does not know I am here."

"So you have your own agenda."

"You might say that. I prefer to think of it as a ... a contingency plan. What do you know about the gate between our worlds?"

"Enough to know that Barthas claims to have a Sorcerer who can open that gate, and I want to pass through it with my Swamp Demon."

"Why would a Swamp Demon want to pass between worlds ...

unless he, too, had been translated between worlds?"

"You're perceptive, lady, but you don't have to be psychic to figure that out."

"But I am psychic, Annie DeLeon."

That stopped me in my tracks. No one here knew my name, much less my maiden name. And Max always called me Mom, or Mombie. Maybe this lady had something worth listening to.

"I seek passage through that gate as well," Irene said. "Perhaps we can help one another."

"And your relationship with Barthas...?"

"... is strained," Irene replied.

"So, it comes to this. What are you offering?"

"I have suggested to Barthas that he must form an alliance with you, in order to beat the Rebels. You only have to play along until the gate is opened. But once it is open, you must swear that I go through with you and your pet demon. Until then I will use my ability to see the future for you, and I will mislead Barthas so he has no clue of our intentions."

"I might be able to manage that on my own."

"But it would be easier with a friend on the inside. Besides, I have already seen part of what is to happen."

"But not all," I challenged her.

"It doesn't work that way. It's not so simple. I see possible futures—there are many of them, believe me. Besides, being blind, I may not be able to get to the gate in time without your help. Please," she added softly. "Please don't refuse my offer. I have seen you there when the gate is opened. All you need to do is bring me with you."

"Why does an important person like the Seer to Lord Barthas want to escape this world? Did you leave the iron on back home?" I couldn't help my sarcasm.

"I am losing my mind, Annie DeLeon, and my conscience. If I help Barthas in his monstrous deeds much longer I will take a blade to my own wrists. I have foreseen it. It creeps closer to me every passing day. I don't want to die in shame. Is that reason enough?"

"Not bad; truly heart-wrenching," I answered. "But I still want to know, what's in it for me?"

"Have you ever heard of a Manticore?"

"Yeah, I think so. It's a mythical beast, it's … isn't it sort of cobbled out of a lion and a scorpion?"

"With the face of a man," Irene answered. "Some people think it is where the myth of the sphinx first originated. But here Manticores are not mythical. The Centaurs keep them as herd animals and milk the Scorpion's tail for the venom, which they use to poison their arrows for hunting. I have been buying that venom from the Centaurs for some time now. I have more than enough to kill myself, perhaps even enough to kill Barthas."

"But how could you get him to take it? Isn't he a Swamp Ogre? It would take a lot of poison to kill something that big."

"Barthas is a glutton. He eats all day, at least when he isn't snorting Pixie Dust to get high, or drinking to soothe his conscience. I could poison his meat, or have Paulette do it for me. She works with the cook when I don't need her. It would be easy to accomplish. A carcass full of Manticore venom would paralyze even Barthas. It would keep him out of our way when the gate is opened. If it kills him, so be it. He deserves to die."

"I don't know that anyone deserves death," I said slowly. "I've seen beyond the veil as a Necromancer, and I now understand the darkness of the long sleep." We both pondered that for a moment, until my old self surfaced. I chuckled. "You must really hate this bastard." I took her silence for agreement. "Okay. So what do you want from me?"

"First, you must keep this meeting a secret. Barthas can never know that we spoke. He is insanely jealous about my time. When you arrive at the Manor, pretend that you are meeting me for the first time. Negotiate with Barthas any way you see fit. But in the end you must pretend to join his cause."

"But that means I would have to fight the Rebels, and frankly, I sympathize with their cause."

"So you lose a few Zombies. You can raise more from the dead."

"But that means I might have to kill some of the innocent Rebels, too."

"Fake it. Make your Zombies hold back. Wound without killing. Just buy us time to get that gate open and get through it. There are only a few days left until the full moon, and they may not even strike before then."

This last part stopped me. "Full moon?"

"The gate can only be opened on the full moon closest to the equinox. The equinox is tomorrow. You have to meet Barthas and negotiate by tomorrow at noon. Oh, and by the way, your threat to Barthas was a nice move. It shook him up and took him by surprise. Don't let up. He is a bully ... and like all bullies, he's a coward. Press him to the wall and demand your price."

"You can't see the extent of my Zombie army, but I can assure you, my threat is not an idle one."

"I believe you. I have seen the extent of your power in my visions." As she turned to go, she added, "Remember, we never met. This never happened."

I got up my courage to say, "Wait. I have my own demand."

Irene stopped and turned back around.

I walked closer to her and said, "You can't see me, Irene, but I am old. Older than the oldest person you have ever met. Old and fragile, except for my Zombies."

Paulette nodded and said, "She is telling the truth, Miss Irene."

I continued, feeling like I was channeling unwavering, pitiless determination from some latent source—maybe every mother in the universe. "If I'm going to meet with a two-thousand-pound Swamp Ogre and come out without a scratch, I'll need a hostage. I'll need someone Barthas values, someone he is close to. You seem to fit both those bills. You stay with Scyssa and Max while I negotiate, and afterwards. If one hair on my head gets mussed, your throat will be opened by a Swamp Demon's claw. Capiche?"

Irene nodded. "Capiche."

"You'd better get going if you want to be back before dawn."

Irene turned to the serving woman at her side and asked, "Paulette? Are you ready?"

Paulette took her arm and answered, "Yes Ma'am. But may I say to the Death Witch, that if she betrays you, I will kill her myself."

I laughed. "Do you see how old I am? Death would be a relief. But I doubt you could get past my Zombies before they killed you first." I had the Trolls move to surround me, and one of them brandished a sharpened scythe in Paulette's direction.

Paulette was undaunted. "Nevertheless, watch your back if you betray my mistress."

"That goes both ways." I left them with this to think on. Was there no one who didn't threaten me in this land? I nodded to Paulette and sat on the edge of my cart while Paulette helped her mistress back onto her pony.

Scyssa wanted to follow them back to Barthas's Manor to make sure that they had not been not tailed by his spies. I agreed and sent Max to help scout the woods along the King's Road. Scyssa was becoming part of our little group, and I was proud to see her take this initiative.

So now I was a double agent. The pain of controlling the thousands of Zombies made it hard to get back to sleep. I planned to get up early, scour the remaining two battle sites, and hit the old town graveyard, then be at the Manor by noon. How would another several hundred Zombies affect my already pounding head? It didn't matter, I told myself. I had to handle it. I had to get Max home and out of that reptilian body. He liked it too much. Beyond that, his relationship with Scyssa was getting closer all the time. I wondered if there was such a thing as a condom for Swamp demons? I went to sleep giggling to myself and on the verge of tears.

Pheek told Barthas his story from the beginning again, and Barthas asked him, "How many soldiers do the Rebels have?"

"Thousands, Lord. And they are ready to march on you."

Barthas laughed out loud. "They filled you with bull crap, you stupid weasel. They are a frightened rag-tag bunch of refugees, and they haven't got a pot to piss in. Go on. Get out of here before I put your scrawny ass on my spit for dinner."

Blina asked nervously, "What if he is telling the truth?"

"Go on," laughed Barthas. "He admitted they kept him blindfolded the whole time. Why would they tell him the truth? They're trying to frighten me, and it ain't gonna work. Not that easy."

Keivitch managed to say, "Keivitch Blunka thunk refugee!"

Barthas rubbed his chin and wondered, "Maybe that Death Witch bitch is bluffing, too."

Irene yawned and said, "She will arrive today. You can see for yourself, José."

"BARTHAS!" he barked.

"My Lord Barthas," Irene corrected herself.

"Everyone get ready. If the Death Bitch arrives today, I want everyone in front of the main stockade to back me up. No questions."

There were nods of assent, and the meeting dissolved.

Patty was trying to get to know the other Pixies and Fairies who were imprisoned with her. They varied in color and type, but the Fairy who fascinated Patty the most was Bart. Patty hadn't known that there were male Fairies before. It had simply never occurred to her. She asked Pink and Tweet about it and while they admitted that it was rare, it was not unheard of. All Fairies and Pixies helped things grow: trees, flowers, vines, fruits, all things botanical. Patty had been to the Botanical Gardens in the Bronx and it had been beautiful. There was an enormous greenhouse filled with orchids in bloom. She wondered if they had Pixies and Fairies on staff.

Bart specialized in making tiny acorns grow into mighty oaks. It was a magic that took an enormous amount of patience. So Bart just said, "All this will pass, too." Patty asked him what he was doing and he said he was working on a spell to un-grow the oak plank bottom to his cage. "Un-grow?" Patty had asked. All Bart would say was that the spell took time. And he urged Patty to have patience and, above all, to believe. "Believe what?" she had asked. Bart just pointed to the wood on the bottom of his cage.

In a way, Bart gave Patty hope: maybe he was right. Maybe the spell would work. Other magic worked in this world. Most of the girls just moped and cried all day. Although Pink, whose cage was closest to hers, gave her a pretty good idea of how things worked in Barthas's Manor. Mornings meant that the creepy Sorcerer Sideous would come and fill their water bottles with sugar water. He was too stingy to bother getting them honey or jam, so he had outfitted their cages with inverted water bottles like the kind you put in a hamster's cage and he filled them with sugared water. Patty had seen a hummingbird feeder that people filled with sugar water and she realized what a dirty trick that was. Natural creatures weren't meant to drink sugar water, they were meant to feed on nectar and pollen from the flowers.

But she needed something to eat, and if sugar water was all there was, what could she do? Still, she felt silly drinking from the bent metal tube like a pet hamster.

After Sideous fed the Pixies in the stone and earthen basement area where they were kept, he walked down the stone staircase to the sub-basement dungeons where he kept his "batteries" and the prisoners he called volunteers. Even Patty knew they were not volunteers. She had seen them drag a Harpy down those stairs. Harpies were horrible creatures with the heads of women and the bodies of enormous birds of prey. That Harpy had scratched the soldiers bloody with her talons and flapped her black-feathered wings trying to get away. It created a horrible stench, and all kinds of dust and detritus flew through the air before they succeeded in getting her down the stairs. Patty and the other Pixies and Fairies had coughed until the dust settled.

Mermaids and Mermen were the saddest, though. Out of water they couldn't swim or walk, and the soldiers simply wheeled them in a wheelchair through Patty's room and down the stairs. They always looked so stoical. Patty wondered if there was some kind of giant fish tank where they were kept between being hooked up to the batteries. Barthas sure was determined to catch everyone and everything and put it in some kind of cage. Tanks. Cages. Patty wondered if he had people on leashes, too.

She began to realize that as bad as the Pixies had it, the prisoners who were trapped down those stairs had it worse. There were screams and moans and groans of pain and horror. It was hard to sleep at night remembering those voices during the day.

One morning Sideous came to them and told them that Barthas was concerned for their happiness. So he had hired a painter to paint a mural of a woodland scene on the wall behind their cages.

As if a painting of trees and flowers would fool a fairy into thinking they were in the forest. If anyone knew how to tell a real flower from a fake one, it was a Fairy or a Pixie. That was their business.

Barthas and Sideous didn't know anything about Pixies.

Patty hoped that Button and Squirt would come soon with her father.

Ben was beside himself. His knapsack was packed with food and his sparse wardrobe. He didn't mind the weight, but the trail down the mountain was rocky and dangerous. He had already fallen several times and bloodied his knee. Hook travelled with him and drilled him relentlessly. Simple defense strategies, like water for fire and earth for electricity, but there were also more complex weaves of some or all four elements. These Hook referred to as spells, but Ben saw them more as patterns in the air. And then there was the elusive weave of spirit, which was like weaving your willpower into the spell. It was all so complex that Ben's head was spinning. He had all he could do to navigate the mountain path. Hook, he thought, must have had some mountain goat in his family. He never missed a step and always managed to balance that damned paper parasol over his head to protect his complexion.

Ben was relieved when they reached the base camp, though full military restrictions were in place. No fires were allowed. The cooks had made biscuits of waybread, which after the long climb down tasted of raisins and cinnamon, and Ben could have eaten half a dozen at one sitting—but each man was rationed to three per day. So he forced himself to imagine what Patty was going through. Gods! It was his fault! Annie had trusted him to take care of Patty and he had failed. She was in the hands of a villain.

Hook appeared out of the crowds of soldiers. There were Dwarves in armor wielding axes and crossbows. Centaurs wearing breastplates with longbows hung over their shoulders and quivers stuffed with sleekly fletched arrows. Humans in great numbers, most carrying swords, some with bows and pikes. There was a contingent of Gnomes, a scattering of Giants. And apparently the Elves had come out of hiding from their refuge beyond the mountains and joined them at this base camp. The Elven archers looked cunning and agile in their forest-colored tunics and hose. Everyone looked sleek, well fed, and well trained by Miss Edna. She had given a speech as they set out. Something about "taking back the land of our ancestors." There were also some distinct aspersions as to the character of Barthas and his minions, which raised cheers on all sides. That was when they had begun the march this morning. But now it was evening and Ben was exhausted.

Hook attempted to drill Ben before bed, but they were sharing a lean-to pup-tent with Dr. Rosenblatt, and after a while even the pedantic Hook let Ben fall sound asleep in his blanket roll.

I started my morning by going to the two battlegrounds marked on our map. There I raised many Rock Trolls and Swamp Ogre Zombies. There were even several Giants. All this added to my power and to my headache. I began to hear a faint ringing in my ears from the pressure.

Max looked concerned. "Hey, Mom, uhm, Mombie, you look kind of pale. I mean seriously, even for you."

"I know, honey, it's these new Zombies. Give me a moment to adjust," I lied.

"Seriously, Mom, be careful. Remember what you told me: 'Be aware of your own limitations. Don't overdo.'"

"Thanks Max. I love you, too."

There was one more graveyard to hit. It was roughly eleven in the morning, so I had time to scour it before my meeting with Barthas. And I did so, to my success. We found five Giants, rare Centaur corpses (most were considered Fairy Folk like the Elves, and did not rise but died forever), two Minotaurs (another rare find), and assorted Humans. We had run out of swords, so we were giving the new troops sharpened wooden spears fashioned by Max and Scyssa from forest saplings.

By noon we reached the plain in front of the Manor. I arranged my Zombie army surrounding myself—frail, little old me—with rows of the largest, strongest, and most brutal of them. Many rows of Zombie archers held a line behind me, ready to release their arrows overhead toward Barthas and his troops.

They sent an advance guard, a horrible, enormous Human who looked as if she had Troll blood, on a black horse and wearing plated armor. She advanced to within twenty feet of my Trolls and I shouted in the paper-thin voice of an old woman, "That's far enough!"

And she halted.

"Tell Barthas this: I know how his operation works. If he wants me to use my Zombies to fight the Rebels, we need to negotiate. And in order to be sure that Barthas negotiates in good faith, he must offer his blind Seer as hostage to my Swamp Demons. Then and only then, he comes forward alone and unarmed. Otherwise I attack and hold your Manor in siege. And I assure you, Miss Whatever-your-name-is...."

"Turdgirdle."

I hesitated a moment to be sure she wasn't kidding. "I assure you, Miss Turdgirdle, my Zombies do not need to eat. We can hold siege to your Manor indefinitely. Offer a hostage and talk, or no talking and a siege. You choose."

Blina turned her horse around and returned to the stockade wall where Barthas and his Shadow Stalker waited with a third creature—Keivitch, though I didn't know it at the time.

Even from where I stood I could tell that the Ogre was throwing a temper tantrum, smashing the ground with a huge spiked club and screaming obscenities we could hear at this distance. Good. I had upset his plans. Men were such babies when it came to giving up control. I had pissed Barthas off. Now let's see what he did.

"Max, you and Scyssa stay behind the line of Zombies and hold the hostage."

"Mom-bie, I ... I don't think he's sending any hostage."

"Give him time, sweetheart. He hasn't got much of a choice."

We waited. He ranted and raved, and apparently Irene talked to him. Even at a distance it was clear even how careful he was about not waving his club in her direction. He valued her. He knew how to be careful. Barthas was just a bully, but he had values. He valued Irene. Maybe she was a better Seer than I had given her credit for. Or Barthas had reason to think of her as some sort of mother figure. One or the other was playing out here, because after a while, a lone figure walked bravely forward swinging a white cane from side to side. I waited till she was almost with us before I sent Max forward to meet her. Max took her back to the appointed area with his claws at her neck. If things went wrong I would let Scyssa kill her, to spare Max the trauma. But right now I had to meet a Swamp Ogre. My Zombie bodyguard comprised eight Rock Trolls and five Ogres, each carrying an enormous pike. I had the Giant Zombie pick me up in his arms and we walked forward with him cradling me like a baby. Now at least I was high enough to look Barthas in the eye.

When we got close enough Barthas stood still. I had the Giant walk forward still surrounded by the Trolls and Ogres.

"Are you Barthas?" I asked.

"Are you the Death Bitch?" he asked.

"You will refer to me as Mombie, the Zombie Queen. Or have you forgotten your hostage?"

"Okay. Okay. Don't screw with Irene. Okay?"

"Watch your mouth and this will go smoother."

"Okay, Lady, this is the way I talk. Are you some kind of grand Lady or something?"

"Yes. I am," I had the guts to reply. "I am the Necromancer and Zombie Queen. You would do well to remember that." I stared at him for a full fifteen seconds until he looked away.

"All righ', all righ'," he grumbled.

"You have access to the gate between our worlds. I want that. You will allow my Swamp Demon and me to cross between worlds on the full moon. In return, my Zombies will fight for your cause." I could only pray that the Rebels would not attack before the full moon. But I wasn't counting on it. My luck wasn't that good.

"You gotta keep the Zombies outside the stockade. My men don't like them. They smell."

"So do you, young man." Something told me that this Barthas was a child; his language, his temper, his irritable mood. It all fit together. He was a rotten foul-mouthed teen.

"Shut up, Bitch."

One of the Ogre Zombies smacked his head with the flat of his pike. "Watch that mouth when you're talking to me if you want a Zombie Army to crush your foes."

Barthas rubbed his head with his big blubbery hand. "Okay, okay. But let Irene go."

"Irene stays with me as an assurance of your good faith. The minute she leaves, you are on your own."

"Hey. Wait. That ain't fair. I need her to foretell for me."

"Fine. You may come alone into my camp to speak with Irene once a day—for one hour at dawn."

"That's harsh," he whined, and I took great satisfaction from the childish petulance in his voice.

"Take it or leave it, or I surround the Manor and starve you out."

"Bitch," Barthas muttered.

"What!?" I demanded.

"Nothin'."

"You may go now," I said making the dismissal clear.

Barthas sputtered; he had meant to ask other things, but I had obviously intimidated him. Must be the parent skills I had gained from having a teenager of my own. He waddled off like a top-heavy water buffalo.

I went back to where Max was waiting with Irene. "You may let her go now, Max. The show is over. Give Miss Sanchez some water and see if she is hungry. Let Scyssa watch her and you go hunt us up some dinner. I'll have Bernice and Klug gather us some herbs to go with it. And you, Miss Sanchez, how do you feel as our hostage?"

"Free, Great Mombie, freer than I have felt these last three years. Thank you for taking me hostage. I have my cards. May I do a reading for you?" Irene inquired politely. "It was a pleasure to hear José, I mean Barthas, spoken to like that."

"His name is José? And he is a kid, right?" I asked.

"Seventeen this past May. I knew him in L.A. He's not all bad."

"Sorry, Irene, but he's a monster, both physically and mentally. He's pressing the simple folk of this Valley to desperate measures. He has prisoners in those buildings within the stockade, *and* he has done murder. He should be in jail."

"Well, you have taken me hostage."

"I have a thirteen-year-old who needs to get back to karate class."

"Max is thirteen?"

"Now you're getting the picture, Miss Sanchez. And I was not always this old. But don't tell Barthas any of that. For now, I am Mombie the Zombie Mistress, and I have just made a deal with the devil. There are two days left till the full moon. God help me. If only this headache would let up."

Sixteen

War Is Not Pretty

Something in Ben was galvanizing. He no longer felt disjointed. Miss Edna had assured him that they were marching on Barthas. They would be at the Manor the day before the full moon. Soon they could storm the dungeons and free Patty. Miss Edna had even sent Button and Squirt ahead on their leaping bullfrogs to see if they could free some of the Wee Folk.

Some weeks back, Edna had scouted the grounds within the enormous stockade on her broom. She had learned that Barthas had separate areas of the dungeon where he kept various prisoners, as well as barracks that had been converted to prisons for Fairy Folk. There were also scores of other buildings to house the inner core of his army. It would be difficult to tell where to find the captives, providing of course that they were able to defeat Barthas and breach the reinforced doors into the stockade.

Everything was in place. Miss Edna had given orders as to which units were to respond and when. Not surprisingly, Planks and Ferny each led his racial unit. What Miss Edna tried to impress on Ben was that his job was to act as Sorcerer and back-up to Hook. Hook would lead the forward unit and engage Barthas's Sorcerer. The real question was whether there would be more than one Sorcerer fighting for Barthas. That's where Ben came in. He was to run cover fire for Hook.

But Ben came into play one other way. Hook had taken him

aside each time they stopped for water and food and begun teaching him an extremely complex weave of elements, which was the key to using the energy stored in Sideous's batteries to open the gate between worlds.

Hook had explained, "If we take out Sideous, I open the gate. If I go down, it will all be up to you to open the gate and get Patty and yourself through and back to your world." Hook paused for a drink of water from his canteen. Miss Edna had them well supplied: there were wagons with huge oaken casks and spigots, filled from the river as they passed over it into the beginnings of the forest.

The old forest was large, dark and mysterious, and it was in that shadowy darkness that they met up with a band of woodland Centaurs armed with bows and morning stars. They joined in the march on Barthas. Miss Edna wasn't kidding: they did number in the thousands. Ben hoped that her ploy in telling Pheek the truth had worked. What they wanted more than anything was to come upon Barthas unaware and unprepared.

Hook returned to his lecture. Ben would have to pull electricity from the batteries, add other elements, and focus it all into a complicated weave. Ben began to wish he had paid more attention when Annie had taken up knitting. At least he could crochet a little.

But here, spatial memories were also involved. "This is what fine-tunes the weave for a specific part of your world. But don't worry about that. Even if you wind up in Singapore, you can get a plane home."

Ben was puzzled. "But how do I make that final piece of the weave? I can see that you're weaving spirit through the loops of electricity, and fire, but what makes the difference in where you wind up?"

"It's like Dorothy's slippers, Ben, like all magic: intention is essential. Click your heels and think of home. The spirit *is* your willpower. So when you add that weave you think of your target, in your case, home. Try the weave again and see if you can manage that last part of it. I'll supply the electricity. You just pull the charge off me as if I were the battery."

Ben tried once more, adding the final twist for destination. He thought he did it they way he should, and asked Hook if it was right.

Hook was guarded with his answer. "The first part of the weave was perfect, Ben. But I cannot read your willpower, or where you are directing it: only that you *are* directing the weave. But don't worry too much. With luck we can get Sideous to open the gate, or I will do it myself. It all depends on how the battle goes."

Ben nodded. So much could go wrong. Patty was still a prisoner, and Ben was a pawn in a war. No; his therapist would never allow that phraseology. Pheek was a pawn. Ben was a player, and everything he had learned was going to make a difference for their side. He had studied hard. He would be ready for any eventuality.

The break was over. The army pulled to its feet. Those with horses remounted. And they made their was through the dark, overgrown old forest—the one path Barthas would never anticipate. Barthas would expect them either to come up the river's tributary which ran close to the Manor, or use the King's Road. He would never be looking for them to appear out of the dense wood of the old forest. That was why Miss Edna had gone light on the horses, but heavy on the numbers of soldiers. With luck they would take Barthas by surprise and overwhelm him.

Irene spent the night in our camp. Max had found some chickens, and Irene had been happy to help pluck the birds. Her dexterous fingers found every last pinfeather, and the birds were as clean as a baby's bottom. We roasted them on a spit with more of the wild parsnips that grew throughout this country. Irene helped with the few pots I had used. It was primitive but wholesome.

Max and Scyssa sat by the fire and whispered in their reptilian tongue. It was all a confusion of sibilant "esses" to me. It annoyed me that I couldn't understand what they were talking about. They laughed, and I saw Scyssa hitting Max in jest when he said something funny. Well, I told myself, they *are* both Swamp Demons. They're bound to have things in common. Still, I worried. Every mother worries about her son's first relationship, and this was a doozy.

Before I could settle down for the night, Irene unburdened herself to me about Barthas's last order to her. He would try to stop her from getting through that gate. Great. How the hell was I supposed to get her through the gate if Barthas tried to hold her under house arrest?

"I trust you, Mombie," Irene insisted. "Many things I have foreseen change when you interact with them. You are a catalyst. There are many surprises to come over the next days. I see you fighting the Rebels. *And* I see you fighting Barthas's army."

"Hey, I can't do both. You're asking too much of me."

"I didn't say they would both come true. But they may. All things are possible. Just try to get me through that gate and I will owe you my life."

"All I can say is that I will do my best." I settled down the Zombies, who as usual had reacted to my emotions, and except for a small guard that I kept awake with my one open eye, I let the other thousands relax and recline. I lay down on my bedroll to get some sleep before Barthas came at daybreak.

Dawn seemed to arrive the minute I closed my eyes. Fried green tomatoes, but I was getting older and older by the minute. I grabbed onto my headache and roused the Zombies. I threw some water on my face and watched the hulking form of Barthas waddling in our direction across the plain. There was a bandy-legged green form next to him. He had brought his Swamp Demon. This sent a chill down my spine.

I gathered my Zombies around me and shouted, "That's far enough. You were to come alone."

"My Swamp Demon wants to speak to your Swamp Demon."

"Not until you finish talking with Irene. He is to keep his distance."

I signaled to Max to bring forward Irene. We knew she wouldn't run, but Barthas didn't. So, for appearance's sake I had Max hold a knife to Irene's throat.

Barthas waddled forward and asked, "How you doing, Irene? You okay?"

"Stay back," I warned.

Irene answered Barthas, "I am fine, José. They treated me fine."

"Okay. So what did you see about the Rebels? And can Sideous open this gate to my world?"

Irene saw Sideous's death again in her mind's eye. "Sideous is capable of opening the gate. And the Rebels are just what you have said: they are a rag-tag bunch of refugees and desperados."

"What about my friends? Will Malik, Hector, and Umberto get through?"

"Yes. This part I have foreseen." Irene remained cool and calm. I hoped this last part wasn't true. The last thing this Valley needed was three more members of the Crips running things. Irene continued her prophecy. "They will come through the gate and they will be changed in the transition."

"Great. We can all be Swamp Ogres!" Barthas was elated by this idea. He seemed satisfied by this and turned to go.

Irene looked tense and quietly said to me, "You had better send both your Swamp Demons. I see conflict—and I mean that I see it as a Seer."

Crap. Up till now I had kept Max out of conflict. But another Swamp Demon just hadn't been on my radar. I couldn't see any way to avoid this. Still, I took Irene's advice and sent both Max and Scyssa, while I waited with Irene and watched from a distance. I had to let Max handle this by himself. There are some things you just cannot do as a mom.

From the first moment that Max and Scyssa approached, the tension was apparent. Scyssa drew off to the side and I could hear her shouting in that strange sibilant language. She started whisking her spiked tail back and forth and hissing. I could see that Max was doing his best to keep his distance from the other male Swamp

Demon. Instinctively he was talking with his hands. This may not have been the best idea. The other Swamp Demon stood near to stick-still, but punctuated his words with intermittent slaps of his thick muscular tail on the dry dusty ground. Scyssa seemed on the verge of tears. Then Max raised his arms as if to say, "I give up!"

Things were not going well. Swords were drawn, and I thought my ancient heart would give out. It was fluttering in my chest like a bird. Eventually, Scyssa pulled them apart, said something final and probably insulting, and pulled Max after her back toward our camp. For that moment, I loved Scyssa.

Max broke into a jog and ran back to me. The words tumbled out of him. "Mom, he's totally crazy. He thinks Scyssa and I hooked up. He's the guy her father promised to ... to marry her to! He insists that he has the right to engage in combat with me. I know that doesn't sound so bad, but he claims one of us must draw blood. I tried to tell him that nothing happened, so did Scyssa, but he's totally crazy. Scyssa told him to flip off and dragged me away. But he's not ready to let go of this issue. He hates me and he said he wanted to KILL me!"

Max paused to catch his breath and added, "Oh, yeah, and he says that Scyssa and I are traitors to our race! And, in case all that isn't bad enough, Shadow says he wants to skin me and wear my skin!"

I struggled with my pounding heart, but finally managed to say, "Max, calm down. We will handle this, even if I have to negotiate something with Barthas."

"Nah, Mom, this is my fight. I'm a Swamp Demon and Scyssa has taught me that we are a proud race. I'm part of this crazy world now. Scyssa and I will handle it. But I need some time to think."

I let him have some time to himself. He went to meet Scyssa, and they walked arm and arm to the tent we had erected. I slipped over to Irene. I wanted to ask her how much of the "foreseeing" that she had done for Barthas was real. I was not the only one playing double agent in this game.

It was past midnight when Squirt and Button rode their bullfrogs to the outside of the stockade, where they left the frogs tied in the bushes. Disguised to look like shiny black boots, they sneaked inside under the legs of a company of guards, and no one noticed them as they safely reached the stairs to the Manor itself. Squirt became the color and shading, even the grain, of raw pine planking, and he crept up the stairs and through the front doors. The main room was empty, except for Nutkin the spit-boy. Staying in the shadows Squirt motioned to Button to follow his lead; quickly they both reflected the firelight dancing on the pine beams. Squirt led the way to the basement, and Button followed.

Patty was drifting in and out of sleep when she heard a familiar voice whisper, "Patty...." The sound was coming from the table beneath the cages, but try as she might, she couldn't see anyone. Then part of the painted mural stepped forward.

"Squirt!" she began to squeak, but he hushed her with a gesture.

"Patty, we've come to help you. I don't know if we can get you all out. But we've brought some real honey. Let's get you out of there."

He threw up a rope, but time after time Patty couldn't reach it. Finally Bart said, "Throw the rope to me." And he caught it on the first throw. With it they hauled up several thimbles full of honey, and by swinging their cages back and forth all the Pixies and Fairies managed to pass them to each other. It was a great relief to get real food.

But Squirt and Button were not sure what to do next. They were not big enough to unbend the wires that locked the doors to the cages. But at that moment—perhaps as a result of his renewed hope—Bart's spell began to take effect. With a strange groaning and squeaking sound the bottom of his cage transformed from solid oak to rotted wood and slowly crumbled in half. Bart flew free with a tiny Fairy's yelp of triumph. "I un-grew it! I knew it would work if I gave it time. See, Patty? Spells work! You should try some. Just believe in yourself."

With Bart's help Button sent a rope ladder up to Patty's cage and climbed up to examine the lock on the door. "It's just wire. Squirt, send up that crowbar and come up here and help me. Bart, see if you can throw some light our way."

Fairies and Pixies tended to glow, so Pink and Bart concentrated on lending light to the situation, while Button and Squirt angled and bent the wire locking the cage door. The Brownies were twice the Pixies' size, and together they had just enough strength to undo the wire wrapped around the door latch. But it was slow work, and dawn was approaching. In time they had three of the cages unlocked, not counting the wreckage Bart had made of his. There wasn't time to free them all, and they agreed that either all would escape or none. They agreed to just leave the doors closed on the cages and hope that Sideous would not notice as long as the girls were still there. Nothing could be done about the missing floor of Bart's cage: the rotten oak had started turning to sawdust on the table below. So they decided that Bart would fly out a window and attain as much height as his wings could manage and then fly back to the Rebel army and tell them the news.

Bart tipped his tiny green Robin Hood hat at the females and flew out into the night like a streak of blue flame. Patty missed him already. He had been right about the spell—and she would never scoff at magic again. In fact, he had been right about everything. Maybe there was something Patty could do by herself. The wooden bottom of her cage had once been alive. Maybe she could coax a flower to bloom out of it, or even better, a vine. That was the answer! She could grow a vine around the lock on the cage and it would look as if the wire were still in place! The honey had given her a burst of strength and hope.

Rays of sunlight were coming in to the dungeon, and Button and Squirt quickly took down the rope ladders and hid. Soon Sideous could be heard clumping down the stairs. But Patty's idea had worked! Her new-grown vine had wrapped itself around the cage door just like the wire that Button had pried off. Pink and Wixy managed to do the same to disguise their opened cage doors.

Sideous would believe they were all still locked in, except for Bart.

But when Sideous arrived and saw the wreck of Bart's cage he was furious. To the other prisoners' amazement, he was not that upset that one of the Fairies had gotten away—but that the day's supply of Pixie Dust had been contaminated with sawdust and rotten wood.

Patty turned and looked at the mural that had been painted on the wall. Amid the paint strokes of leaves and flowers she could see two pairs of tiny eyes looking back at her. Sideous did not notice the hidden Brownies; people never did, which was how they "borrowed" so successfully. Instead, he made a great show of cleaning the table and throwing away all of the contaminated Dust. But he never even checked the wires on the girl's cages: the vines had worked to confuse his preoccupied mind.

Well, at least they knew that Button and Squirt were nearby, and the honey had given them all strength. There would be plenty more Pixie Dust by evening. It was going to be a long wait. But Bart was on the way back to her dad with some news. At least Daddy would know she was alive and fighting back. That made Patty proud.

I demanded to know the truth about Irene's visions. Apparently, Sideous the Sorcerer was in for a violent death. Crap. How the heck were we going to open the gate back to our world without him? Would he die before or after he opened the gate? Irene couldn't say. More than that, Irene saw the Rebels attacking sooner than she was telling Barthas, and in force. As for Malik, Umberto, and Hector, they would make it through the gate, but not as Swamp Ogres. Barthas was in for several surprises, which Irene was keeping to herself. But right then, I was struggling with the notion of bringing my Zombie army to bear on the Rebels, with whom I sympathized.

It was nearly dawn on the day before the full moon when a scout came to me to inform me that the Rebel army was pouring out of the old forest in force and moving across the plain toward the Manor. There wasn't much time. I had thought this all out beforehand, but putting it into place was another story. I had to get into the stockade and get my Zombie Gnomes and Dwarves with bows up on the stockade wall. There were a lot of keystone cops fumbling with fingerless hands on steep ladders. A few Zombies broke off arms in the process, but there were always others to take their place. I arranged Human Zombies with pikes behind a front row of Zombie Ogres, Trolls, Giants, and Swamp Demons. I wanted a powerhouse of a frontline to discourage the Rebels.

I ordered Scyssa to stay with Irene in our tent. Irene was still a hostage but safe from the fight, and from Barthas's thugs. Blina, Keivitch, and Shadow Stalker headed cavalry divisions. They were there to observe the fight and lend a hand when my Zombies needed help. Looking sullen, Sideous appeared on a horse and joined Blina and Shadow. Barthas came out dressed in a clean bearskin hide, carrying his enormous spiked club, and glared at everyone with equal malice.

We held our ground without firing while the Rebels appeared to be doing the same thing as I. They were arranging rows of Elven archers (I had no Elves—they were Fairy Folk and not resurrectable), and Centaurs with morning stars and bows on their backs. I noticed that the tributary river which ran up to and through the stockade as a canal was filled with Mermen and Mermaids brandishing swords, and some of them carried shields.

I brought a large contingent of my Zombie Humans with pole arms to fend off the Merfolk. Thank heavens I had raised large numbers of Ogres and Trolls, because the rebels looked to outnumber us. A woman—no, a Witch—on a broom floating through the air above the rebels appeared to be shouting orders to them.

Damn. I didn't want this fight. But it was about to begin and if I didn't make a good show of it, Barthas would not let Max and me pass through the gate. I called Max over to me and reiterated for the umpteenth time that he was to stay close to the stockade and behind the forward force of Zombie Ogres and Trolls. I finished with, "Stay close enough that I can see you at all times."

Max was embarrassed and indignant. "I can fight better than most of these bozos. They don't even know karate."

"Max, I have the utmost faith in your fighting ability, but just stay close until we know how things are going. Okay?"

The reply was sullen but affirmative. "Okay, Mom-bie."

Things were not going as planned for Miss Edna's Rebels. They knew the formations they had to take: archers to the back, pikemen forward, Sorcerers surrounded by companies of armed Humans with shields for protection. But the minute they began to pour out of the old forest, the scouts came back with reports that the Necromancer had joined forces with Barthas and the Manor was teeming with armed Zombies. They were not just fighting Barthas, they were fighting the Necromancer and her Zombie army, too.

"Cat's Cradle! We're trumped before we begin. We haven't the reserves to fight off those Zombies *and* Barthas's mercenaries!" fumed Miss Edna.

Hook alone, fending off the bright morning sun with his parasol, remained calm. "Are you advising retreat or do we proceed? It was a long march, and it would be a shame to cancel the party."

Ben looked panicked and began to choke on his words. "But Patty ... Patty's in there. What about the prisoners? What about the gate back home? What about...?"

Edna put her arm on his shoulder. "Don't despair, Ben. We came to show Barthas our strength and our intent. And we came to free those prisoners, and somehow we will. But this just turned from a turkey-shoot to a free-for-all. This was the one eventuality I had hoped would not happen. Barthas got to the Necromancer before us and she is fighting for his side. Soon we'll see just how tough that old broad is."

Just then a blue Fairy came floating down from a great altitude and fluttered into the space between Ben and Edna's faces.

"Bart!" Edna exclaimed. "You're free! Tell me, did Button and

Squirt get through? Tell me everything."

Bart nodded his tiny head, but first turned to Ben. "Patty wants you to know that she is fine. She is still in a cage in Barthas's basement, but Button and Squirt have been hiding in plain sight nearby. Sideous never notices them. Tonight they will unlock the rest of the cages. When they are all free they will leave together."

Ben was dumbfounded. "If Patty's cage was unlocked why didn't she leave?"

"Sir, they have all promised one another to leave together or not at all."

Ben frowned and asked, "Then why are you here?" Patty's loyalty to her new friends touched Ben, but worried him.

"Well, Sir, I used magic to destroy my cage and there was no faking it back together like the locks on doors. Besides, they needed someone to take a message back to you and Miss Edna."

Miss Edna asked, "Bart, what did you do? How did you escape? Is it a magic other Pixies or Fairies could create? Tell me everything."

Bart looked rather proud and glowed a little brighter in the morning light. "Well, you know that turning acorns into mighty oaks is a specialty of mine. So you might say that I am the patient type. Miss Edna, I un-grew the oak bottom of my cage. Mind you it took a few days instead of a few years, because I did use magic. But it is the same magic involved in turning an oak tree back into soil, a simple compost spell. After a week of concentrated work the oak plank simply rotted and fell away. And I flew free."

"You hear that, Ben? That is ingenuity. It's the genius of using the obvious to override the impossible. You have to think outside the box to accomplish what seems impossible. And that is what we are going to do today when we fight that Necromancer's Zombies." She turned to the others. "Now, places everyone. Ben, get behind your shields. And Hook, move some earth and create some hillocks for my archers to shelter behind. Those Zombie Trolls look like they're coming our way."

Before I could launch a volley of arrows, the Witch got off her broom and a Sorcerer began moving earth to form bulwarks for their archers to hide behind. I decided I had to make a first move, so I sent out a group of Zombie Ogres and Trolls I had armed with heavy war hammers. Of course they were clumsy, but each of those hammers weighed close to seventy pounds, and the ground troops they sent forward had heads smashed in, arms ripped off, and were generally decimated. It was gruesome. But I had better get used to carnage. This was war.

A second Sorcerer came forward surrounded by a guard of men with shields. Flame flew from his fingers and lit the dried corpses of the Trolls into huge torches. The first Sorcerer moved earth beneath the Ogres until their hulking top-heavy forms fell over and rolled down the incline. I was happy to see that their massive weight bowled down enemy soldiers like bowling pins. I took advantage of the flames and sent the flaming Trolls into the area that looked like their main encampment; I set fire to one of the flags they were waving.

But soon the smoldering forms of the Trolls no longer obeyed my mental commands. The Sorcerer's flames had consumed them, and there is nothing deader than a dead Zombie. So I brought forward many more Trolls and Ogres from the rear and armed then with pikes and halberds. Meanwhile, the Rebels' Elven archers rained arrows down on us, flaming arrows that lit my Zombie Gnomes and Dwarves on fire. And they were dangerously close to the flammable stockade wall.

Hindsight is twenty-twenty, and had I thought of the danger of fire to a Zombie army I would have been more prepared with reserves of water.

I called out, "Blina, Keivitch, form a bucket brigade before the Zombies and the stockade both go up in flames."

They seemed startled to be given orders from me, but they obeyed and started a relay of buckets from the canal that ran up through the compound. But that canal was now filled with Merfolk who sprang from the water with swords and chopped off hands., arms, and even heads. Soon the air was filled with the screams of Barthas's Men as they lost both buckets and limbs. I stationed Human Zombie archers about the edge of the canal, but a Zombie's aim was not the best, and their reflexes were only as fast as I could think them. So the elegant Merfolk dove deep underwater and eluded the archers' arrows while causing desperate damage to the bucket brigade. The burning Zombies on the wall began to crumble and fall. I lost mental contact with them as they disintegrated.

In the meantime the two Sorcerers were making their way up the incline to the stockade and directing bolts of lightning or electricity into the cavalry led by Blina Turdgirdle. I saw her convulse and fall from her horse. This was turning into a rout, so I quickly brought out a band of Zombie Ogres with clubs to chase the Sorcerers back down the hill. I sent forward a group of Human Zombies with bows to fire a volley into the air and toward the heart of the Rebels' main encampment, where I was certain the Witch was hiding. Hundreds of arrows shot down on the Rebels, but in the center, where their command center was, the arrows simply stopped against what seemed like an invisible dome, and after their momentum broke, they fell harmlessly to earth. What the hell was that Witch capable of?

I couldn't let up. If I failed, Max and I would lose our ticket through the gate and back home. So I brought forward a large force of mixed-race Zombie pikemen and had them charge the enemy force en masse. The cries of pain and death haunted me as Rebel soldiers fell to my fighters. But many of the Rebels carried swords, and each time a Zombie lost a head it was lost to me. There were already hundreds of bodies on the field, and the sun was only halfway to noon.

I had many large Zombies as well as Trolls, Ogres, Giants, Swamp Demons, and a few Centaurs, but I needed to make the hard decision. I was a Necromancer. It was my business to deal in carnage and horror. I wasn't proud about what I was about to do, but I had a thirteen-year-old boy to get back to his family. Maybe

God would forgive me. Someday.

I turned my attention to the battlefield between us and began raising the dead Rebels and making them pick up their weapons and then walk back toward their former colleagues and attack.

I could see at once the Rebels' revulsion and terror. The whole front line pulled back. Good. I had regained the upper hand. They were appalled by the idea of fighting their own dead.

Now where was Max?

Max duels Shadow Stalker

Seventeen

A Change of Plans

"Miss Edna," Ben complained. "This is a crap storm. If that Witch keeps sending back our own dead to fight us, the men will lose their nerve. I think I saw Ferny's corpse out there, fighting our own men. It's a horror."

"I can see that, Ben. None of us were prepared for this. But if we don't keep fighting, Button and Squirt will never get Patty and the girls free. Take your choice. Hook, get out there and lay down some fire and lightning. Give me a chance to think. And Ben, I want you covering the Merfolk in the canal. The more we stop Barthas's troops from dousing our fires, the more Zombies we can burn."

Miss Edna took a deep breath. "But it might be time to request a parley. We need anything to gain us time."

Ben took off after the soldiers assigned to him, each carrying a shield and a morning star and ready for close-quarters combat. Ben followed them to where the canal emptied into the tributary river, trying to figure out how to give the Merfolk a respite and protection. Apparently there was a company of Swamp Demons who were not only strong swimmers, but armed with vicious claws and teeth, preparing to attack the Mermen and Mermaids.

When Max saw the Swamp Demons forming up around the town canal, he wanted to be part of whatever was happening. Any chance to speak in his native language and be part of the Swamp Demon community appealed to him.

"So what's happening?" he asked in his best dialect (Scyssa had been drilling him in the nuances).

"Big group move on the Water-Fairies. Stopping the bucket brigade, and Barthas wants them dealt with," replied the other Demon. Max couldn't help but size himself up. Maybe Max was big for a Swamp Demon. He was sure bigger than this guy. But Shadow Stalker had been at least as big as Max. That was another worry.

"Okay. I'm in. But I work for Mombie the Zombie Queen. So I'm only doing this to help her Zombies."

The other Swamp Demon shrugged, unconcerned with Max's political affiliations. Then Shadow Stalker came forward blowing a whistle, and the disorganized fist of Demons dissolved into two neat lines. Shadow noticed Max.

"Sssoo, you are here, traitor."

"Not a traitor. I work for Mombie. I'm just volunteering."

"Volunteering to do what your people have sworn to do, to uphold Barthas's laws. Is that what you mean, traitor?"

Now everyone was looking at Max. "Yeah. For the moment."

"I will deal with you later, Maxsswell." Shadow Stalker spat on the ground. "Enough. The Water-Fairiesss have taken control of the canal. Our people are aquatic. Ssshow them who rules these waters."

Shadow Stalker dove into the canal and the rest of the Swamp Demons slid in behind him. Max hit the water and a whole new world opened up to him. He had a third eyelid, which was clear and had always seemed extraneous until now. Now it slid into place like a pair of racing goggles. The webbing between his claws and his toes acted like scuba fins to propel him effortlessly. And with his tail he could slither forward—like an alligator, he thought with a grin. He could see the Mermen and Mermaids fleeing further down the canal toward the river. They were armed with swords and shields, but they stood no chance against the extreme speed and predatory nature of Swamp Demons, who were raking deep bloody grooves into the fish tails of the fleeing Merfolk. It was a massacre. Max followed the others but took no part in the carnage.

As they breached the tunnel under the stockade wall, the Mermen and Mermaids hauled themselves up on the riverbank and turned to watch a lone man who stood further up the riverbank wearing blue satin pajamas, a floppy red-and-white striped hat, and a goatee. He seemed to concentrate and gesture, and an enormous wall of water rose up out of the river and smashed into the Swamp Demons, pushing them back up the canal and washing them back out onto the grounds of the Manor.

Max managed to splutter one astonished word. "Dad?" And then he ran to find his mother.

I was beside myself. I could see what animating their dead did to them, and still they fought bravely on. These Rebels had guts. I sent Zombie Trolls, Giants, and Ogres after them, and a Sorcerer appeared on the hill to set them on fire. I was busy trying to get the Zombies to chase the Sorcerer down the slope when Max ran up to me breathlessly.

"You're all wet!" I managed to admonish him.

"God, Mom. I saw Dad! He's here fighting for the Rebels. I think he's a Sorcerer!"

I was gobsmacked. I began by doubting my own son. "Are you sure? Did you see him up close? How can you be sure?" And then because maybe it just wasn't obvious enough I added, "That's crazy!"

Max was indignant. "Mom, I know my own dad." He crossed his arms, swung his tail in the dirt and stood his ground.

I had to think. How did I go about verifying this? What did this mean? Was I fighting my own husband? I nearly lost control of the Zombies. So I called the largest of my decrepit attackers back up the hill. I told Max to search for a large sheet or a tablecloth to use as a white flag. I had to have a parley.

Damn. How was I to going to keep Blina, Barthas, Keivitch, and Shadow Stalker out of this? Sideous seemed to have gone

AWOL. He complained that he had to keep up his strength for the ceremony. Meanwhile we were being roasted by hostile Sorcerers, one of whom might, or might not, be my own husband. I had to come up with a reason for attending this parley alone. Maybe, I thought, I could take Irene as both hostage and representative of Barthas. Yes. That should work.

Max was already waving the white flag. I could see Blina on her black gelding approaching at a clip.

"What do you think you're doing?" she demanded.

"This is a massacre." I added, as arrogantly as I could, "So far I've been fighting alone, mostly with my Zombies. When you add the full force of your soldiers the Rebels will be overwhelmed."

"But this way we keep casualties to a minimum. Zombies can be replaced."

"I'm glad you think it is all so easy, Miss Turdgirdle. I'm calling a parley to give them a chance to bow out before they are massacred. I need a break from fighting, and now is the time. I want to see who it is I'm fighting."

"I will go with you," Blina said bluntly.

"No. I am taking Irene. She can meet the leaders of the rebellion and see their futures. I want nothing to interfere with her psychic sensitivities. You stay here. I'll take several of my strongest Zombies and they can bring their own honor guard, their Witch and a Sorcerer."

"I don't trust you," Blina said bluntly again.

"And I don't care!" I retorted. "I'm the one who's been doing all the fighting so far. When you can say the same, you can start having a say in things. Until then, keep your half-Troll ass right here on your horse, and wait until I return from the parley." I knew Blina outranked me in Barthas's eyes, but I had to hope my bluff would work.

Max arrived leading Irene by the arm. He had told her about the parley, but I wasn't sure how much else he had said. He had been pretty excited about seeing Ben, and those Swamp Demon eyes of his did not lie.

I had one Zombie Giant pick me up in his arms and another carry Irene. Max came along because I wanted him to. To my relief, Blina obeyed my orders and stayed seated on her horse. Eddie flew alongside.

We approached slowly, and so did the Rebel party. The Witch flew her broom, slowly, but the others approached on foot carrying their own white flag. There was only one Sorcerer and it was not Ben. I had the Giant Zombies put Irene and me down. If there was going to be an ambush, I was sure leaving myself open for it.

Their Witch spoke first. "Why have you called for a parley? We have come to free our imprisoned comrades." She was defiant in the face of disaster.

I decided to be direct. "You have a second Sorcerer. Why is he not here?"

The Witch was curt. "He is not part of our ruling council."

"Well, fetch him. I have reason to believe that he and I are acquainted." A servant was sent to fetch the Sorcerer. "Your situation here is tentative, to say the least. If Barthas adds the full force of his army to that of my Zombies, you haven't a chance. Run. Take this chance to flee to the woods and the hills."

"What shall I call you, Necromancer?" asked the Witch politely.

"I am Mombie the Zombie Queen."

"Well, Mombie, we have come out of those woods and those hills because Barthas has taken our friends prisoner, and has taxed us out of our own homes. And we are not going back like a pack of frightened mice."

I had to give it to her, she had guts. "And your name?"

"Miss Edna will do."

It was at that moment that a familiar form in blue pajamas and a floppy red-and-white striped knit hat that I remembered from our trip to Stowe arrived. He looked tired and dirty, but I knew that face. Max cried out first, "*DAD!*"

"Ben." I was overcome with emotions and my ancient heart was fluttering. This would be the perfect time to die of a stroke.

Ben was guarded and, of course, did not recognize either of us. "How do you know my name? Aren't you the enemy Necromancer?"

"Oh, God, yes. I suppose I am. But I'm also your wife, Ben. I'm Annie DeLeon Prockner." Irene gripped my hand and I knew she was sensing all sorts of possible futures. "And this strapping young Swamp Demon here is your son, Max. We fell through a gate into this world and it changed us as much as it seems to have changed you. I don't remember you shooting fire from your fingertips back in Middleville."

Ben stood his ground and asked, "Is this some kind of a joke, lady? My wife is my age, and you look older than Grandma Moses. And my son has red hair and freckles. If this is a joke, it's in very poor taste. I've just lost my daughter to Barthas's thugs, and the mention of my family is not amusing to me."

"Jesus Christ! Barthas has Patty? How the *hell* did you let that happen?"

Ben just stared. "We're working on that...." He looked at me intensely, especially at my wrinkly, tired eyes. "Where was our first apartment?"

"The Upper West Side, Seventy-fourth Street, around the corner from the original Fairway. Ben, it's me, but I really am this old, and I ache in every bone in my body—and Max really is a Swamp Demon. And this is Eddie." I pointed to the raven on my shoulder.

"Caw," said Eddie.

Ben screwed up his courage and asked, "Max, where do you study karate?"

Max replied, "At Mr. Kyuke's Dojo!" He stepped through some karate forms and thrust his fist out into the empty air.

Miss Edna interrupted and said to Ben, "I told you it was possible. It happens from time to time. Related individuals arrive apart but in the same world."

"Answer me one more question. Why are you here at Barthas's Manor helping him to fight us?"

I blurted out, "Because he controls the gateway between worlds and I'm trying to get Max and me back to Middleville."

"Well, we have to free Patty first, and these people are my friends. Annie, you're fighting for the wrong side. How could you?"

I had known this was coming, and I had no real answers. "Because I did what I had to. You have no idea what it is like to live in this ancient body. Max has been such a help to me."

"Yeah, well, I assume an army of Zombies is some help, too. Do you know that this whole Valley has been following your every move and praying that you would not align with Barthas—and here I find you fighting for him! You're the great Necromancer, Mombie the Zombie Queen? Where the hell did you even come up with a name like that?"

"Max made it up, because he kept slipping and calling me Mom. So we turned it into Mombie. So sue me. I made some mistakes. But we're both alive and we are going to get Patty out of wherever she is, and then we're getting the hell out of this crazy world and back home—tomorrow night, on the full moon."

I turned to Miss Edna and asked, "Couldn't you just pretend to withdraw into the woods and wait until tomorrow night to attack in full? Then I would turn my Zombies on Barthas and we can take control of the gate and get home."

Miss Edna smiled at Ben and said, "So this is really your wife? The woman who has held a knife to Barthas's throat, terrorized the Valley, and sent our own dead to fight us?"

"Shucks," said Ben. And with a touch of pride, "That's my Old Lady." Suddenly we were all laughing, though just for a moment.

Now we had to come up with a plan to fool Barthas. Irene and I would swear that we had bartered a truce. The rebels would withdraw deep into the woods where the Centaurs could hide them. Then they would return tomorrow night as the full moon rose and help me storm the Manor. The hard part would be to keep Blina out of my face until that time. We took one last moment to shake on the deal and to swear on our lives that we had each other's backs. It felt strange when I kissed Ben goodbye. He couldn't help but recoil a little at my withered geriatric kiss. Well, I had seen myself. I was no beauty. But it hurt.

I had the Zombie Giants carry Irene and me back to the stockade. We talked quietly between ourselves. Irene wondered why she hadn't seen the connection between Ben and me. But she did point out that she had seen me fighting both the Rebels and Barthas. I was more than a double agent: I was a complete double-crosser. And I had to make Blina believe that I was Barthas's savior.

When we got back to the top of the hill, I said to her, very formally, "They have seen that their cause is hopeless. I have offered them the mercy of retreat."

"That was not your place to offer," Blina snapped.

"Well, considering that you have all been sitting on your hands while I've fought this war almost singlehandedly, I don't think you or Barthas has very much to say about it. The bottom line is that I have brought an end to a very badly timed attack by a Rebel army. It frees Barthas to open the gate in safety tomorrow night. Have you done that much for Barthas lately, Miss Turdgirdle?"

Blina held her peace, but turned her horse to report back to Barthas. My Zombie Giants carried Irene and me to the Manor, where we found Barthas was pretty far gone into his drug haze. Blina, intruding meddlesome creature that she was, ratted that I had negotiated a truce with the Rebels.

"On the contrary, Lord Barthas, we beat the pants off the Rebels and they were glad to take the chance I gave them to run for the hills. I have saved the Manor from being burnt to the ground by their Sorcerers, and have opened the way for the ceremony under the full moon tomorrow night."

Barthas eyes were unfocused as he thought of his old friends. "I'm gonna get Hector, Malik, and Umberto, and we gonna all be Swamp Ogres. Irene, you saw it, right? They're coming through the gate, right? Right?"

Irene's calm cool nature helped the ruse. "Yes, Lord Barthas, your friends will come through the gateway with Sideous's help, and they will transform. Mombie must be present at the ceremony so that she can pass through the gate with her Swamp Demon."

"Shadow wants to duel with her Swamp Demon."

Crap. He would remember that detail. "My Swamp Demon is not of their tribe. They have no claim on his loyalties."

Barthas yawned and drank some wine. "Let them work it out. Be here at dusk if you want Sideous to work the spell to get you through. Sideous, bring me more Pixie Dust!"

The Sorcerer appeared from a side door where he had been skulking and listening to our conversation. He carried a crystal sugar bowl full of iridescent Pixie Dust and smiled, commenting, "The Pixies and Fairies are much happier now that my Lord Barthas has seen fit to provide them with a mural of their natural woodland habitat. They are producing more Dust than ever."

Now that I knew my daughter was being held captive by this monster, I wanted Barthas dead. There wasn't enough Manticore venom in the world to satisfy my thirst for revenge. I looked at Irene and my face remained steady. Paulette had better be ready to help Cook tomorrow. There was meat to be poisoned. I had the Zombie Giants lift Irene and me and carry us back to our encampment outside the stockade.

Patty had waited all day long. The rest of the Pixies and Fairies had tried to keep conversation to a minimum while Squirt and Button were camouflaged within the mural. They didn't want to draw any attention to themselves or their rescuers, so only in secret had they eaten the honey that the Brownies had brought. With good nourishment they had been able to produce plenty of Pixie and Fairy Dust, and Sideous had been happy to collect it, encouraging them to "continue to do their best for the cause."

When night fell Button threw up the rope ladders again. This time Patty caught them. One by one, using the single crowbar, they wedged back the wires that held their cages closed. They had to take breaks and hide in the mural whenever the night guard came up the stairs from the dungeon to check the basement door. But that happened only every forty-five minutes or so, and they could always hear him coming. Still, it was near dawn before all the doors were opened. As agreed, they let Button and Squirt get a head start on their bullfrogs, but as their hour of waiting passed and dawn approached, all twelve of them opened their cage doors, took to the air, and flew through the crack in the basement window. When they were all high enough in the air, Pink and Wixy led the way to the forest, where Button had told them the Rebels waited.

Pink found Miss Edna first, and the Witch told Patty where to find her father. Ben was awash with tears when he saw her tiny, glowing form alight on his bedroll. "Patty, Patty, my baby. You have to promise never to disobey me again."

"Oh, Daddy, I promise. I made a terrible mistake and there were some really mean people. I was wrong, Daddy. I'm sorry."

"Well, Punkin, learning to do the right thing is hard work. But I have good news: I found your mother and your brother. They're here, in this same Valley. So is Eddie."

"Oh, Daddy, Mommy and Max are here? Where?"

"Well, Punkin, that's the hard part. You know how you and I have changed since we got here? Well, Mommy and Max have changed even more than we did. Mommy is the Necromancer that everyone has been talking about."

"Mommy is the Zombie Queen?"

"Yes, Punkin, but she's only pretending to help Barthas, so she can really help us."

"I want to see her. Does she really have Zombies?"

"Yes, Patty, lots of them, thousands of them. But listen to me, Patty. First of all, you wouldn't recognize Mom. She's grown old. She's older than Grandma. But more than that, I am not letting you out of my sight. Do you understand me, young lady? You're not going anywhere. When we go back to the Manor..."

"Oh Daddy, I don't want to go anywhere near that place ever

again!"

"Well, I wish it were that easy, Punkin. We have to go back there because there's a gate that we have to open to get back home. So I want you to hide in my pocket and stay there, no matter what happens, until we're through the gate. I want you to swear to me that you will stay in my pocket."

"Daddy, it's stinky in there."

"Patrice! Swear you will obey me and stay in my pocket!"

"Okay, Daddy, I do. I swear it."

"Okay. Now get some sleep. We have to march back through the woods again tomorrow."

Ben watched her lie down on the pillow he had made with his clothes. He spent the next few hours watching her breathe and thanking Kwan Yin for her mercy. Sleep was not an option.

I was exhausted. I had single-handedly held off the bulk of the Rebel army. I had lost many Zombies and gained some new ones. However, out of respect to Ben and his friends, I let most of the Rebel corpses slide back into oblivion.

I wanted Irene to tell me one more time the way she intended to poison Barthas; I needed to be sure the plan was foolproof. She had several of Barthas's old hypodermic needles that she would use to inject the Manticore venom into a haunch of meat—hopefully venison, and not Gnome. We went over the plan step by step.

I also took some time to talk to Max and Scyssa. I needed Max to understand how important it was for him to stay close to me when the gate was opened. He had to say his goodbyes to Scyssa tonight. I took her hand, or claw, in mine and told her how grateful I was to her for her help. How sorry I was that Max had to leave her. Maybe I sounded stupid. Maybe Ben would say I was being a fool. But Max had lived as a grown-up all this time. He had hunted and scouted, and protected me like a man. He deserved to be treated as an adult for once in his life. I gave them my blessing and let them wander into the woods to spend the night.

"I want you both back here in the morning, understand?"

"Fair enough, Mombie." Max took Scyssa's hand in his and they meandered into the woods.

Max and I had grown a lot during this time together. Maybe, just maybe, I wouldn't tell Ben this part. Max was entitled to a few secrets of his own.

Eighteen

Treachery

I woke up late, taking the time to rest and recover some of my strength. But the constant headache of the Zombies was always there. The sun was halfway into the morning sky when a pair of Fairies flew into my tent and hid behind the canvas flap. We were far enough from Barthas's main stockade for them to be fairly safe, but nothing would put a Fairy at ease this close to the Ogre. I closed the tent flap and urged them to sit at the ceramic outdoor table Irene and I used for tea. I searched around and found a bit of jam we had gotten from Barthas's kitchen and offered it to them. Miss Edna had told me that they liked sweet things, and Ben had nodded emphatically in agreement.

They introduced themselves as Bart and Wixy and said they had come directly from Miss Edna. Her army was to return to the woods surrounding the Manor at dusk. Ben would call down a bolt of lightning from the evening clouds. If there were no clouds he would send up a fire-bolt. But I had to be facing south, because Ben and the Rebels would approach from that direction. My part in the effort was to have my largest Zombies throw open the gates and use some of the others to guard the Rebels. I think Barthas had a gun, but mostly we were talking about arrows, crossbow bolts, pike arms, and swords. Things could get bloody once again.

Once Sideous opened the gate to L.A. things could get even messier. I had to try to get Irene through, but only after he pulled in Barthas's three thug friends. Sideous might close the gate as a punishment for my throwing Irene through.

All bets were off if I defied Barthas's order. Hopefully, though, he would be so poisoned and appear so drugged that he would be out of the way—or completely out of it. Both Hook and Ben felt that they were capable of either opening or holding open the gate for Max, Ben, Patty, Eddie, and me. Miss Edna had hinted that she had another plan involving the gate. But she wasn't about to tell me what it was. She was a cagey one, that Miss Edna, and she still considered me "the enemy."

All in all, it would be a crapshoot. We would have to fight off battalions of Barthas's men. And Barthas had living Trolls and Ogres and Swamp Demons, not just Zombies like I was working with. Miss Edna said the front force of the rebels would be Elves armed with long bows. Elven archers were said to be fast and accurate. They would try to take out the soldiers who were present at the ceremony: My concern was that they might mistake Max or Scyssa for one of the enemy Swamp Demons. Wixy suggested that they wear red sashes. But how was I to get Max or Scyssa to wear a red sash? And where was I going to get such things?

I woke Irene and asked her if she had any red cloth. She said she would find some, but that she and Paulette had to get to the Manor to "assist the cook." She was right: it was growing toward midmorning, and noon was around the corner. I asked if she needed any help, and she declined in that polite, controlled way of hers. Then I asked her, more directly, if there was enough of the Manticore venom.

"Depends how much I can get him to eat. There's enough venom," she replied calmly. Irene had hardened her heart to Barthas.

I wish my own resolve had been so firm. My conscience was already aching.

I said goodbye to Irene and told her I would see her that evening. Max and Scyssa sauntered back into camp. I gave Max a look.

The tips of his red crest flamed brighter red, and he shook his head in embarrassment. "Don't worry, Mom. Nothing happened. We just talked."

Irene took Paulette's arm and began the long walk back to the Manor. The ground was dry and she could feel the dust coming up as she swung her cane from side to side in front of her. Irene never let go of her self-control. It was counting steps and memorizing the placement of buildings that got her through the day. Paulette had become her trusted friend over the three years of Barthas's rule. She had seen the toll Irene's foreseeing had taken on her spirit: Barthas had slowly crushed her. But his forbidding Irene to leave was the final straw.

They stopped at the guardhouse room that Irene had moved into, and Irene took the five tiny vials of Manticore venom from the secret space between the floorboards. She lifted the loose plank and replaced it carefully the same way, so the scuffmarks would line up. Then with the precision of a chemist, she coaxed the viscous liquid from the vials into five waiting hypodermics. Paulette remained absolutely silent. There was no going back from here.

They walked back to the Manor arm in arm. Irene wasn't even counting her footsteps, just letting Paulette lead her into the hall where Barthas was waiting.

"That bitch let you go or are you still a hostage?" He was already high and his "kit" was on the table. "I can't get an appetite no more, without a hit or two," Barthas complained.

"Whatever, you need, Jo— Lord Barthas. It's your life. In fact you're in control of this whole Valley tonight. Mombie just made the rebel forces retreat. The Valley is yours, my Lord. It's time for a celebration. Why don't I have Cook fix something special for you?"

"Okay, but make it meat, just meat. That's all I have an appetite for," growled Barthas as he sniffed some more Fairy Dust off a greasy mirror with rolled paper tube.

Good, thought Irene. *All the more reason everyone else will think he's just self-medicated as usual.*

"I'll go consult with the cook about a special haunch of meat for you. How about a nice leg of venison?"

"Yeah, great. Have them put it on the spit and we can take slices as it roasts."

Irene found the hallway to the kitchen with her cane, and counted the fifteen steps to the doorway. It kept her calm.

"Do you need my arm, Miss Irene?" Paulette asked politely.

"No, thank you Paulette. I know my way by heart."

"Cook, Lord Barthas has requested a special haunch of venison to celebrate the routing of the rebel forces. I am to select the haunch."

"We just got in a lovely doe which the butcher has sectioned and hung in the cool room. Why don't you and Paulette pick out a nice haunch and I'll have it spitted for you? Do you need help or do you know the way?" asked the rotund Human. Although it was said that Elves made better cooks, Barthas wouldn't have them in the Manor.

"No. No. You know me, Judy. I know my way. Twelve steps to the cool room and watch your head for hanging meats. Paulette and I can manage. I'll call you when I've made my decision."

Irene walked the twelve steps as calmly as possible, and she could hear Paulette behind her. As she entered the marble-lined cool room, she raised her right arm to feel for the hanging pieces of meat while she swept the floor for obstructions with her cane. There was a moment when she ran her hand down a severed arm and felt the cold fingers with her own warm ones. But Irene kept her cool. She knew Barthas's vile taste.

It didn't take long to locate a plump haunch of drying venison. Irene handed two of the hypodermics to Paulette, and she pierced the remaining three into the fleshy part of the meat and pressed the plungers. It took little time for the venom to ooze into the flesh, and there was a slight hissing sound; soon they were both done and Irene had stashed the hypodermics back in her pocket.

"Judy?" Irene called. "I think we found just the right one. Would you come in and help us?" Irene called innocently.

Judy came bustling in and whistled for Nutkin the Spit-boy. "Hey, Nutkin, help me get this haunch of venison on the spit for Lord Barthas." Irene could hear the Gnome's long thin feet slapping the marble floor. Then she heard the Cook wrestling down the haunch, and Nutkin grabbing the heavy end of it, as they waddled out to the roaring fireplace to skewer the meat on the spit.

Irene and Paulette were done. Now they had to find some red fabric and get back to Annie before the evening's festivities.

Twelve steps back into the kitchen....

Sideous was as close to hysterical as he ever got. When he had collected the Pixie Dust that morning he had discovered all the cages unlocked and empty. Someone must have helped the Fairies and Pixies escape—someone small enough to enter undetected, and strong enough to pry free the wires that locked the cages. What was Sideous to do? He knew, none better, what Barthas's temper was like.

He would have to focus on the fact that Barthas needed him to open the gate and pull through his villainous cronies. He paced back and forth repeatedly in the dungeon, now with its cartoon mural of a woodland scene. It had taken the last three years to collect enough Fairies and Pixies to supply Barthas's growing habit. Barthas would freak out when he discovered the truth. But Sideous could not delay much longer. Blina had already learned about the escape, and she was sure to blab.

Better, Sideous thought, to be the one to tell him, and face the music while Barthas was alone. Best of all to blame the faulty guard work by the night patrols. Guards could be replaced, but Barthas couldn't do without his principle Sorcerer.

Barthas was alone in the Main Hall, slavering on slices of roast meat, which the cook had sliced and placed on a platter for him. He seemed oddly slow and distant. Maybe his mainlining of Pixie Dust had relaxed him, thought Sideous. Good.

Sideous began slowly, "My great Lord Barthas, there has been a breach in security during the night. Prisoners were allowed to escape under the very noses of the night guard."

"Prisoners? Which prisoners, Sideous?" Barthas demanded.

"The Pixies and Fairies, Sir. Not one other prisoner; only them."

"What the eff!? Are you crapping me, Bonehead?" roared Barthas. "Why don't you just open all the prison doors and let them ALL go free? You are a total jack-wad! I should just kill you now and put you out of your misery! What the hell do I need you for if you can't even supply me with Dust any more?"

"Sir," drawled Sideous with a supercilious smile, "it's not my job to guard the prisoners, only to make use of them. Whoever was in charge of the guards must have been ... lax. At any rate, the ceremony is tonight. I have to focus the spell on your friends, Malik, Hector, and Umberto. Soon they will rule at your side and bring peace and order to the Valley."

"And that's the only reason you are still living! Get the hell out of my sight, you moron. And find a way to get more of that damned Fairy Dust. I ain't going through withdrawal because you can't keep your eye on a few freaking cartoon Fairies!"

"Sir, we are working on the problem as we speak. I have sent a large military force to the waterfall. The Rebels have run like cowards to the forest and the mountains. And the Necromancer Mombie sent them into retreat with their tails between their legs. They don't have the resources to guard the Fairy Folk who are hiding in and around the waterfall. The escaped prisoners should be recovered in no time."

"You had better hope so, Dung-brain." Barthas took a generous dripping slice of the venison haunch Cook had plated for him. He dribbled the juices all over his chest and sighed deeply as he swallowed. Sideous thought with relief that Barthas's eyes were very glazed for this early in the day.

Miss Edna brought Ben out to a clearing in the forest. There was a series of stepped bedrock outcroppings, and a huge boulder had fallen down the hill to land in the sunlight in the middle of the clearing.

Ben spoke first. "Miss Edna, I don't think I have to tell you how nervous I am about tonight's activities. I've finally found my wife and son and I can't hold them or speak to them. So much depends on the opening of that gate."

Edna smiled kindly toward him. "I know how much pressure you feel, Ben. But consider this: unless Sideous had created those infernal batteries, none of this would be possible. It's the combined magic of our Fairy Folk which is stored in those batteries that will get you out of the Valley. Once we get you and your family through the gate, the batteries should be destroyed. But first I have an idea I need your help with."

"Me, Miss Edna? Why not Hook?"

"Because if all goes well, he will be holding open the gate for your family to pass through. I saw you swat Hook with that woven shield the day Patty got lost. You have rather a talent for creating a large shield." Miss Edna turned toward the center of the clearing and pointed at the gargantuan boulder. "See the boulder, Ben? I want you to help me lift it and move it."

"Wha...? That thing must weigh over three thousand pounds."

"I know. I want you to weave your shield *under* the boulder, like those silicone furniture-moving pads they sell on TV. I used to love watching those infomercials back in Tampa. But I don't have any here, so I'm going to have to push it with telekinesis, and I'll need you to raise it up for me."

"I hate to be negative, Miss Edna, but I have a lot on my mind. It would help if you let me in on your plan," Ben said plaintively.

Miss Edna plopped herself down on a rock and motioned for Ben to sit next to her. When he was close enough, she whispered in his ear. Soon he was laughing, glad to join in the effort to move the stone, though it took some practice. First, Miss Edna had to get an edge of the boulder lifted, which brought a cold sweat to her normally calm brow. Then Ben needed time to weave the shield and slip the corner of it under the rock. After that Miss Edna had to rock its main weight back onto the shield while Ben maintained it under the enormous pressure. Once they finally got the bulk of the boulder in the right position, Edna was able to slide it along the invisible edge of the shield as Ben shaped it into a sort of wedge. It took some serious teamwork and timing, and it was an enormous effort, but four times they moved the boulder, between ten and twenty feet each time.

Miss Edna seemed satisfied. "That ought to do it, Ben. If you can help me do that tonight, after we crash the party, this Valley may have a chance to heal and recover from Barthas's brutal damage. Let's get back to camp. It's already after noon, and we need to start marching back toward the Manor. I'm going to have the bulk of the army hold back in the forest until we've sent the signal and Sideous has begun the ceremony."

"But Miss Edna, Annie said that Barthas was planning on pulling in three of his friends from the L.A. Crips. What are we going to do about them?" asked Ben earnestly.

"Honey, this Valley is all about balance, and since Barthas has arrived he has created some serious imbalance in the natural order of things. Let's just say that this beautiful magical land I call home has its own sense of order, and we will all work to restore that order. It brought you and Annie, Max, and Patty to us at just the right time."

"You forgot Eddie," mumbled Ben. "That was a cryptic answer. But I get the idea. Yin balances Yang. Karma's a bitch. Let's get back and start marching."

As the hours ticked toward evening I began to get increasingly nervous. So much was at stake. I would have Max and Scyssa bring Irene as my hostage to the ritual. We would all be wearing red sashes. Irene had taken a set of scarlet velvet curtains from her old bedroom in the Manor, and Paulette and I had turned them into sashes for all of us. We were representing a different diplomatic faction from Barthas and his men, and I wanted the Rebels to be able to identify us.

I also wanted to be sure Irene understood that my family came first. I would not dare to attempt her transfer through the gate until Barthas had pulled his friends through. It was just too dangerous. I liked Irene and I trusted her, but I wasn't going to endanger the welfare of my family for her happiness. Irene seemed okay with that; she told me I was the catalyst. All things would change because I was here, and she had faith that I could get her through.

Time would tell. Even Max was nervous. I had told him about the Manticore poison and Irene's treachery. The main thing would be that he obeyed me when I told him to jump for the gate. Patty would be with Ben and I would be carrying Eddie on my shoulder. It helped my look. I was wearing the wolf-skull crown with the pheasant feathers tonight. I carried the gnarled walking stick that Dendra Mossy's husband had carved me. Everything was about impressing Barthas that I was a team player. At least until halftime ... when the teams would change.

My greatest challenge was bringing enough Zombies to guard Irene, Max, and myself without annoying Barthas. He didn't like the way they smelled. Still I would need some of my largest Zombies to open the gates to the stockade and let the Rebels in. After that I could call in as many as I needed. I had gathered them around the stockade and they felt the restlessness of my mood. They were milling about and mumbling with broken jaws and desiccated lips, awaiting my commands.

It was late afternoon when we proceeded to the stockade. Sideous had moved the batteries into the main courtyard, and Irene had arranged braziers of incense about the perimeter. It looked properly mysterious. Barthas had arranged to have his huge wooden throne brought out from the Main Hall in the Manor. As the light began to fade we saw him wobble out unsteadily and plop into his enormous chair. His bearskin was crooked and there were meat stains all over the front. Irene was thrilled to see that he had slid the haunch of venison from the spit and was ripping chunks of flesh from the bone and swallowing them.

I whispered to her, "What are the symptoms?"

She could have been a ventriloquist, her lips moved so slightly.

"It's a neurotoxin. There are varying degrees of paralysis, slowed heartbeat, difficulty breathing, lack of coordination."

Barthas caught sight of her, "Irene, Irene, my lucky charm. I'm glad you're here tonight to ... you know ... welcome my old friends." His words were slow and getting slurred. He slumped in the great wooden throne. "This meat is awesome! I feel great. Nice and relaxed."

Barthas seemed drunk as he chanted, "I am the King. It's my thing. I rule 'cause I am cool." There was drool sliding from the corner of his mouth. "Hey, I can't feel my legs."

Irene was cool as a cucumber. "My Lord Barthas, it is all the meat and wine. Just relax and enjoy it. You spend half your life getting high. There's no point in complaining that you feel high. Relax and enjoy the show, José."

It was going to be some show, too. All of Barthas's followers had come out to see the magical gate opened. There were Men, Gnomes, Trolls, Ogres, and more soldiers than I could count. They were all out of their barracks for an evening's entertainment. Some soldiers carried weapons, but many did not. I hoped my Zombies would be able to handle a counterattack, if it was needed.

Nothing could begin without Sideous—and he was not there yet. Keivitch was standing near Blina, who was throwing me the evil eye. I had to get onto the north side of the enclosure so I could see the signal Ben was to fire. So we inched our way through the crowds and stood behind Barthas's chair.

"Nice to feel the night air, eh, my Lord Barthas?" I asked for no reason.

"Uh-huh," he managed to grunt. But the poison was having more effect by the minute. Soon he would have trouble talking. Hopefully everyone was so afraid of Barthas that no one would question his physical or mental state.

Sideous arrived in a garish red-and-white striped robe. He

was going to milk this for all he was worth, what with the loss of the Pixies this morning. I rejoiced in his loss. So, this was the skulking monster who had held my eight-year-old child prisoner. I wanted him dead. But right now I needed to see that gate opened. I motioned for Max and Scyssa to stay close and pretend they were holding a knife to Irene's back. My head was aching as I held the Zombies under control both within the walls and without. This was one of those moments when I wondered how much more of this stress my ancient body could handle. I could feel my hands trembling with the tension. Even my hips and knees hurt.

Sideous waved to the crowd and motioned for quiet.

That's when Shadow Stalker stepped forward.

My heart froze.

"I demand the right of combat with my mortal enemy, Maxsswell Prockner. He has kidnapped my female and is a ssscoundrel and a traitor to his people!" Shadow stood with his hands on his hips glaring at Max. "I demand thisss by tradition. It is witnessssed by members of my tribe." The Swamp Demons who stood behind Shadow, in various leather gladiator costumes, grunted and hooted in unison.

All I could think was *sheisse*. I'd learned it in college: German or Yiddish for crap.

Max handed his knife to Scyssa and took off his sword belt. Oh Lord, I thought, he can't be meaning to go through with this!

Shadow laid down his weapons; at least there were not going to be knives involved. But I had seen what Max's claws could do to filet a slice of sushi. Shadow had those same claws. Oh, gods. Where was Ben? I wasn't equipped to handle this much testosterone! Slowly Shadow and Max approached one another. Shadow had a hungry look in his eye. On a positive note, they looked to be roughly the same size and muscle weight. They were prime mature specimens of Swamp Demons. Only one of them was my son.

Shadow circled Max slowly, but Max took the gentle relaxed stance I had seen Mr. Kyuke teach him. He was sizing up Shadow, who clearly was a savage warrior of his people. Shadow lunged for Max with his claws extended. Max rolled onto his back and took Shadow in the gut with his foot, rolling Shadow over his head and onto his back. Max sprang back up. Shadow got up out of the dust and dirt and took another look at Max. I said a little prayer of thanks to Mr. Kyuke. Use your enemy's weight against him. Be the bamboo. Bend in the wind.

Shadow came at him suddenly and clenched Max, pummeling him with punches. Max caught Shadow's fist and twisted his arm under to flip him or break the arm. Shadow flipped.

"I don't want to hurt you," said Max calmly.

"You? Little boy? You don't want to hurt me?" scoffed Shadow.

Shadow slashed sideways at Max with his muscular tail. Max countered easily with his own.

Scyssa shouted something that sounded like, "Sligh niss toe sylba heeba, Maksssss!" The group of Swamp Demons snorted in derision and shouted back, with their own sibilant sassing.

Oh, great. We had a peanut gallery. And this comment clearly pissed off Shadow Stalker. Pressing my finger to my lips, I motioned to Scyssa to be quiet. I think she got it, but to me she still looked smug—as much as a lizard face can.

Shadow began circling Max again, feigning little jabs and punches. Max crouched slightly and held his arms gently at attention. Shadow jumped up from where he was and hurled himself feet-first at Max. Max turned slightly to the side and grabbed onto Shadow's feet as he flew by, twirling him so he fell face-down in the dirt. Max straightened his red sash. "And I fight for Mombie. I am not a traitor."

"Tunis mah, Thessnah! Gulvissa!" shouted Scyssa, shaking her hand at Shadow. I rolled my eyes. Eddie fluttered his wings and resettled himself on my shoulder.

Max began to circle Shadow, alternating between little jabs and wide high kicks, which were not easy on his shorter Swamp Demon legs. Still he landed quite a few blows. Shadow was off balance. And that's when Max did the move he had showed me that night at Dendra's house. His leg rotated around him to the back and his foot took Shadow in the chin, his right arm followed with a sharp jab, and he finished by slashing Shadow's face with the sharp scales on his muscular tail.

Shadow fell backwards and staggered. The crowd of swamp Demons hooted and cheered him on. And he came forward, although I could see that he was a bit punch-drunk, and tried to land his own tail flip on Max. But Max was way ahead of him: he pulled the same rear kick behind his back and took Shadow on the chin. In a second he followed with a snap punch to the gut and his tail took Shadow in the chest with a resounding "Thump!" Shadow went down on his back.

"Gulvissa!" heckled Scyssa.

But Shadow was nothing if not stubborn. He was snarling and in a rage and hurled himself toward Max, torso first. I saw his claws rake into Max's shoulder. Max threw him off and drew his own claws. No more Grandma Nancy's rules. This was serious now. *Sheisse!*

Max circled and dodged Shadow's swipes with his claws. He took a back kick at Shadow with his toe claws extended and left a streak of blood on his cheek. Shadow lunged in fury again, but Max was ready this time. He rolled onto his back, taking Shadow in the gut with his toe claws and followed with two sharp jabs of his upper claws, raking Shadow's midsection. Shadow was wounded and bleeding.

Scyssa spoke up, this time in her broken English, "Contest finished. Gulvissa!" Her claw pointed at Shadow Stalker. She took Max's arm and held it above her head and called out. "Sstrykass!! Sunkinlap!"

The crowd of Swamp Demons roared with agreement. This had been a whole new form of fighting, one they had not seen before. Shadow was no longer top dog. Gods, was I proud of my son! Max returned to me and said, "Scyssa says I am the new tribal warrior. That's second only to chief and the chief is her father." He was beaming with that dreadful, canine-filled grin.

Patty had begged her father for time to say goodbye to all her new friends in the Fairy world. Most of all she wanted to thank Squirt and Button for saving her life.

It was so hard to explain it all to Daddy. How do you explain the feeling of being a magical creature? Feeling so filled with magic that you literally overflow with Fairy Dust? The world looks so beautiful when you see the growing process of flowers and vines. Wildflowers were just as beautiful as the blooms you buy in a florist shop. The old Patty hadn't realized that.

Maybe she could study botany when she got home. Home. That world had always seemed so comforting. But the idea of an ordinary life as an ordinary elementary school student seemed so mundane, so utterly lackluster. Cynthia McGowan would never believe this whole story. She would think that Patty was making it all up. And why not? Patty wouldn't believe Cynthia if she told the same story. But what was the use of all this joy if she couldn't gloat a little?

Daddy couldn't understand being so filled with joy. Patty would just have to remember this so that she NEVER EVER forgot it. She would always carry this joy inside her that, once upon a time, she had been a Pixie.

She saw all her friends ahead in a tree, free as birds and flying all about. There were Bart and Wixy, Rose, Dahlia, and all the others. Dido and Coco had flown back to the waterfall, where hopefully they would be safe. Miss Edna and Daddy had to stop Barthas tonight. Even Patty understood that he was ruining this beautiful Valley. It needed to be alive with Fairy Folk and regular folk just living side by side. Maybe that had been what the teacher had been trying to teach them during Martin Luther King Day. There are places in the world where one kind of person is mean to another kind of person, but the Valley shouldn't be one of them. Patty was just as much a person as Barthas was. Barthas needed to take a civics class and grow up.

Soon it was time to go and meet her father, and she had promised to stay in his pocket. But he never said she couldn't peek out and watch. They were in the forest surrounding the Manor. That place scared Patty, and she snuggled back down into the pocket of Ben's coat. Miss Edna had sent forward silent scouts, and once the guards had been blindfolded and gagged, the scouts brought them back alive. Now they had only to wait until Sideous began the ceremony to open the gate.

Sideous opens the gate

Nineteen

Transitions and Transformations

Once the battle between Max and Shadow Stalker had ended, Sideous looked anxious to begin the ceremony. The moon was over the horizon and as full and white as a great shining plate. Maybe the moon was closer to the Earth here. For that matter, who was to say if we were on Earth any longer?

I wondered if Ben was out in the forest waiting for things to begin. I assumed that he and Hook could sense the spells being woven by Sideous and would time things accordingly. Irene had become Barthas's tool again—at least for the evening. She sat cross-legged on a carpet between the braziers of incense and concentrated on Malik.

"I sense his presence in a Tacoria in South L.A. He is in a red vinyl booth." Irene held both her hands palm up and made her voice sound hollow. I had to remember that she had been doing this since her days in Los Angeles. What's the term, a shill? Irene knew the routine.

Sideous began to pull energy from the batteries and weave the spell to pull Malik from the old world into this one. Arcs of electricity snapped and crackled in the evening air as he concentrated on the vision Irene was describing. A wavering sort of hologram formed in the air between the batteries at the focus of the energies. It was the image of a tall thin black youth in his late teens. He was eating a taco and slurping through a straw on a large soda in a gigantic paper cup. The booth he was sitting in was indeed red vinyl. Irene was good.

Barthas was stupefied by the Manticore venom but managed to nod his assent to Sideous. The Sorcerer began weaving patterns with his hands, and something I could not see began to change the hologram: it shifted into a portal to draw Malik into this world.

The image shimmered like water in a shallow pool. Shapes blurred, and the picture shifted into that of a Faun, not unlike Ben's satyr friend Porkchop, but younger and without the horns. It became more solid as Malik came through. A Pan flute hung on a leather cord about his neck, and he took an unsteady step forward on his new goat's hooves.

"José?" the Faun queried, sounding bewildered. His long pointed ears focused on the sounds in the camp.

Barthas tried to rise but slumped back into his chair slurring his words. "What the eff?! Wadda hell's dat?"

"Looks like a Faun to me," I ventured.

"Each individual is affected differently by passage through the gate," Sideous said tensely.

"He was s'pose' to be an Ogre, like me!" grumbled Barthas. I could see that he could hardly lift his head, yet he kept eating chunks off the meaty leg of venison. "Do better with Hector, Dung-for-brains!" he barked.

Irene resumed her air of dignity after Barthas's spate of hostile obscenities. She lifted her palms to the heavens and began to speak, "Hector is at home in his mother's apartment eating a Hot Pocket from the microwave."

Once again Sideous began to pull energy from the batteries, and again they arced and fused in the middle to form another hologram of a Latino youth, this one with the nearly Asian eyes that indicated South American Indian heritage. He was, indeed, eating a Hot Pocket, the processed cheese visibly oozing from it.

Sideous concentrated and sent waves of energy into the image; it wavered and blurred and the shape shifted. At one moment I thought I was seeing a horse, then a man, then both.

Hector still looked like Hector. He had the same shining blue-black hair and tilted eyes, but he was a Centaur, with a longbow slung over his shoulder and a blue-black mane flowing down his back and into his horsey parts. He took a tentative step forward and then pranced about the ring of incense braziers like a prize-winning stallion. "Bitchin'!" he shouted.

Of course, the problem for Barthas was that neither the Fauns nor the Centaurs were allied with him. Things were not going his way.

"Bloody crap. Make the next one an Ogre—or die, Sorcerer," muttered Barthas as he took another bite from his poisoned haunch.

"My Lord Barthas, I have no control over the whims of the gate. Allow me to bring through your last friend and I will close the gate."

"Whoa there, Slick. You promised to get me through that gate with my Swamp Demon," I said assertively. Max and I had a home to get to.

Now Blina spoke up. I think she could tell that Barthas was losing his grip on the situation. "Get the Death Bitch through. We'll be glad to be rid of her and her pushy ways."

Hmm, I had pushy ways, did I? And that was coming from Blina Turdgirdle, as pushy a broad as I'd ever met. I actually felt rather proud of myself for shaking up her world.

Irene looked at me and said, "Umberto remains in the human world. I see him at a Maroon Five concert in a sea of faces. The crowd is roaring with applause."

Sideous took this as his cue to act and began forming an image of the selected importee. Umberto was a tiny, bone-thin Brazilian youth, covered with tattoo sleeves, eighteen-gauge loops in his ear holes, and a green Mohawk. He was jumping up and down and waving his arms to the beat of the music. Sideous concentrated on the holographic image and began weaving invisible threads of power to bring Umberto through the gate. Once again the image wavered, and this time bright lights filled the space between the batteries—until at last Umberto morphed from tattooed youth into something tiny and bright in the evening moonlight. Umberto was a tiny glowing green Fairy, a boy Fairy like Bart.

"Crap, crap, crap, crap, holy blessed crap! How the freak did that happen? I oughtta—"

Barthas was suddenly silent as a fireball lit the night sky. I simultaneously gave my Zombies the command to throw open the stockade walls. The Rebels had disarmed all the guards and were outside the walls. Elven archers stepped through the gates and began picking off the soldiers surrounding Barthas first. I pulled Max and Scyssa close to me, afraid they might be caught in the barrage. Blina charged forward on her huge black gelding and took the head Elf in the throat with her sword. Keivitch rallied the Rock Trolls to him and stood back-to-back with his soldiers to mow down the Rebels who came through the gate.

That's when I saw Ben shooting an arc of pure electricity into Blina, and Edna began doing something to Keivitch with her Witch skills. There was blood everywhere. A troop of Dwarves and Gnomes came through brandishing swords and crossbows: bolts began flying through the air. But something caught my eye as the door to the Manor opened and a dark, shadowy little figure came flying down the stairs toward Sideous, jumped onto his back and plunged a dagger in, out, and back in again and again. The batteries fell silent as Sideous slumped to the ground clutching at his chest. The dagger had come all the way through from his back.

Pheek stood over Sideous, looking satisfied. "They were right," he said.

Sideous collapsed in a heap muttering, "A Clerk. Finished by a Clerk."

Barthas seemed overwhelmed and unable to get up—only Irene and I knew why. But it was helping to slow things down so the Rebels could control the situation. Blina and Keivitch were doing their best to regain their army, but Rebels kept pouring through the door in great numbers.

Hook stepped forward and began to pull power from the batteries. They began to snap and crackle and arc with power. The strange magic mirror image began to form a shimmering reflection of the carnage going on within the stockade.

"Mrs. Prockner, I encourage you to step through the gate while I can hold it open," said Hook with tight control, concentrating on maintaining the spell.

"Sorry, not without my family. Besides, I can help." I began shielding the Rebels with rows of Zombies as they fought. And I brought my Zombie Ogres and Trolls to smash into the fist of Trolls that Keivitch had formed. I had a dog in this fight. I was not leaving without my family.

That's when I saw Ben and Miss Edna standing together and concentrating on Barthas's paralyzed bulk.

Miss Edna, as always, was in control. She spoke calmly and firmly to Ben. "That's it, we have time. Just weave the shield under him as we practiced. I will lift."

Ben saw the slumped form of Barthas in the great wooden chair and wondered what was wrong with him—he knew Barthas for a drug addict, but his inertness was beyond that. They had been planning on tipping a standing Barthas onto the shield; now Edna had to lift his limp form so Ben could get the shield under him. Still, he weighed less than the boulder they had practiced on. If Ben could get his shield under him, Edna could slide him into the gate.

"Hook," called Edna, "keep that gate open, we have another volunteer."

A limp Barthas was difficult to lift, but they were making progress. He was off the chair and sliding toward the shimmering gate. Though he couldn't move, and as doped as he was, he realized that something was happening to him. "Hey, what the eff? Who's doin' this?"

Annie realized that something important was happening, and she surrounded Ben and Edna with a protective ring of armed Zombies. The sweat was pouring down Ben's face, and Edna was steely cold with the effort, but foot by foot they moved Barthas's massive bulk toward the gate.

"Hurry!" urged Hook. "The batteries have limited supply and there is much that has to be done."

"I assure you, Mr. Hook, Ben and I are hurrying." With that, Barthas's inert form became vertical and tilted toward the gate.

"Make the gate bigger, Hook. He's got to go through."

"Madame, I am making it as large as I am able. I need Ben's help but he is busy with you."

"Go on, Ben. I can hold him. You weave with Hook and enlarge that gate." Miss Edna was clenched in every muscle, and she gritted her teeth as she held Barthas upright by some invisible power.

Ben concentrated and wove the spell with Hook until the shimmering mirror became large enough for Barthas's elephantine bulk.

"Here goes nothing," cried Miss Edna with some satisfaction as, with a final mental heave, she shoved the gigantic Swamp Ogre through the gate.

Barthas barely had time to moan, "Shi—" before the gate shimmered and he was gone.

"Good riddance to Bad Rubbish." Miss Edna dusted off her hands as she spoke, then quickly turned and tried to assess the battle going on in the courtyard. The archers and the crossbows had put a bolt or an arrow in many of Barthas's men. Zombies chased stragglers and hit them on the head with pikes or swiped crudely with their rusty swords. Barthas's army was in chaos.

Hook and Ben shut down the gate, Hook explaining, "We have to conserve what is left in the batteries."

Edna gave orders for her cavalry to pursue Blina and Keivitch, who had fled when Barthas disappeared. The rest of the soldiers lost interest when they realized that Barthas was gone. It reminded me of when Dorothy killed the witch. None of these soldiers had fought for Barthas because of love. They were ditching their weapons and running.

Irene motioned for me to join her. Things seemed to have calmed down a little, and I dared change positions only when I had found a Zombie Giant left. I had him carry me to where Irene sat.

"Is he really gone?" the blind woman asked me quietly.

"All two thousand pounds, thanks to Miss Edna and my husband, Ben." I took real pride in saying that. Clearly Ben had learned how to manage his new talents. We would have a lot to talk about when we got back.

I kept my Zombies on duty just in case. If I got through that gate and regained my middle age, I would drop my undead guardians like an old coat. But until then I was keeping myself protected and safe. I was still frailer than Ben realized. But then if we stepped through that gate everything would go back the way it had been. Or that was the theory. How could he understand the decisions that I had been forced to make? Would he ever forgive me for working for Barthas? Time would tell. I had to hope our relationship could handle it. Heck, he had lost Patty. He would understand my mistakes.

Miss Edna came over to me. "What did you do to him? That wasn't just Pixie Dust."

I cleared my throat and spoke. "Manticore venom. It was Irene's idea." I felt a little embarrassed. It was yet another treachery which I had admitted to. What did Max think of me?

Miss Edna laughed. "So you immobilized him for me, which by the way made him heavier to lift, but at least he didn't try to run. And the irony is that I may well have saved his life. Manticore poison does not exist in ... well, your world. Of course, that world is no longer my world. No more Florida for me." She paused, then said with a smile, "We could use a few brave women like you here. Any time you're bored with your world, come on back for a visit, Mrs. Prockner."

I was beginning to feel anxious. "Hadn't we ought to get back to open a gate back into that world?"

I had the Giant carry me out to see Ben. I had never seen Patty as a Pixie.

Ben was standing with Hook. They both wore silk pajamas, Hook carrying a paper parasol. I had to wonder about its significance— just one more mystery to unravel when we got home. I had the Giant put me down.

"Ben? May I see Patty?" I asked simply.

"I suppose it's safe by now. I've made her promise to stay in my pocket."

Just that concept blew my mind. She must be so tiny.

"Okay, Punkin, come on out and meet your mother."

Out of Ben's pocket came a shining figure carved of pure light. It was a joy to behold her. She shimmered, and her tiny dragonfly wings buzzed and fluttered as she hung in the air before me. And then she spoke.

"Oh Mommy, you look terrible! And your Zombies stink!"

That hit me right in the gut, but I reminded myself that she was still only eight. "I know, Sweetheart, but I'm okay and the fighting is over for a while. It's time we all got home. Ben, you round up everyone and let's get that gate opened back up."

Ben took a deep breath and then said, "That's the thing, honey. I think the list of those going has changed. Irene has been talking to Miss Edna and they've realized that they want the same things for this Valley. Now that Barthas is gone, Irene is free. Not only that, but she would have a chance to use her foretelling gifts for good."

"Irene?" I asked.

Irene smiled at me from where she sat with Miss Edna. "All I ever wanted was to get away from José. Really, this place is full of beauty, and it is a chance to start over. Doing something good without having to pick customers' pockets by telling fake fortunes. I'm sorry, Mombie. I know you were willing to help me leave, but now I think I'd rather stay after all."

That's when Scyssa said, "I go. You my family now. Scyssa go with Max and Mombie."

"Max?" I hollered, not knowing where he was. But Max had found his dad and begun his reunion, and he turned immediately to me, anxiety in his eyes.

"Mom, Scyssa is an outcast, she's been disowned by her entire tribe. And unless I go back with her as head warrior, she'll still be taboo."

"Well, isn't that a conundrum?" I asked sarcastically. "Just what do you think is going to happen to her if she goes through that gate with us?"

"I s'pose she'll change, somehow, like us." Max didn't want to look at me.

"And what are your Father and I going to do with a teenage female ... something?"

"We can pretend she's an exchange student and enroll her in my school!" Max replied.

"So, you two have already been thinking this through. It might have been helpful if you had shared this with me."

"Come on, Mom. Dad was cool with it."

Ben interrupted. "I said I would discuss it with your mother. Come on, Annie. We have to get out of here while the moon is still full. We have to make our decisions. The batteries are low and we have to go through all at once."

Well, it didn't look like anyone was really interested in my opinion. This was a lot to process. I would miss Irene: at least she understood what it was to feel like a survivor. It looked like I had survived the worst of the potential violence. Max was still here, and I had found Ben and Patty. Eddie had stayed with me and been a good dog-raven. I might as well take what was left and make a meal of it.

Ben was waving me over to where our little group was gathering. I heard Miss Edna settling some final disputes. Apparently the Cook refused to deny her alliance with Barthas. Finally Miss Edna decided that if her wish was to be taken prisoner, she could work off her indenture by cooking for the Rebels. That seemed to satisfy Cook's personal sense of honor. I imagined there would be many more such confrontations as the days went by.

Miss Edna was telling the truth when she said she would need help. Someone would have to replace Barthas and run this place. Roads had to be kept in repair. Bridges built. Taxes would have to be paid. But Barthas's methods needed to be replaced with some sort of simple democracy. I suppose elections would have to be held, as Miss Edna had mentioned.

I felt a little sad. As old as I was here, this place had awakened my sense of wonder and adventure. Things would have to be different between Ben and me from now on. Scyssa was standing with our little group. Eddie was on my shoulder. Max was between Scyssa and his dad. Patty flitted about in the air by their heads.

So this was it. Down the rabbit hole and back out. Ben smiled at me—though I knew I looked like his great-grandmother. He nodded to Hook to begin weaving the spell. The batteries crackled and snapped, and I could see Ben helping shape the spell: he had that concentrated look that I hadn't seen since his hippie days as a potter. He looked happy.

"Patty, stay with us!" was all I heard as the shimmering mirror opened in the air. "Hurry everyone, through the gate!" There was a weird static sound like a theremin. I felt extreme pain as my bones straightened out and my spine seemed to reconstruct. I imagined the process was equally painful for Max and Scyssa. We had been unconscious on the way in.

Then it was over ... and I could see light and feel gravel under my feet.

We were on the shoulder of some country road, under a streetlight. Eddie barked and leapt onto my lap. Patty was back in her pink jacket and purple starred leggings. Ben was still wearing that silly hat. And there was a naked adolescent girl standing next to Max. His eyes were carefully averted. Ben came to the rescue and placed his sheepskin jacket over her shoulders. She put her arms through the sleeves and said. "Thanks you, Mr. Prockner." She looked like a Mongolian girl, with deep hazelnut eyes and silky reddish black hair framing her high rosy cheekbones.

I had the funny feeling that she spoke mainly Mongolian. The language barrier had to be managed somehow. Magic had its price.

I wondered vaguely what Edna was going to do with all those limp Zombies. By now, without me, they were really just loads of corpses. What a strange talent, raising the dead. I would never be the same. None of us would.

That's when we noticed a tall, skinny Hispanic kid standing outside the light of the street lamp we had gathered under.

"Who are you?" I finally asked.

"Who the eff are you!? I'm Barthas!"

I almost felt sorry for the kid by the time we all stopped laughing at him. He looked confused and humiliated. He kept staring at his arms and legs and feeling himself.

Ben flagged down a police car. We told them that we had been carjacked: that story seemed to fit as well as anything else. By the time we got home, we discovered that none of us had keys, so I used the spare we kept hidden in the rock garden. Only the gods know what happened to our cars. Ben and I decided to call the insurance company and reinforce our story about both being carjacked. Sure, it was a coincidence, but there were weirder ones, and our cars truly had been stolen. They would never find them in this world.

I put Scyssa in the spare room, on the convertible sofa. Ben and I would have to deal with registering her for school, when we managed to get Max and Patty back into class.

One good thing was that Max and Patty seemed to share mutual respect for each other's experience in the Valley. Max listened to Patty's enraptured stories of being a Pixie, and she listened to him tell all about being a Swamp Demon. Scyssa sat by his side and interjected with her growing English vocabulary.

In time, people learned to excuse her talk of "her tribe." "She's Mongolian," we would explain.

José-Barthas was turned over to the police. He was wanted in California on a series of misdemeanors and felonies—including murder.

But after a while, the kids began asking us about going back. "Maybe for summer vacation?" And I wondered all over again if I had done the right thing. Ben and I had been offered a second chance at life, bizarre as it may have been, and had chosen to come home. Did we have a choice? Didn't we do the adult thing? Who was to say?

One day I came home and there was a letter on my dresser. Not in the mailbox, but inside the house, on my dresser. It was from Miss Edna.

Dear Ben and Annie,

Things have been going well here.

We had elections last week, and Irene was elected Governor of the Valley. It has been decided that each racial tribe will elect one representative to sit on a governing Council. Even the Trolls and Ogres are represented now. There will be no more partisan decisions without Barthas.

All the female Centaurs have been vying for Hector's eye. That silky black mane is the envy of the community. Umberto is learning some patience spells from Bart, and seems to have taken a liking to being a Fairy. Bart says Umberto is working on the cultivation of some special mushrooms. Malik is having the best time as a Faun, chasing Nymphs near the waterfall. It took him some time to learn the basics of the Pan Flute, but he seems to be getting better. And one of these days he might just catch himself a Nymph.

The batteries were NOT destroyed because we may fill them through some honest volunteering and keep them as an emergency fund of energy to be used by appropriately designated

Sorcerers.

I wanted to thank you both, and your children, for your parts in ridding the valley of Barthas. We couldn't have done it without you all. And even though we met under some curious circumstances, I have faith in your moral convictions.

Hook can get a message through for me now and then, and I promise to stay in touch. It may be possible for one or more of you to come for a visit from time to time if we are able to fill the batteries and the conditions are right.

Magic and science are funny things. Both have their rules.

Oh, and Annie, the council recently voted to charge you for corpse and Zombie clean-up. Your carefully constructed army collapsed like a wall of rotten meat the minute you passed through the gate. It took volunteers nearly a week to fully clean out the Manor.

And I am sorry to have to tell you that while the council was understanding of your dilemma, the deaths of Ferny Willowbranch, and Sylas' brothers, Willem and Jon Fairhaven, will be charged upon you if you return. The council has promised clemency for your cooperation in Barthas' removal. But a trial must be held. It was your Zombies who caused their deaths.

We are using the Manor as a Governor's Mansion and Town Hall. All the barracks come in useful when we have major votes and many folk come to town. Serving in our standing army is going to be mandatory for all races. Everyone has to serve for a period of six months to two years. After two years we feel it is good to change directions. We don't need any more Blina Turdgirdles, or Keivitch Krakowers. Who, by the way, have been reported as far away as beyond the mountains at the Elven havens.

We are hoping that they never blow back this way.

Max solved the problem with Shadow Stalker. He has been taken down a peg in the tribal standing. Scyssa's mother sends her love and is negotiating with her father for forgiveness. I hope she is well. Please send word. Hook will check from time to time to see if you have left us a letter on your dresser. Please do write back when you have time.

Patty, the girls all say hey and hope you will come back some day. Wixy and Bart say that there are many more spells for you to learn. Perhaps you will discover a talent like Bart has.

Ben, thank you for your courage and faith in our rebel band. You made remarkable progress as a Sorcerer and Hook misses having a student. We hope to show you a new Valley when you visit next.

Love and best wishes,
Miss Edna P. Eastman

So I wrote this all down, knowing that I would never be believed. And I returned to life as a suburban mom to a family that had grown by one Mongolian Swamp Demon. Ben and I had some long talks about our decisions and have been getting along better than we had in years. The kids all get along, and Scyssa is making progress in public school, after some remedial classes to catch up. And maybe, just maybe, one day we might all go back, even though I'm now a wanted criminal.

Annie DeLeon Prockner

About the author

Barry Burgess grew up on Long Island in a time when the vineyards were still potato farms. He and his brother raised pet crows and were often seen cawing at the sky.

Barry attended Vassar College, where he explored his interests in biology and ballet and made lifelong friends. He then enrolled in the Harkness School of Ballet, where he studied with Elena Tchernichova, and later became a designer in New York's garment industry.

Today he lives in an enchanted cottage with a secret garden filled with hummingbirds and Pixies—a home disguised as a post-war bungalow hiding behind a row of ancient arbor vitae in suburban Yonkers, NY. There he and his beloved rescue pit bull, Daphne, honor the Goddess by planting dahlias in the garden and preparing delicious meals for visitors and family.

About the illustrator

Jake LaGory is an illustrator and art teacher based in Asheville, NC. Raised in Chicago on a steady diet of canoe trips, monster movies, and Saturday cartoons, he uses art to connect his curiosity about the natural world with his interest in imagining the oddities that could inhabit it.

Previous work includes writing and illustrating a Cryptozoology-themed coloring book and individual illustrations that offer whimsical interpretations of sci-fi and pop-culture figures. He exhibits his work at Studio ZaPow, an illustration and pop-culture gallery in downtown Asheville. The full range of his art can be seen at http://cargocollective.com/jakelagory.

9 781942 016038